WEAK
AT THE TOP

WEAK
AT THE TOP

THE UNCENSORED DIARY OF
THE LAST CAVE MANAGER

GUY BROWNING

London ● New York ● San Francisco ● Toronto ● Sydney ● Tokyo ● Singapore
Hong Kong ● Cape Town ● Madrid ● Paris ● Milan ● Munich ● Amsterdam

PEARSON EDUCATION LIMITED

Head Office:
Edinburgh Gate
Harlow CM20 2JE
Tel: +44 (0)1279 623623
Fax: +44 (0)1279 431059

London Office:
128 Long Acre
London WC2E 9AN
Tel: +44 (0)20 7447 2000
Fax: +44 (0)20 7240 5771
Website: www.business-minds.com

First published in Great Britain in 2002

© Guy Browning 2002

The right of Guy Browning to be identified
as Author of this Work has been asserted by him in accordance
with the Copyright, Designs and Patents Act 1988.

ISBN 0 273 65682 1

British Library Cataloguing in Publication Data
A CIP catalogue record for this book can be obtained from the British Library.

10 9 8 7 6 5 4 3 2 1

Designed by Kenny Grant, London
Typeset by Northern Phototypesetting Co Ltd, Bolton
Printed and bound in Great Britain by Bookcraft, Midsomer Norton, Bath

The Publishers' policy is to use paper manufactured from sustainable forests.

For Esther
Top Totty

About the Author

Guy Browning writes for the *Guardian* and *Management Today*. He is also a business consultant specialising in communication, and creativity. He lives quietly in Oxfordshire.

Acknowledgements

With thanks to Rufus Olins, Rachael Stock, Fiona McAnena, Andrew Lane, Clive Digby-Jones, Eileen Seymour-Watkins, Suzie Dowdall, Alison Coudray, Ushma Patel, Anne Braybon, Rebecca Hoar, Russell Fairbanks, Tom McLaughlin, Jeremy Lee and the great Graeme Wilkinson.

John Weak first appeared in a monthly column also entitled Weak at the Top in *Management Today* magazine, where his continuing mastery of cave management can still be followed. *www.clickMT.com*

JANUARY

Monday January 1

Opened diary. Wrote 'John Weak' across the top in black ink which flowed smoothly from a pen which costs more than my secretary's entire wardrobe, lit cigarette and made a list of New Year's resolutions.

- Give up smoking
- Engage with women on a new level (groin)
- Show ex-wife magnitude of her error
- Make a big splash in new job
- Get six pack (from exercise not off-licence)
- Work smarter not harder. (Or just take it easy whatever's easiest)
- Be myself

Stubbed out cigarette. Lit up new cigarette. If I'm going to stop smoking I'll need to get rid of all temptation. Especially the 50 cartons from Calais.

Wandered down to the Blue Boar. All the usual suspects were there. Barney with The Terminator, his bloody great Alsatian to keep everybody clear of our end of the bar. Barney has a very pukka accent but a brain of solid concrete. Naturally he's something in the City which means he gets paid twice as much as I do and works half as hard. Old Farmer Mike was standing next to him with his head two millimetres from the ceiling and whinging like the miserable sod he is. Three foot below him Evan, who's something in IT too dull to mention, was looking round with his furtive look of being in the pub when he shouldn't be. He was drinking like there was no tomorrow which, knowing his wife Beryl, there might well not be. I got the bevvies in and we discussed how bad our various Christmases had been. I got extra points for the divorce of course. At ten to eleven on the dot, Beryl marched in and dragged Evan off, giving us her look of complete withering contempt. When he'd gone we agreed that Evan had probably had the worst Christmas this year and all the other years he's been married.

Tuesday January 2

Tackled totty issue by composing personal ad for myself.
Started with 'tall, dark, handsome and rich'. Bit clichéd that.
People might think I'm taking the piss. I'm not on the list for
council housing but if you have to work, you're not rich.
Handsome. Well I've never had any complaints. Tall. Anything
over six foot is tall and I'm well over six foot. Also well under
six foot two, but what's an inch between friends. 'Would like
to meet absolute fox for shunting round carpet at regular
intervals'. Had to translate that. 'Would like to meet
attractive, free-spirited woman'. Free spirit is a bit dangerous,
as you could end up with some raddled old hippy wearing a
flower in her hair on her way to San Francisco. 'Gorgeous
vixen'. Now we're talking. That'll sift out the po-faced
feminists.

The question is what do I want in a woman. Perhaps I'll
write down a list of all the things you normally get with a
woman, cross off all the things my first wife had, and what's
left will be what I want. Basically I want a woman who knows
how to use a washing machine and who goes like a spin
dryer. Changed into running gear then had a fag by way of
warming up. Ran out of the front door and then walked
briskly down to the Blue Boar. Had a few pints with Evan and
we agreed what a funny lot the Scots were.

Wednesday January 3

Woke with the lark. Let it lark about while I went back to
sleep. Thought about my new job and dug out the original
advert again. *International Marketing Director, Global
Manufacturing Company, Six-figure salary with benefits.*
That's me. Globe trotting, big-hitting director with big
package. In fact I think I'll put that in my personal ad. Walked
to newsagent for cigarettes. Was seized by fit of virtue so
diverted to Blue Boar which is a slightly longer walk..

Barney and The Terminator were there taking stock of the
new blonde barmaid. We were placing bets on which dominion
she came from. I turned on the high-octane Weak charm and

we quickly discovered that her name was Angela, she was from Australia, she was 21 and she had a boyfriend thank you. Got me thinking that I should specify blonde in my personal ad. Let's be honest, I want a blonde. Brunettes are OK for first marriages but it's now time for a blonde. Gentlemen prefer blondes, blondes have more fun and this particular gentleman is in the market for fun with a capital F.

Thursday January 4

Visit from my sister Karen and her new boyfriend who is a trainee Anglican vicar. Something to set the blood racing obviously. I was expecting a limp-wristed invertebrate but they showed up in his Austin Healey 3000 so he can't be all bad. We all went down the Blue Boar for lunch. Barney let The Terminator slip off the leash when he saw the dog collar (pardon the pun) but the Rev gave him some kind of death stare and he went trotting back to Barney. If that's what the Church of England are teaching these days, count me in.

When Karen was in the loo I asked him why a normal bloke like him was going into the church. He said, 'For the women' and winked at me. Before I could get to the bottom of this Karen had returned. I don't know exactly how women empty their bladders but I've noticed it always requires refreshing their lipstick afterwards.

Friday January 5

Changed into my kit, jogged up to the postbox (250 yards) and posted my personal ad. Well that's my new flat-stomached, high-totty life sorted out for this year. Suddenly remembered the detritus from my old life i.e. my two ankle biters Leah and Kieran who were conceived after two memorable but ultimately disastrous drinking binges four and six years ago. Wouldn't surprise me if they'd both been born with a hangover. Took them to the cinema which keeps them quiet for an hour or two. Means I can sit in the car for a couple of hours on the mobile. When they'd finished I took them back to their biological mother as I refer to her (makes her sound one up the evolutionary chain from a cabbage).

Her parents were with her so I had to weigh up whether I would like to spend the evening under the full weight of their moral disapproval or in the Blue Boar with a couple of straight ones. Difficult decision but I found myself in the Blue Boar with my hand round a pint of Speckled Hen and my eyes glued to Angela's contour-rich top. Got talking to Mike the Miserable Green Giant. He's a farmer, he's big and he's a miserable bastard. We agreed that the Welsh were a funny lot. Went home rather happy and broad-minded.

Saturday January 6

Drove down to Dorset first thing to spend the weekend with big brother Matt and his Anglo-Saxon wife Camilla. She has hair braided down to her backside and slaughters chickens with her bare hands. She thinks I'm an utter lightweight because I can't strip down a Land Rover and reassemble it with a blindfold on. I can strip down certain other things with a blindfold but that kind of thing isn't required in the country. Or it might be as she seems to have another screaming baby every time I visit.

Went to the local pub with Matt and drank some of the local brew. After three pints even the locals appear normal. I've noticed if you get further than two hours from London the gene pool tends to silt up considerably. Got to bed very late after a spot of cow tipping which Matt does to annoy the neighbours.

Sunday January 7

Woke up with the worst hangover ever. Matt said that a lot of pesticide gets into the local beer although it didn't seem to affect him. We had a chat about various things while I had to help peel every vegetable known to man. They asked an annoyingly large number of questions about Kate and the kids, most of which I had to pass on. They offered to put them up in the country for a week. I said I would send them down but couldn't promise to come with them. Camilla announced she was pregnant again which she does every time I visit.

Managed to get back in time for rugby training. Really good session although Martin Padley got one of his fingers broken in a nasty ruck. Stayed in the bar until closing time and then we took Martin to casualty. Went to bed relatively early because it's first day of new job tomorrow.

Monday January 8

Arrived at Smokehouse *plc* rather late due to hangover-induced navigation/parking/steering/focusing problems. Parked in handicapped slot. Until I get my own dedicated parking space I'm effectively handicapped so no problems there. First meeting of first day and I lose my rag with Giles Renton-Willets, weirdo HR Director. I want to talk company cars, he wants to talk company culture – communication, team playing, coaching – usual bollocks. Let him talk for a good minute until he said Mondeo. Spelt it out for him: if I don't have my Porsche, he doesn't have his job. He jibbered for a while and had some sort of minor nervous breakdown. Not very supportive on my part, but first day in a new job and you've got to show who's boss. I'm all for a coaching style of management but he's got to realise I'm from the Brian Clough school of coaching.

Tuesday January 9

First big team meeting went extremely well. I talked through most of it and everyone very impressed and quiet. Obviously not used to strongly held views, powerfully expressed. It was final meeting on major business re-engineering project. Told them that their initial thinking was poor and they'd have to start again. Some woman – project director I think, can't remember her name – tried to make a fuss about all the hard work they'd done already etc. Quite a shrill voice so I had to shout over her. You've got to put your foot down. Left work early to try out new gym membership. Totty-rich zone with lots of well packed, heaving lycra. I'm clearly going to be spending a lot of time at the gym.

Wednesday January 10

Have decided that office needs redecorating. Good for staff morale etc. Called in the office manager, Mrs Tooley (General Pinochet in knickers). Told her to start with my office and get some quotes for knocking down the intervening wall with Ken Carmichael, Research Director. She started bleating about 'open plan' and asking a lot of foolish questions. No point delegating if people don't do as they're told. Suddenly remembered I haven't sacked Carmichael yet. Probably best to do that before I have his office.

Had to take emergency phone call from Chief Executive Sir Marcus Rigby asking where business re-engineering project was. Told him we were doing major rethink, I wanted to get personally involved, new broom, new thinking etc. He said if he didn't get it tomorrow, *he* would be doing major rethink. Not sure I like his style – unbelievably insensitive and arrogant. I told him we'd work through the night and he'd have it first thing. Kind of challenge we love etc. Called project team and told them to work through night. Went to gym for work out i.e. working out which totty's lycra I need to get inside first.

Thursday January 11

Had long lunch with headhunter to say thank you for the Smokehouse job and to keep me posted on any big marketing jobs located in the Caribbean. We did grievous bodily harm to three bottles of red. Got back at four and found crowd of sullen teenagers outside my office. They had been waiting since two for their induction talk so for a couple of hours I talked to them passionately about marketing with very little slurring. If that doesn't induce them nothing will. Hayley (my Secretary) kept interrupting to say I was supposed to be somewhere else. But you've got to give time to youngsters. They're the future. Although with this lot, the future better not come too quickly. Called Renton-Willets again about Porsche. Says he will facilitate it in Board meeting tomorrow. I said sod the facilitation, just make sure it's parked outside Board meeting. Probably not culturally sound. Must be careful after long lunches.

Friday January 12

Have been savaged by a woman. Just getting into my stride at Board meeting and she pipes up asking what my point is. I told her I can make points without her help thank you *very* much. Didn't faze her a bit. Just kept on saying we had to stick to agenda. Shouted at her twice and she still asked what the point was. Scary looking woman. (Found out afterward she's Clare O'Keefe, Operations Director – just my bloody luck.) IT Director Gavin Smedley made an arse-achingly dull presentation about integrated systems and Internet Protocol. Might just as well have been talking Serbo-Croat. Told him I just wanted a computer on my desk that worked. (NOTE Must ask Hayley how to switch on computer.) Board ganged up on me and lectured me on car allowances. Turns out Smedley runs car purchasing committee. Mondeos all round then. Just before we finished Ken Carmichael asked about restructuring plans. Bit embarrassing. Told him we had to be flexible, responsive, right size etc. He didn't seem very happy. Probably best if he goes. We can't have unhappy people on Board.

Saturday January 13

Wanted to tell my wife all about my week at work. Realised I didn't have a wife so made a mental note to reprioritise totty search. Went to Blue Boar for lunch. Disappointing barmaid totty factor. Only Becky from the village who clearly fell out of the ugly tree at birth, and hit every branch on the way down. She's obviously from the shallow end of the gene pool but it's probably not her fault. She grew up in the village so her parents are probably cousins. Barney said she probably had tinted windows on her incubator. Evan said he'd been reliably informed that the doctor at her birth slapped her mother when she was born. The poor girl doesn't do herself any favours though because she was wearing those tight fitting lycra trousers that looked like a duvet stuffed into a pillow case. Mind you, by the time I left the pub I felt quite fond of her.

Sunday January 14

Papers, hangover, fried breakfast for lunch. Got myself down to rugby training. Fortunately bagged myself the wing so I didn't have to get too involved in all the argy-bargy. Martin Padley got rather badly raked in a scrum and had stud marks all over his face. Didn't seem to affect his performance in the bar, although his finger is still giving him a bit of gyp. Got rather badly plastered and accidentally went home to the first wife. She was massively underwhelmed and told me so with a selection of the expressions that made our marriage such a hot-bed of Anglo-Saxon studies.

Monday January 15

Have managed to meet all the new directors apart from a Bill Peters in Chemicals. Hayley called him four hundred times but we've never managed to speak. He's probably working night and day in the laboratory trying to bring the IT Director to life. Continued my rolling programme of lunches at Mr Bojangles wine bar with Clare O'Keefe Operations Director and Hannibal Lecter's love child. She's one of those women who don't feel they're getting equal opportunities unless they've got their foot on your throat. I thought we were having a nice lunch and she gave me a worse grilling than my interview. By the end of lunch I felt I probably wouldn't have got the job. She insisted on putting the lunch on her personal credit card. I tried to protest that it was a business lunch but I felt she was on the verge of calling in the fraud squad so I kept my mouth shut. Bloke eating next to me with ginger hair winked at me. Didn't know him from Adam so I was a bit suspicious. Didn't look like a mattress muncher though.

Tuesday January 16

Had lunch with Polly Trip, junior spod in the department. She's got quite a nice little body on her but didn't say a single thing throughout lunch. I think she might actually be in a permanent vegetative state which is a shame given her physical assets. Classic case of Ferrari chassis, moped engine. All she did was look longingly at the single flower in the vase. I wondered for a moment if she was being suggestive but I concluded that she was just checking whether it was a wallflower like her. I kept trying to think of things to say to her but she only had one answer and that was 'Kind of'. I finally ask her what she's responsible for in the department and she said internal communications. Naturally.

In the end I spent more time looking at the bloke next to me who was the ginger nob who winked at me yesterday. He was about my age but he looked amazingly like Henry VIII. Orange hair, no discernible neck, just great bearded rolls of fat. He might not have been much to look at but the woman opposite him certainly was. She was laughing at everything he said and it looked as if they'd polished off two bottles of red already. Felt like asking him to swap places so I could have a crack at his bit and he could try talking to my young Miss Trappist Monk.

Wednesday January 17

Henry VIII was in Mr Bojangles again having lunch with another tidy piece. Perhaps they were his six wives. I was having lunch with Gavin Smedley IT Director, a quiet orange juice kind of a guy. Smedley was talking in a calcifying kind of way about how he made his heroic leap from accountancy to IT so I tried to eavesdrop on the conversation next door. Henry was in the middle of this fantastic story of how a chicken was used to tell the weather in an African village he'd been in. I didn't manage to catch the middle part because Smedley asked some arse-aching question about the IT marketing interface. I said 'what do you think Gavin' to keep him blathering and just managed to catch the last bit about how Henry had swapped chickens before an inter-village football match. If you can laugh a woman into bed, this one already had both feet under the duvet. I managed to drag my attention back to Smedley who was telling his own rip-roaring anecdote about a rare programming language he'd encountered. I paid the bill and got out before my will to live drained away completely.

Thursday January 18

Was supposed to be lunching with Bill Peters but he didn't turn up. Got talking to Henry VIII and said I'd been stood up four times by one bloke and asked him if he'd stand for it. He asked me how upset I was. Not much I replied: his secretary said he was the most conscientious hard working person in the company. He then laughed like the flush of an old toilet and admitted he was Bill Peters. We agreed that he had a very good secretary indeed. Bill admitted that he avoided meetings and the only reason he was still in the company is because his first wife had been a top lawyer. This had meant that he had the tightest employment contract in the universe and also that he'd been hit harder than any man alive in his divorce settlement. Bill said that his whole purpose in life now was simply to serve as a warning to others. I mentioned I had a meeting with the CEO Sir Marcus Rigby the following morning. Bill warned me that Sir Marcus was a bit of a seagull manager – flying in, making a lot of noise, crapping on everything and then flying out. Arranged another lunch with Bill for tomorrow.

Friday January 19

Meeting with Sir Marcus. He said he'd heard I was having lunch with Bill Peters and felt he had to warn me that he was a bit of a company albatross in that he wheeled around all day doing nothing but it was considered bad luck to shoot him. Began to think I was working for the RSPB.

At lunch with Bill I asked him how he managed to keep his relaxed lifestyle amongst all the vicious young workaholics. He told me that the thickest trees reach the greatest height. Shortly afterwards he fell off his chair in mid-sentence so I didn't get to probe him on what he meant by this. No one in the bar seemed to notice or mind and he was back in it after a few seconds. He said he was just doing a quick gravity check, something he liked to do after his fourth bottle of red.

Our lunch finished as the sun was rising on Saturday morning. I don't remember much about it but I seem to recall that we were both at the gym at one point. God knows what we did there. Then we went on to somewhere shady in town. I can't remember a thing about that. But I think I'm going to like Bill Peters.

Saturday January 20

Got home at 11.00am. Slept until Sunday morning.

Sunday January 21

Death's door throughout Sunday. Thought about getting last rites. Just in case. Took a bottle of aspirin and decided to end it all. Felt better after the first two. Managed to get down to rugby training. I got roped in as a prop which was a bit rich because I was the one that needed propping up. Don't remember much about the session apart from the fact that Martin Padley got his ribs badly cracked in a lineout. He probably couldn't see much of the play because of the bandaging on his face. We got him to the bar afterwards to dull the pain. He dropped his first pint because of his dodgy finger and got some glass in his foot which was pretty funny.

Monday January 22

Brand Manager recruitment week! This is where I play God and toy with other people's lives. Got a whole stack of CVs dumped on my desk which I rigorously pre-sorted. Looked at photos first – don't want anyone aesthetically challenged scowling round the office. Then checked interests. I will not work with anybody who thinks rambling is interesting. Found one who had skydiving and ski-extreme under interests. Crossed him off – can't have people working for you who have more interesting lives than you do.

Had long lunch with Bill Peters from Chemicals to discuss modern recruitment methods. He says he takes them all to lunch, cracks open a crate of red and anyone that can make it back to the office without medical attention gets recruited. (Possibly explains disintegration of Bill's department – and Bill.)

Tuesday January 23

Got e-mail from Clare O'Keefe, Ops Director (hairy-legged nut cracker) who is also on the interview panel. She suggested we use 'assessment grid' plotting core learning skills against emotional intelligence. No idea what she meant but told her it was an excellent idea. She can fill that out while I assess totty rating for women and rugby potential for men. Ideal candidate would be accountancy trained prop forward with large breasts.

Giles Renton-Willets (weirdo HR Director) will be the chair. Very appropriate as everyone sits on him. Told me that he judges candidates by the colours in their aura. I suggested he may be working too close to his marker pens. Told him that the acid test I always use is would you really want to sit next to the candidate at the company Christmas bash.

Wednesday January 24

First interview day. O'Keefe got her emotional intelligence/learning quadrant out and Renton-Willets lined up his coloured felt tips for recording their auras. I put my cigarettes and Porsche keys on the desk. The first person to say, 'Let's go outside for a fag and discuss company cars', gets the job. Which wasn't the first person in – a chinless little twerp with a Double Ego from Cambridge. I didn't understand 90 per cent of his first answer; picked up a few phrases like 'matrix management', 'empowered stakeholder base', 'endemic discontinuity' etc. I only asked him how he was. He regurgitated business books for half an hour and I wished him a very pleasant future in management consultancy. Renton-Willets showed me his aura – yellow and pale blue. Intellect the size of Denmark, personality of a baking tray. Pretty much summed it up.

Thursday January 25

Arrived late for interviews because of over-enthusiasm at gym – they've now started doing proper cooked breakfasts to work off all the exercise. Burst into the room and said, 'What poor little sod have we got today?' O'Keefe pointed to chair at other end of room containing the day's poor little sod. So small and timid I didn't even notice her. Mentally crossed her off and sat down for the interview. Renton-Willets used tippex on her aura – not a good sign.

Afternoon candidate's CV said he played rugby for London French. Thought I'd try old trick and throw him something to catch. Threw O'Keefe's handbag which burst open, showering tampons all over the room. Incredibly embarrassing mostly because he didn't manage to catch it. Renton-Willets said afterwards his aura stopped at the neck. Had to remind him we were looking for a marketing man not a Zen Buddhist.

Friday January 26

Last candidate had excellent qualifications. Her CV wasn't bad either. I took over and gave her some high-octane questioning to show her who was boss. As I'll be her boss, best to show her straight away. 'Accidentally' offered her job at end of interview.

Said she would have to think about it. (Why can't women ever just say yes straight away?) Got an absolute roasting from O'Keefe afterwards about undermining process etc. Told her she needed to use her emotional intelligence more. Heard later that the preferred candidate had called O'Keefe to decline job. Apparently she liked the company but wouldn't want to sit next to me on a bus let alone at the Christmas party. Which proves to me what a good test that is. Obviously not the sort of woman we want.

Saturday January 27

Woke up with a feeling of impending doom. Checked to see if my ex-wife was in the bed next to me. All clear thank God, but reminded me that I had to see her later to take the ankle biters off her hands. You would have thought with the amount of maintenance I pay, I wouldn't have to see the kids as well. When I got to Kate's, both her parents were there with their Justice of the Peace faces on. They're perfectly polite but the subtext of everything they say is, 'we told you he was a wanker'. I never thought there'd be anything worse than a mother-in-law but an ex-mother-in-law is the dog with the muzzle off. Took the kids for a pizza which they complained about because they don't do burgers. I explained to them that when I want a burger they can have a burger.

Sunday January 28

Papers, breakfast, shower, shave, shit. Rugby match against Garford. Close run thing but we ended up losing 64–3. Martin Padley was taken off ten minutes into the match because of a dislocated collar bone. But he played a blinder in the second half. After a few in the bar afterwards got down to the Blue Boar to finish the job. Big Becky was on duty. She'd obviously made a big effort as she was only looking moderately rough. Bar maid is a good job for her because you can see her chest above the bar but the lower half which is the size of Glamorgan is kept well out of sight.

Had a few straight ones with Barney and we agreed that the Dutch were a funny old lot. Bit of excitement when The Terminator attacked some hippy who'd wandered into the pub. The Terminator's an ex-drug squad dog and tends to get over-excited when he smells something suspect. Probably the main reason why we don't have many young people in the pub.

Monday January 29

Came down the mountain with tablets from Sir Marcus (CEO). Apparently we have to innovate or die. Creativity and new thinking top priority. Does this mean we can ditch quality I asked. Probably shouldn't have especially as he's looking for me to lead fresh thinking. Good opportunity to make early impact with him.

Lunch with Bill Peters to get creative juices flowing. Got back just before four. Never felt so creative. Suddenly had fantastic big idea for major innovation and phoned agency immediately to do it up in colour (if there's one thing agencies are good for, it's doing things up in colour). Also have ordered two big sofas for my office. Gives the place a more creative, informal feel and good for sleeping off lunches with Bill Peters. Possible totty hands-on management zone as well. In a non-sexist nurturing supportive way of course.

Tuesday January 30

New receptionist called Shirley. The old one was incredibly good looking but the world's worst receptionist because she behaved like visitors' only purpose was to come and stare at her. I had to go down there virtually every day to assure her at great length that she was imagining all this.

Summoned marketing and research teams for a meeting. Told them that creativity and innovation are required from senior management but they can all relax as I already have big new idea. Unveiled big new idea on agency boards. *The soap that dries your hands.* Everyone shocked into deep and reverential silence. Obviously weren't expecting their Marketing Director to be taking a creative lead. Deborah Wills (Brand Manager – nice body) asked me what the thought behind it was. Pretty obvious to me but I explained that you have to dry your hands after washing them so why not have a soap that dries them for you. She said we needed to get the idea into research as soon as possible. Smart girl. Better chase up sofas.

Wednesday January 31

Lunch with weirdo HR Director Giles Renton-Willets. Don't know how he got in my diary. Must tell Hayley that lunches are strictly by my invitation only. No point getting squiffy with someone who wants to talk business. Hayley told me that word was out round the company about my big idea. No surprise there. Probably first big idea they've heard since original sliced bread concept.

Over lunch I was tucking into very good filet mignon when Renton-Willets piped up about risk culture and innovation funnels. Hadn't a clue what he was talking about but made encouraging noises. Apparently he thinks whole company should be innovating night and day, taking all sorts of risks and not getting blamed when they all go pear shaped. I've got a good mind to report him to Sir Marcus and get him sacked for stirring up the workforce. He liked my sofa idea though. Said he could advise on fabric. Got bill quickly as I didn't want to be seen in a public place discussing sofa fabric with another man.

FEBRUARY

Thursday February 1

V. bad day. Clare O'Keefe, Operations Director volunteered to join the innovation task force I'm apparently setting up. Told her in no uncertain terms a) task forces are just committees in combat trousers and I wouldn't be seen dead in one; b) I was handling innovation personally and she should keep her fat snout out; c) if there were ever to be a task force I would decide who was on it, thank you very much. She ignored all this and then said she loved my joke about the soap that dries your skin. I assumed she was joking about me joking.

Went to see Timothy Smallwood (Finance Director) about non-appearance of sofas. He kept saying 'cool' and 'fab'. He's the same age as me for crying out loud. Said there was no budget for sofa as I have already spent it on redecoration, new desk, chair etc. Gave him an absolute roasting about how vital it was to make people feel comfortable. He said he'd look at his spreadsheet. I said that was 'groovy' and left him to it.

Friday February 2

Called marketing team in after detecting distinct lack of enthusiasm and action behind my mould-breaking Hand Drying Soap concept. Just getting into my stride about lack of teamwork, risk taking etc. when Sir Marcus popped in to congratulate me on setting up of new innovation task force. My confusion covered by appearance of delivery men carrying in two bloody great sofas. Quickly explained to Sir Marcus that they were for the innovation task force meetings to help encourage an informal, blame-free risk taking culture. Smiles all round from Sir Marcus until he spotted Hand Drying Soap concept boards and got all grim faced. I explained it was a spoof from the agency. He then asked whether choice of sofa fabric was also a spoof from agency. Much laughter all round. Bit too much from some quarters. Must set up headcount reduction task force.

Saturday February 3

Woke up at the crack of dawn for some reason. Before I knew what was happening I had put my kit on and was out of the door jogging. Had got about half a mile and was ready to call it a day when I bumped into this rather pert little number also out jogging. She said hello and we got talking. I had to speed up to keep up with her and soon found it pretty difficult to talk. I could feel my cool points slipping so I managed to say a cheery goodbye and peel off down an alley. I spent the next five minutes bent double, wheezing like a horse and coughing up most of my internal organs. Finally recovered and realised I was in a dead end with an electricity sub-station. Walked out of the alley and bumped into the totty coming back. She waved. I tried to say something funny, clever and explanatory but just managed to dribble down my t-shirt.

Sunday February 4

Woke up at the crack of dawn again and turned over. Got up and went to the Blue Boar for lunch. Conversation was a bit inhibited as Evan's wife Beryl had made an appearance and we all had to be on our best behaviour. We couldn't say much about anything interesting while Beryl was there but we all enjoyed the sight of Angela pulling pints. There's something about young women pulling those big levers I find strangely exciting. I know Evan feels the same but he was too scared even to look in case Beryl gave him a thick ear. Barney arrived with The Terminator who immediately started whimpering when he smelt Beryl. Bit of a Saddam Hussein in knickers, old Beryl.

Big rugby match in the afternoon against arch rivals Hinton. We started brightly but got completely shut out for the last 75 minutes. Found part of an ear on the pitch after the match which turned out to be Martin Padley's. He didn't seem terribly bothered, so I threw it in the bin.

Monday February 5

Arrived slightly late due to difficulties opening Rice Krispies with double vision. Said hello to Shirley, got into a lift and found myself face to chest with the world's largest woman. She looked at me as if I was edible. I was bloody glad to get out I can tell you. Hayley gave me the post she thought I'd be able to cope with and informed me that a top financial journalist wanted to interview me. It's nice to be taken seriously especially if she's some smoking hot totty.

I've got women on the brain at the moment. Apparently your average man thinks about sex every nine seconds. I'm well above average in that department as the only time I'm not thinking about it is when I'm actually doing it. In fact that's just about the only time I think seriously about business. That was the situation with the ex-wife though, which doesn't really count as sex.

Tuesday February 6

Bumped into the big woman in the lift again. Bit of a salad dodger that one. Don't know who she is but I wish she wouldn't look at me like I was a tub of chocolate chip ice-cream. Prepared for interview with top financial totty – bought a nice tie and had my hair primped at my favourite salon where they specialise in resting their breasts on your head when doing your hair. It's a great business proposition; you pay through the nostrils and you could come out of there looking like Friar Tuck but you'd still be one delighted customer.

Had lunch with Bill Peters – a couple of bottles of red thickened with steak and chips. Bill let slip that he quite fancied Hayley which came as a bit of a shock. That's my secretary for crying out loud! If anyone's going to fancy her it should be me. Bill was surprised I hadn't already had some personal assistance from her. Returned to office and for the first time looked at Hayley as a woman rather than a photocopier. Had to admit, if push came to shove, I wouldn't mind her changing my toner. Trouble is of course, if I wanted to have a little extra-curricular with her, she would be the only person capable of organising my diary so I could squeeze her in, as it were.

Wednesday February 7

Got in slightly late as my duvet was rather badly twisted. The Big Friendly Giant was waiting for me in the lift again. Apparently she works for me and wondered whether we could have lunch together. I nearly told her I don't do lunch with any woman who can bench press more than my bodyweight but I didn't in case she tried it. Gave Hayley my gladdest of glad eyes and told her how much I liked her new dress. She said she'd been wearing it once a week to the office for the last five years.

Then kept financial journalist waiting for half an hour just to show her exactly where she was in the food chain. Braced myself for some swamp donkey with big glasses but she nearly broke the tottometer. She asked about relationship marketing so I honed in on the relationship part and told her a few choice stories from past relationships (reassuring her of course that past results were no guarantee of future performance). We finished by talking about the role of women in marketing and I agreed that you can sell anything with an attractive woman perched on top. She wrote a lot after this. Good interview all round.

Thursday February 8

Took stairs to office just in case the Honey Monster was lurking in the lift. Binned my post, deleted my e-mails and then called up the überbabe journo and asked her out for some 'background' research. She suddenly got very hormonal and said my behaviour was 'inappropriate'. Probably best out of it – these career women are ball breakers at work and crying to their cats at home.

Switched to plan B. Told Hayley I really appreciated the job she was doing, loved the way she'd done her hair and asked her out for dinner to discuss a more hands-on style of management. She gave me a look she usually reserves for the times I ask her to type up the Rugby Club minutes. But then she suddenly perked up, suggested tomorrow night and said she would organise everything. Good girl! I love a woman who takes the initiative.

Friday February 9

Holy Mother of God!! Godzilla assaulted me in the lift! She just grabbed my arse and tried to snog me. Who does she think she is, I'm her boss for God's sake!! I should have her for sexual harassment. Let me tell you, it's going to be bloody difficult working with her from now on. Hayley had scrubbed up well and didn't look quite as cheaply dressed as normal. She must be looking forward to our little session this evening. Found newspaper on my desk with my interview titled *Last of the Cavemanagers*. I like it!! I'll have to distribute that round the office. Good PR never goes amiss. Spent rest of the day happily anticipating new working relationship with Hayley.

Got to restaurant slightly late which was lucky because I spotted Godzilla inside applying anti-perspirant to top lip. Reversed out in top gear and promised myself never, ever to mess with Hayley again or ask her to organise my social life again. Women!! Can't get them in the sack, can't sack 'em.

Saturday February 10

Have decided not to dip my pen in the company ink for now especially as post was chock full of replies to my personal ad. Some of them had sent photos of themselves which puzzled me because some of them were clearly grizzly chickens of the first order. But one was a little blonde number who would go well with my duvet cover so I gave her a call and arranged a date. Spruced myself up, made sure the bedroom was ready to receive and then went off on my date via a quick stop at the Blue Boar for a couple of pints of charm enhancer.

Got to the restaurant late and found the little blonde in the corner. I was only half an hour late but she seemed to have aged 20 years in the interval. She was nearer 60 than 16 and even the two bottles of red we finished couldn't persuade me to take her home. She offered to walk me home but I said I had a headache. Have decided to dip my pen in the company ink at first available opportunity.

Sunday February 11

Changed into my kit and walked up to the shop for the paper. Walked back, read papers, took off kit. Blue Boar for lunch. Mike the miserable farmer was in there. We've never discovered why he's so miserable as apparently he trained as a legal expert on European agricultural subsidies and is one of the richest men in the county. Becky likes him though and is always showing him the full measure of her cleavage which is really not what you want to see before you've eaten. Evan slipped the leash and showed up for a quick one. We got talking and agreed what a funny lot the Spanish are.

Excellent rugby match against Stanton. Martin Padley scored a superb try but managed to smash his head on one of the posts and had to be stretchered off for 15 stitches in his head. His try was disallowed as well which upset him.

Monday February 12

Arrived late at Board Strategic Planning meeting as I had completely forgotten all about it. Hayley told me it'd been in my diary for years. I reminded her that I don't read my diary years in advance. She started muttering and went for an early lunch. Probably hormonal. I wonder whether we can withhold pay when she's like that. Worth looking into.

Big speech from Sir Marcus about importance of planning ahead, important challenges in year ahead etc. I switched off at this point. Nothing difficult about strategic planning: add 5 per cent to your targets and 50 per cent to your budgets. Then give ground on everything except entertainment because people are our greatest asset and people need entertaining. After work went down the gym with Howard, an old mate from school whose attitude to life is still stuck in the upper fourth (probably explains why he's got such a flash job in the City). We did a bit of circuit training where we go from one machine to another deciding we don't really like the look of any of them.

Tuesday February 13

Called Hayley in first thing and told her to update last year's strategic plan, adding any good marketing ideas she could think of. Having successfully empowered her I then settled back with trade press to look at the jobs page. Always a good idea to check what's out there, what the other buggers are earning and to make sure your job's not being advertised. Also worth remembering that all vacancies advertised have driven the previous occupant to early retirement or suicide.

Bugger me rigid!!! The rugby is coming up in Cardiff and I haven't organised my complete and total absence from office! Talk about taking your eye off the ball. Told Hayley to stop messing about with strategic plan as getting to the rugby was going to take real planning. Organised immediate top level strategic planning lunch with Bill Peters. As luck would have it he was already in wine bar doing 'product scoping'.

Wednesday February 14

Arrived in office first thing after rush hour to do planning. Obviously too late to sponsor match itself but called organisers to see whether we could sponsor boots, ball, jerseys, tracksuits, stand, anything. Told them that we didn't mind sponsoring inside of jock strap if it came with box (which I thought was bloody funny!). She said sponsorship was all taken care off and would I be interested in Women's Ping Pong. Told her that nobody, me especially, was interested in women's bloody ping pong.

After another long planning lunch with Bill Peters, have decided to transfer our entire manufacturing capability to

Wales in Cardiff area. This will entail week long scoping study that Bill and myself are prepared to undertake. As lunch wore off we realised that this would need approval from Operations and Clare O'Keefe. As she doesn't know the difference between Jeremy Guscott and an expandable gusset, we scrapped that one.

Thursday February 15

It came to me in a dream! Well more of a nightmare really. We've been bogged down in this bloody Investors in People thing (cultural revolution where you have to treat your employees like human beings for crying out loud. If you don't shout at anybody for six months you get a plaque in reception). I have now decided this is a good thing and I am going to champion Investors in Welsh People, starting with familiarisation in Cardiff for a week.

Called Renton-Willets (weirdo HR Director) with Investors in Welsh People suggestion. He said the company had won the award last month and I had taken my people out to lunch to celebrate. Of course, how could I forget. This then gave me another brilliant idea. Teambuilding in Welsh mountains! Marketing department up to their necks in mud, crossing rivers on oil drums etc. for entire week. When they've built the team they can come and pick me up from Cardiff.

Friday February 16

Have decided to put all agency business up for review. Need to see evidence of fresh thinking, cost efficiency, corporate entertainment etc. with special emphasis on the period of the Rugby match and the location of Wales. Failing this will organise special test marketing of hair product in some area of the country like for example Wales. Getting desperate so had another strategic planning lunch with Bill. We decided to put all our ideas in strategic plan and hope that something sticks.

Called in by Sir Marcus. Very impressed with depth and scope of my proposals and encouraged by my commitment to detailed planning but sadly will have to reject all my proposals. In recompense he asked me and Bill to join him for the rugby in Chairman's box in Cardiff for 'extended briefing' of City analysts. Had it planned for years apparently. Now that's what I call leadership.

Saturday February 17

As some kind of punishment for ever having been married I have got the ankle biters for the entire weekend. Went to collect them first thing. Kate's dad Arnie was there. He always talks to me as if he were cradling a shotgun. I have to be very polite to him as he is non-executive director of Smokehouse. If I'd known that before, I never would have taken the job. But he seemed very jolly apparently because Kate has got a date with some pathetic loser tonight. I asked who he was and how much he earned but Arnie wasn't saying. Probably delivers pizza.

Took the kids to the Blue Boar. There's a special room at the back where you can just throw in chicken nuggets every half an hour and not see them until closing time. Barney had just got back from the Far East and we were all agreeing what a funny lot the Japs were. Evan let it slip that Beryl had once had a date with a Jap which stunned us into silence. Tokyo Beryl came in shortly afterwards to take Evan back to his cell and it was impossible not to imagine him as an extra from *Bridge on the River Kwai*. Had a fair few sherbets and went home very happy. Then had to go back straight away because I'd left the kids in the back room.

Sunday February 18

Got the kids up early and cooked them eggs, bacon, sausages, beans etc., all the foods that were forbidden fruit in my marriage. I don't want them growing up not being able to look a sausage in the face. Took them on the coach for rugby away match and they joined in some of the singing without (hopefully) knowing the exact drift of some of the songs. We had a good match in difficult circumstances, such as them having 15 fit skilful men in their team as opposed to our 12 unfit, unskilled men. However, Martin Padley rushed in at the last moment fresh from his physiotherapy to make it 13, which was a bit unlucky for him as shortly afterwards he had his retina detached by an accidental jab in the eye somewhere in a ruck and maul.

Dropped the kids back at Kate's and asked her about her date with the pizza delivery boy. She tried to pretend she'd only just come down from the peak of carnal ecstasy which I knew meant the furthest they'd got was probably having a second cup of coffee at the end of the evening. Managed to get down to the Blue Boar for last orders and a quick discussion on why the Swiss were a rum lot. Becky was trying to be all flirty but accidentally managed to wedge her arse in a serving hatch. She really needs to put herself down for genetic modification if they're ever going to breed the arse out of that family.

Monday February 19

Got in before eight and was shocked and appalled by how many people were already at their desks. I can only think that they must find work very difficult. Put my phone on divert, worked hard all morning, had lunch at my desk, worked hard all afternoon. Had a cup of coffee at five and then worked right through until eight. Went home feeling rather pleased with myself at job well done. In fact, that is my job done and I won't have to work again this year.

Jobs at my level are pretty simple really: decide what you're going to do, tell agency to do it and what'll happen if they don't. Above all don't tinker. Most people's jobs are just tinkering and the reason why they have to tinker is because some tinkerer has tinkered somewhere else. JFDI – Just Fucking Do It – and then JLIA – Just Leave It Alone.

Tuesday February 20

This week we relaunch our entire women's cosmetic range. It's a massive project but I've already done the hard work. I got five agencies to tender for the job in the first place, which meant we got five lots of top thinking for nothing. I then took the best thinking from all their pitch documents and made it into the brief for the cheapest agency who we naturally gave the business to. Didn't have much to do in the office so I deleted all my e-mails and then spent a few hours walking the talk which I have interpreted to mean walking round the building chatting up anyone with passable charlies.

After work went to the gym with Howard where we had one too many warm up G&Ts and then lifted an exceptionally heavy weight onto the chest of a nasty little man with a headband who we've never really liked.

Wednesday February 21

Sir Marcus popped in to see whether I was confident that the cosmetic relaunch would be a success. We both knew that was Sir Marcus's way of telling me that my cock was well and truly on the block. Actually I'm pretty confident about it all as 90 per cent of the work we've done so far is to provide armour-plated covering for my arse. We've researched the market to death; we've asked more consumers about whether they would buy it than we expect to buy it when we launch it; we've generated more 'concepts' than the Tate Gallery; we've got more storyboards than Marvel comics; and we've developed advertising worth more than the entire overseas development budget of the UK. And rightly so. The Third World are more likely to see our cosmetics than they are a sack of rice from Her Majesty's Government.

Thursday February 22

Sir Marcus dropped in one more time just to let me know that he'd promised the City boys a 'Category Killer' in cosmetics that would blow the market wide open. Which meant the Smokehouse share price, his bonus, my options, perks, career trajectory, future happiness etc. all depended completely on tomorrow's presentation. No pressure there then.

To steady my nerves I went to Mr Bojangles with Bill Peters and had a couple of bottles of red. Bill's advice was that nothing is ever as bad as it seems at the time except for first marriages and IT presentations. Over another bottle we started to develop a theory that your presentational skills were an accurate reflection of your performance in bed. At that point the waiter came to talk us through the dessert menu and we quickly agreed that he was a definite left footer.

Friday February 23

Disaster. The agency presentation was pathetic and their Category Killer was more of a Category Flopper. As they finished their presentation, two paramedics walked past the window pushing a body bag on a trolley. A policeman outside told us they'd just fished a suicide out of the river. When we sat down again the words 'Category Killer' were still on the screen. Cosmetics, marketing, business all suddenly seemed totally superficial. Just to add to the mood the policeman told us the body bag was a special breathable fabric just in case the body came round and needed some air. I suddenly thought about a make-up that covered you up but let your skin breathe. Bingo!! We had our 'Category Killer'. The agency recognised my brilliance, said it was what they had meant all along, I signed it off, the project went live and everyone was happy. Marketing – it really is the stuff of life.

Saturday February 24

Another hot date from my personal ad. I have spent a lot of time staring at the photo and it seems relatively recent, unretouched and not bad looking. Nevertheless I have booked a restaurant where they have the world's lowest lighting. They also have semicircular booths which are good for shuffling round when you're getting buying signals. Went to the Blue Boar first for a couple of warm up drinks. I told Barney I was off on a hot date and he told me that the secret of getting into a woman's knickers was getting into her head first. It wasn't clear whether he meant getting head first into her knickers but I promised to bear it in mind.

Arrived at the restaurant, installed myself in the booth and braced myself for an absolute swamp donkey. Anthea arrived with a shaggability factor of about seven out of ten which is about six points over the threshold as far as I'm concerned. I poured her a glass of champers and started in on the spade work. She then interrupted and said she wanted sex at the end of the meal. I said I wasn't particularly hungry and was happy to skip the meal but she insisted on eating. The meal dragged on but I finally got her home and got to work. When we'd finished she suddenly burst into tears. She couldn't explain it but said she always did it. Fantastic. I knew there would be catch somewhere.

Sunday February 25

Anthea hadn't deteriorated too badly overnight so I got to work again. All went well until we'd finished and then the blubbing started again. Not what you want at all. In fact what you want is total silence from the woman ideally because she's already gone to get the bus. Had a bit of breakfast, gave her one last go and got the blubbing again. Told her it was lovely to meet her and that I had to go for lunch. She went on her weepy way and I got down to the Blue Boar.

I discussed Anthea's condition with the boys and they all agreed she was weeping with frustration because my technique was so pathetic. After three hours continuous piss taking I was beginning to feel like blubbing myself. Thankfully Beryl came in and fished Evan out. I then veered the conversation around to who would be doing the blubbing in their marital bed.

Monday February 26

Week's skiing holiday with Howard and a few mates from college. Met Howard and the lads at airport carrying my three grand's worth of skiing equipment. I didn't see why we couldn't get the kit out there but Howard is the big expert so I've got three tons of spanking new gear. I notice Howard didn't have much more than hand luggage and the world's longest pair of skis. I suggested to Howard just for a laugh that we should try and take our skis as hand luggage. See if flashing our gold cards would swing it. He said he didn't have a gold card which got holiday off to a bad start.

Landed in Milan and took coach up into the Alps. If I can find a chalet girl as well built as the Alps, I'll be happy. Finally, arrived in chalet. Greeted by Emma our chalet totty, who had everything you want in a woman all in exactly the right place. I asked her whether she fancied some après-ski before the skiing. She gave me a big smile which told me the lights were on but no one was home. Lovely girl but clearly not an intellectual.

Tuesday February 27

Howard and the lads disappeared up the mountain. Couldn't admit to the boys that I was a novice so I said I'd join them a little bit later as I wanted to give Emma some chat. Talking to her was like dropping stones into a well and never hearing the splash. Her wheel is spinning but the hamster's dead. But absolutely cracking bod. Gave her minimum amount of conversation required to cover the fact that I drove a Porsche and had a six figure package and then went out, leaving her to draw the obvious conclusions.

Looked at the map of ski runs and decided that as I couldn't turn yet I should take one of the straightish black routes. Got into the cable car thinking I'd get off at the first stop. Other people in the cable car all had white lips, reflective goggles and what looked like oxygen masks. Began to feel that I may have slipped up somewhere. Got out at the top of the mountain. Not a tree in sight. Edged over to the start of the run which looked like a vertical wall of ice. Spent rest of the day edging down on my backside. Stood up on my skis once, leant forward like I was picking up something and found myself at Mach 2 within seconds, heading for thin air. Stopped myself by snowploughing with my face for 50 yards. Got back to the village in the dark. Had to admit to boys that I couldn't ski for toffee. Orgy of piss taking followed.

Wednesday February 28

Emma looking fantastic at breakfast. Really wouldn't mind getting my hands on her moguls. Tried the nursery slopes. Packed full of children and old women with walking sticks. Edged over to the ski lift, a little button on a rope job that you put between your legs. Had to shove my way through swarms of school kids. Grabbed the button, shoved it between your legs and sat down. The bloody thing couldn't take my weight, I fell over and it dragged me by the nads all the way to the top. Possibly lowest point of my adult life.

Brushed myself down and started slipping down hill. Sat down on back of my skis and started gathering speed. Found myself heading directly towards party of school kids half-way up slope. Tried digging in pole like rudder but couldn't turn in either direction. Shot through middle of school party, wiped out 15 kids and the ski instructor and finally came to a stop in a snow bank while one of my skis carried straight on to the village. Pulled off goggles and found Emma laughing at me uncontrollably. New low in adult life. Pretended I found it funny as well and managed to crank out world's most stilted laugh.

MARCH

Thursday March 1

Howard went off at crack of dawn for some heli-skiing. I checked to see if Emma was impressed by this but she was too busy scraping burnt eggs off the hob. She actually said she was very impressed by my stunt skiing. I died inside but every pig's ear has a silk lining because she volunteered to coach me on the nursery slopes. As she was wearing what seemed to be a fur-lined swimsuit this was a major incentive to keep on my feet and follow her tight little curves (in the snow).

Once we were on the slopes I started chatting her up again but every time I was on the point of delivering a famous Weak bit of chat, the tips of my skis crossed over and I went arse over salopettes into the snow. She seemed to find all this a lot funnier than anything I said or did to deliberately impress her, as if I was just being a total nob for her entertainment. At the end of the day I was bruised from head to foot and seemed to have underpants full of ice. Emma said she'd never laughed so hard in her life. Only bright spot was that Howard had been dropped on wrong mountain and was now in Switzerland.

Friday March 2

Howard called Emma on his mobile to say he was being dropped at the top of the mountain again and would try to go down the right side. Talked on the phone a little bit too much for my liking. I spent all day practising those nifty little stops where you go from 60–0mph with a quick side skid. Just before tea I saw Howard and the boys sitting having a drink at the ski bar. I went in pretty fast, realised as I approached that I was slightly out of control and that the snow became brown slush next to the café. Had to stop somehow so did massive side skid and sprayed entire café with brown slush. Had to buy everyone drinks to avoid returning home with entire body in plaster cast. Emma thought I was just the funniest person she'd ever met. She likes a part of me I never knew I had i.e. the great steaming idiot part. But if this idiot can get his hands on her charlies then I can take the pain.

Saturday March 3

Spent all day on the slopes with Emma. Have perfected crashing into her so we both end up in the snow with me on top of her. Missed her once and ended up skiing backwards in front of an oncoming snow plough. Finally stopped myself with a neat crash into a tree. Howard suddenly swooped down out of nowhere on his snowboard and started chatting to Emma in what I could see he thought was a suave kind of way. It took me half an hour of frantic herringboning to get back up and join them.

In the evening went into town for dinner with the boys and various assorted totty we'd scraped together over the week. Howard admitted to me in the loos that he had a bit of thing for Emma and was going to try and get his leg over. I didn't like the sound of this and realised I better start moving my leg in her direction. On the dance floor Howard said I danced like I skied. I did an impression of me ploughing at full tilt into Howard and he did a very realistic impression of falling over and breaking his leg. In fact he had broken his leg and had to be rushed to hospital to have it plastered. I told him he wouldn't be getting his leg over anything for a while and gave Emma a good snogging on the way back to chalet.

Sunday March 4

Got the coach back. We were all in high spirits partly due to the crate of wine we had on the back seat and partly because I had Emma's phone number in my pocket and knew that I was well on the way to some serious après-ski boffing. I felt like a bit of a teenager again. Emma also felt like a teenager I can tell you, which makes a change from the biological mother.

We all took it in turns to write obscenities on Howard's plaster. I wrote 'Finally you've got a part of your body that

stays stiff'. I remembered to write it on his ankle so that his
trousers wouldn't cover it up at work. We sang the entire
flight back, taking requests from the whole aircraft apart from
ones to shut up and grow up. I bought some duty-free
perfume and only realised when I got home that I was acting
as if I had a girlfriend. Went to bed very happy despite the
news that Martin Padley had been airlifted from the pitch
with possible broken neck after nasty tackle by half opposing
team.

Monday March 5

Decided to have marketing department conference to launch
new dandruff shampoo (Scalpure) and to show department
full power of leadership (me). Foolishly got Renton-Willets
(Human Remains Director) involved who suggested fully
interactive day with brainstorming, syndicate working,
teambuilding, open and honest feedback and motivational
speaker. Switched off after he said interactive and didn't
really catch the rest. Anyway he can do the donkey work so I
told him it was his baby and he could run with it.

Have also decided to make Hayley more of a PA than
secretary, give her a bit more responsibility and show her
she's more than just a glorified tea maker. After work went to
gym with Howard. Sat on our favourite bikes just behind the
treadmills where lycra is tested to destruction. Cycled for 40
minutes but the little computer said we'd cycled just over a
mile, most of it down hill. But it's all good fresh air, that's the
main thing.

Tuesday March 6

Called in Renton-Willets for conference update. Told him I
liked the interactivity bit and I could be interviewed
interactively by serious newsreader or that fox from Channel
5. That would show the troops I wasn't afraid of a real
grilling (all questions pre-prepared obviously). Hayley
brought in tea that looked like gnat's pee. Told her to start

again and treat the tea bag is if it was the body of Ricky Martin.

Bill Peters sent over great new screen saver of missile-eye view of destruction of Iraqi bunker. Loaded it myself but couldn't get it to run properly. Called IT Helpdesk and asked them to send over low-level nerd to install it. IT No-Bloody-Help-Whatsoever-Desk said they didn't have anyone spare as the whole network had frozen.

Wednesday March 7

Conference update with Renton-Willets. Updated him on brainstorming thinking – I talk for an hour or so about innovation, creativity, leadership etc. and then after the conference they can brainstorm what they've heard. He didn't seem to catch on, so I spoke a bit louder (shouted actually) and told him to go away and brainstorm the precise instructions I'd given him. Hayley brought in some tea that looked like Mahatma Gandhi's urine sample (she's obviously not a fan of Ricky Martin). Accompanying biscuits included pink wafers. Told Hayley that Board Directors do not eat pink wafers. She said it was for Renton-Willets. Couldn't argue with that.

Got back to my desk and called IT Apathy Desk to demand one of their cyber-geeks come round at the double and get my screen saver up and running. Told me that network was still frozen. I don't blame it: if I had those anoraks fiddling with me, I'd freeze up pretty smartish.

Thursday March 8

Had very short meeting with Ken Carmichael. Terrible smell in room. Found out later it was his fruit tea. Told Hayley that I don't want meetings with fruit tea drinkers. Renton-Willets still plaguing me with ideas for team building trust exercises. I told him that I wasn't going to close my eyes, fall backwards and trust that I'll be caught by someone who'd just had one of my thermo-nuclear appraisals.

Had marathon brainstorming lunch with Bill Peters with a frightening amount of red. (Discovered afterwards Bill was so cabbaged he tried to go back to work in a company he'd left eight years ago. They probably just assumed he'd been away on an extra long lunch.) Came up with brilliant new idea for teambuilding – instead of holding hands and skipping we can have video of great rugby teams in action – with *Simply the Best* in the background. Got back and found IT nerd at my desk tinkering with my computer – informed me that my screen saver had caused whole network to freeze. Told him to get the screen saver up and running before he started fooling about with the network.

Friday March 9

Had long chat with Hayley, told her I was thinking of increasing her responsibilities, letting her use her initiative etc. Then took her down to kitchen and showed her how to make a proper cup of tea. Told rest of the Board about conference with my speech, interview with me, rugby video and motivational speech from me. Clare O'Keefe (Ops Director – Boadicea in a skirt) said conference sounded like an evening in the pub with me. Thought this was spot on until I realised it wasn't a compliment. Threw my rattle out of the pram at that point and told her if she could do better she was welcome. Bloody woman slid proposal across the table which I had to read there and then. To pacify the Amazon hordes I said it all looked rather good and we should go with it. Then I saw that it was written by Giles Renton-Bloody-Willets. That's the last time I interact with him.

Saturday March 10

I woke up with a song in my heart and a tent in my duvet. Date with the divine Emma today who is back from being chalet totty. Thank God. The thought of her spending every week with people like me makes me shudder. Have booked the swankiest restaurant I know. Very exclusive, very dark and very louche. It's basically a glorified waiting room for the bedroom. Had a good old session in the bathroom sending my flannel to remote parts of the body; you never know who's going to be visiting those places next once you get stuck into marathon acts of darkness.

Met Emma at the restaurant. I started telling her a bit about myself and before I knew it the coffee was being served. Jazz band started up about then with these trashy looking spongers making a hell of racket. Emma suddenly got all excited and said the pianist was her ex-boyfriend Colin Gilbey. He came over and a ranker, more wrecked looking piece of crud it would be difficult to imagine. I got up to say hello and his handshake was like taking a sock out of the laundry basket. He then rolled cigarettes so thin you might just as well have smoked the paper by itself. I offered him one of my Marlboros and he pocketed it. He'll probably make four hundred roll ups from it. We ended up giving him a lift home in our taxi. I was so off my stride I dropped Emma off as well and went home alone.

Sunday March 11

I was in such a bad mood I volunteered to take the kids. I went round to Kate's and then we went to the Victoria and Albert museum to see the dinosaurs. Realised I'd got the wrong museum and had to make up something about dinosaurs hibernating some of the year. Took them with me to rugby training where they witnessed Martin Padley getting his metal neck brace caught in the wing mirror of a passing Range Rover. He got dragged a couple of hundred yards and most of the stitches on his head popped open but was priceless entertainment for the kids.

When I got home there was a message on the answerphone from Emma saying she'd had a really good time and that Colin thought I was really sweet. That's all I need. I can't believe Emma would get within spitting distance of a bloke like that, let alone go out with him. Went down to the

Blue Boar and had a good few pints with Mike the Miserable. Bad mistake as everything you say that's bad he has something far worse which has just happened on his farm. Got home very late and completely cabbaged and then stupidly left long, tortured message on Emma's answerphone. My mother phoned shortly afterwards saying she'd got the message and was I all right. Want to bed angry, confused and shockingly bladdered.

Monday March 12

Arrived latish after an early meeting with my duvet ran over. Shirley on reception asked me whether I worked for Smokehouse which she does without fail every time I arrive after 9.30am. I sometimes think she's going to check behind my ears for dirt.

Found my desk weighed down by huge glossy brochure from HR Department – 'Your Behaviour is Our Business'. Inside it told us we were all the brand and that we should behave in a way that reflected the core values of the Smokehouse brand. I binned it in a decisive way that reflected the Smokehouse reputation for immediate, forceful action. At that moment Giles Renton-Willets (weirdo HR Director) popped into my office and asked me what I thought of the big new initiative from his department. I said there was certainly a place for that sort of thing.

Tuesday March 13

Got in slightly late because of appalling traffic which forced me to wait at home until it had completely cleared. Was crossing the car park when Bill Peters started shouting from his window that I wasn't walking in a way that was consistent with brand values. He finished by shouting 'Report to HR! Report to HR!' I didn't know which was funnier; Bill Peter's shouting or the look on the face of Sir Marcus Rigby (CEO and God's representative on Earth) standing outside reception with important business contact.

Shirley's acid remark of the day was to ask whether I was paid undertime – money for coming in late. I'm beginning to wonder whether having someone that sarcastic sitting on reception is reflecting well on the company. That afternoon Bill e-mailed me suggesting we should write a response to HR brochure called 'Our Behaviour is None of your Business'.

Wednesday March 14

Arrived late and told Shirley I hadn't heard the alarm. She recommended turning it on. At Board meeting I asked whether Renton-Willet's pony-tail was consistent with Smokehouse brand values. Or come to that whether Renton-Willets himself was consistent with brand values. We were ahead on points until Bill suggested a programme of selective breeding of graduates to fit the brand. (I'm all in favour as long as I can select and breed them.)

There's something about this new HR offensive that's got right up Bill's nose. We went for lunch which extended into dinner and then I can't remember anything much after that apart from Bill asking the entire wine bar where the company was going and why it was in a handbasket.

Thursday March 15

Arrived slightly late because of bad two-leg-in-one-trouser-hole situation at home. Noticed a police car outside reception. Apparently there had been some kind of break in. Shirley asked if it was me coming to work early. Len on security called me down to see the CCTV footage. It showed someone shockingly like Bill Peters weaving across the car park. The next bit showed him arriving naked in the HR Department. He took a copy of 'Your Behaviour is Our Business' and rolled it up very tightly. Anyone who plays rugby knew what was coming next. He inserted one end where the sun never shines, set fire to the other end and then goose-stepped round the office with the flaming brochure behind him. He then stood for a minute flicking V-signs at Renton-Willets' office. It was Bill's version of constructive feedback.

Friday March 16

Emergency board meeting started with a thermo-nuclear bollocking from Sir Marcus while Bill nodded his head sagely as if he was talking about someone else. Things were looking bad for Bill when I suddenly had a thought. I interrupted Sir Marcus (which is like handing him your P45 for signature) and asked why we had cameras inside the office. Were these spy cameras consistent with our brand values of openness and honesty? Renton-Willets muttered something about transparency before going redder than a dotcom. Sir Marcus told Renton-Willets he would be facing a disciplinary procedure if he weren't already in charge of disciplinary procedures. Then in a Solomon-like masterstroke, he punished Bill by telling him to write new staff behaviour guidelines. We decided to crack them over a few bottles of red with some top totty. As we left for lunch Shirley said, 'Goodnight'. There's a woman who understands business behaviour.

Saturday March 17

Big date with Emma. I said I would cook her dinner at my place so I had to get half of yellow pages round to tidy the flat, wash the sheets and cook the dinner. Made sure I had everything required for epic shunting session including half a hundredweight of rubberware, my best Cuban thong and various oils, creams etc. Checked the old Weak bod in mirror which was a bit of a mistake as some fat bastard had left their beer gut on my six pack. Went down to the gym to firm up a bit. Bumped into Howard and had a couple of G&Ts to relax before the workout. Got so relaxed decided not to bother with workout at all.

Emma arrived an hour late but she had a little gift for me. It was a slim volume of Tibetan poetry. Oh goody. I immediately simulated life-time admiration for all things Tibetan especially poetry of which sadly I couldn't get enough. Emma is so good looking she doesn't actually look real. I cracked open a bottle of red and we got relaxed together.

Sunday March 18

Woke up with profound headache and empty bed. Tried to remember what happened last night. Half a hundredweight of rubberware, creams etc. still intact so not sure if I got anywhere useful. Emma came back from a jog and into the shower. I thought it would be good to get in the shower with her but it was fantastically crowded and I managed to get a shower head in the eye and nothing else anywhere that mattered. Finally, got her into bed and we got down to some traditional country pursuits. I held my end up nicely (as it were) but she seemed a bit languid. Maybe she was worn out by all that jogging. Still, bloody nice to look at.

Suddenly remembered it was my turn with the kids so rushed round to Kate's to get them. I wanted to lock them in a room with a video so I could get my batting average up but Emma insisted on playing with them. What a waste of a cracking bod. But at least the kids will report presence of world class totty in daddy's bed back to their biological mother. Fitted in some early evening rugby training on the scrum machine. Just before we left Martin Padley was doing a few last pushes when the machine was hit by a white van which pushed the scrum machine and Padley about four hundred yards across the pitch. Martin was OK apart from a shattered sternum but the scrum machine was a write-off.

Monday March 19

Got in rather late thanks to delayed bout of postnatal depression. Binned my post, deleted my e-mails and had an extended stroll through the totty-rich zones. Went to the canteen for lunch and found myself sitting next to a vegetarian. Urgent tightening up of interview and recruitment procedures obviously required. I'm not going to make a big effort to mix with the troops in the canteen if it means sitting next to some goateed weirdo nibbling a UVO – Unidentified Vegetarian Option. They should bring back the executive dining room where red-blooded males can eat red-blooded meat (and nap undisturbed for an hour or so).

Got back to the orifice to find another bloody sponsorship form clogging up my desk. Cycle against Third World debt for Pete's sake. Why not just sell the bicycle and send them the proceeds. If I get any more sponsorship forms we're going to have to start worrying about First World debt. Got priority e-mail telling me to attend crisis meeting tomorrow with Sir Marcus Rigby. All very hush-hush.

Tuesday March 20

Very bad morning. Sponsorship form from Gavin Smedley for marathon in aid of ozone layer. Told him the CO_2 he'll be breathing out will knock a hole in it the size of a swimming pool. Promised him £10 for every minute he does under a time of three hours. No sooner had I got rid of that one when I got petition for more pot plants in office. Had to put my trotter down on that one. I know what happens – say yes to a rubber plant and in two weeks you're working in a rainforest.

Hush-hush crisis meeting with Sir Marcus. Turns out that one of our 2-in-1 shampoo and conditioners kills otters. What the hell are otters doing using our 2-in-1 shampoo and conditioners in the first place? At least they die with a lovely shiny-looking coat. Sir Marcus gave me poisoned chalice of sorting it all out. Had to go to gym to work off otter-induced stress. Howard was on rowing machine so I coxed for half an hour with several large G&Ts. Soon felt positively loving towards otters.

Wednesday March 21

Otter damage limitation exercise underway. Smokehouse now sponsors largest Otter Conservation Centre in Europe (only Otter Conservation Centre in Europe). Shampoo has been withdrawn immediately for further testing (not on otters). All primary schools to get otter colouring kit. For every otter picture submitted we put 3p towards otter therapy, nurturing, self-expression etc. Am thinking of registering as an otter. Not a bad life if you don't wash your hair too often.

Called in consultants for Environmental Audit. Was expecting bearded sandal-wearers with divining rods but they all seemed relatively normal. They recommended benchmarking environmental performance against best in sector. Lucky they came actually. Turned out crayons for colouring competition have more lead in than a church roof and would have decimated school population. You can't bloody win with all this environmental stuff.

Thursday March 22

Went to office in otter costume this morning. Nobody knew who I was. Hayley warned me to take it off because 'That Weak bastard doesn't have a sense of humour'. Returned an hour later minus costume and asked her to remove staples from 10,000 surplus company reports 'for recycling as part of our environmental effort'. Green revolution in full swing as Sir Marcus is now backing petition for greenery in every office. Bill Peters (Chemicals) is going to astroturf his office and if all right-minded directors do the same we can have a half decent putting course.

Initial results of Environmental Audit showed that we were slightly below Polish coal mining but well above Porton Down Chemical Warfare Establishment. But no room for complacency obviously. Apparently Bill Peters and Chemicals are responsible for 99 per cent of the damage. Not surprising considering he hasn't made a management decision of any sort for the last 22 years. But you can't knock him. Used to play rugby for London Belgians.

Friday March 23

Cycled to work. Only kidding. If we don't drive big cars with big engines the big oil companies won't make the big profits needed for the research into alternative sources of energy. Which is why cyclists and their ridiculous helmets are the main obstacle to tackling environmental issues. I cut up a couple on my way to the office just to do my bit for the environment.

Lunched with Bill Peters to alert him to the fact that he is a one-man Chernobyl. After second bottle of red he admitted that he had forgotten he was in charge of Chemicals. We had a couple of cigars and through the smoke I told Bill it was time for a clean-up. The smoke cleared and Bill wasn't there. He'd gone to siphon the python. Bill is a first rate bloke obviously, but will have to be sacrificed to the Otter. No doubt he'll be 'promoted' somewhere where competence isn't at a premium. Client Services Director is the usual resting place. Blokes like Bill are a threatened species. I'll have to organise a sponsored bike ride.

Saturday March 24

Went to the gym with Howard to get the old Weak musculature honed. That's the price you have to pay for going out with an überbabe. I looked at all the lycra'd totty in the gym and me and Howie agreed that the sixties were a massive cock-up. You had free love which was good but you only had raddled old hippies with flowers in their hair to lift your kaftan for, instead of hot working women with bodies like a sack of nuts.

Managed to get down to the Blue Boar for lunch and showed the boys a picture of Emma. They accused me of cutting her picture out of a catalogue and couldn't believe I'd pulled such a gorgeous looking piece. Had hot date with gorgeous looking piece that night. Took her to top restaurant and every head in the restaurant turned. Going out with her is just the same as driving a Porsche and, given what I paid for the meal, about as expensive. She said she'd like me to meet her family. I instinctively asked her if she had any sisters but that was probably not what she meant. We got back to her place for a bit of headboard hockey but it wasn't as good as you would imagine given her looks and my technique.

Sunday March 25

Spent the day in the park with Emma. I got a little bit soupy and asked her what she was looking for in a man. I had my mental checklist ready: tall, dark, handsome, Porsche, experienced, man of the world, great sense of humour etc. She started talking about sensitivity, empathy, intellect, passion for the truth, frailty. I began to lose the drift when she got to sensitivity but once she started talking about frailty I thought she might have misheard the question. Then she said it was everything that bloody Colin was. Naturally, I spat my dummy out on that one and asked her why she'd ever bothered to split up with him if he was so bloody perfect. Apparently he's too frail to commit. He'll be a lot frailer when he's got my knee wedged in his gonads and my Porsche hitting his bicycle at 150mph.

Took her back to my place for an extended duvet derby. Not brilliant if I'm honest. A little bit too much lying back and thinking of England from Emma. Can't help thinking that she might be thinking of that little runt Colin. The sooner I kill him the better it will be for everyone, including him. Rugby training cancelled because floodlights had all fused after Martin Padley accidentally short-circuited main generator and diverted 50,000 volts through his kidneys. Lights should be up and running by next week hopefully.

Monday March 26

I am on paid leave this weak or training as it's sometimes called. I've discovered that Smokehouse insists that all staff do 20 days training a year. Someone's obviously been trained in throwing money down the toilet. I have called up a list of training and you can do all sorts of vital industrial things like emotional intelligence and synchronised skipping. I thought it might be funny if I did an assertiveness course and scared the pants off all the little weeping girlies on it. Bill Peters and I tried to get on interpersonal skills together so we could get interpersonal with some fit graduate totty but Obergruppenführer Prothero from HR told us we could do that in our own time. In the end I picked creativity training, whatever the hell that is.

Met Howard at the gym. His leg is still in plaster but it meant he had all the lycra'd totty fawning over him and writing long messages that stopped a couple of adjectives short of his groin. He didn't have to bother with all the sweaty weight-lifting stuff either. I'll have to break the other one for him.

Tuesday March 27

Long drive to country house for creativity training. Should have checked whether they had a golf course as my back swing needs a bit of lateral thinking. Thought about getting arty: I've always fancied cutting a cow in half and shoving it in a perspex case. Probably make more money than I do currently and get some of that red hot arty totty who all go like Black and Decker sanders apparently. Have to be careful though: the day after you've shunted them round their studio, you're likely to find a plaster cast of your John Thomas on display at the Tate Gallery.

Met the other delegates over dinner. Nobody I recognised. Pale-faced IT and logistics types coming up for a drop of ultraviolet light most of them. Wouldn't know creativity if it burst through the wall of their stomachs. I had to fancy someone so I began to take a shine to one woman who was a bit of a BOBFOC – Body off Baywatch Face off Crimewatch – but I was getting very creative in imagining what I could do with her below the neck.

Wednesday March 28

Wore casual clothing as this is vital for creativity apparently. Bacon rolls for breakfast. Now that's what I call creative thinking. Some slaphead came out of the meeting room at 9.00 on the dot and barked at us to get inside. Not very free flowing and creative if you ask me. Tables arranged in primary school fashion with bucket of coloured pens on the table. No cows or chainsaws.

Slaphead started in by telling us that creativity was basically about making new connections. I decided that I was going to give him a hard time. Trainers love it when you give them a bit of feedback. He asked us to write down everything we knew about the Pope on one side of a piece of paper and then everything we knew about chocolate on the other side. He asked for two difficult aspects to connect and I gave him Polish and Hazelnut Whirl and then asked him whether he could make the connection. Slaphead said he could but more to the point could I. Of course I could but actually couldn't think of a damn thing and the rest of the group began to titter. Slaphead suddenly said. Polish, shoe polish, application in little swirls, hazelnut whirls. Before I could come back he'd moved on leaving me feeling a bit of a twonk.

Thursday March 29

Slaphead gave us an example of how we could be creative called Corporate Takeover, where we thought about how other companies would solve problems. The task was to develop a whisky aimed at women. I was given the task of tackling it as if I was Boots the Chemist. I was paired up with this half-wit from IT who was bleating on about serving it in white coats. I ignored him and thought about the fact that women generally don't like the taste or smell of whisky but it feels great when you've got it inside you (same old story). I thought why not make it in pill form so you can just swallow it and get the hit. Call them Snifters. I was very pleased with this idea. My IT half-wit didn't like it, but if we start listening to what IT have to say, we might as well all pack up and go home.

When we had to present our ideas to the group I gave them the full sales presentation on Snifters along with packaging and advertising concepts. Everyone was impressed. Slaphead suddenly got a roll of twenties out of his pocket, peeled one off and gave it to me for having a top idea. Boy did that focus the rest of the group for the rest of the session. Have to try that kind of incentivisation in my department. Later on had good night in the bar with all the delegates and tried to persuade BOBFOC to come to my room and get creative. She said she would rather eat pig's vomit which I thought was unnecessarily graphic but I took it as a definite maybe.

Friday March 30

Woke up with a gang of dwarves trying to saw the top of my head off. Took a handful of Anadin Full Strength but what I really needed was a hair of the dog. If I'd had a Snifter I would have taken it. On the drive back I couldn't stop thinking about my idea for Snifters. The idea of having an emergency G&T in your back pocket for those arse-aching IT presentations was a cracker. You could have variety packs which would be like having a whole pub with you or vending machines in railway stations. The possibilities were endless. I could see all the advertising already taking shape. I was thinking about it so hard that I missed my turning and ended up in Kettering – somewhere I'd hoped to pass my whole life without visiting.

Saturday March 31

Extraordinary day. I woke up early and started developing a business plan for Snifters. Whichever way I looked at it, it was a winner. I just couldn't understand why nobody had done it before. I decided I would have a word with the lab rats in R&D when I got back to work to see whether there were any technical obstacles.

Went down to the Blue Boar for lunch. Barney and The Terminator were there. He was chatting with Evan and Mike the Miserable about what a funny lot the Chinese were. I told them my idea and they all said they would drink to it. Evan especially liked the idea of smuggling a few Snifters back home to help him cope with Beryl the Peril. I met Howard at the gym that evening and he said it was possibly the daftest idea he'd ever heard in his entire life which as far as I'm concerned is a green light for the whole project.

APRIL

Sunday April 1

Was slumped in the sofa reading paper with one hand and scratching scrotum with the other, when there was a ring at the door. I just hoped it wasn't Emma as I hadn't exposed her to the more relaxed side of my personality yet. Bugger me rigid!! It was the little toerag Colin who wanted to talk to me about something. At first I thought he was going to do the right thing, apologise for existing as such a mucky little specimen and volunteer to do away with himself. But no. He started talking about how I was a man of the world, had been around the block, knew a thing or two etc. etc. I'd almost got my chequebook out when he suddenly dropped the bombshell that he was going to propose to Emma and wanted to get my advice on what the best approach would be. If ever there was a time for a quick Snifter that was it. I told him it was a big step, I would think about it and get back to him (my usual reply in business when I've been caught with my pants well and truly down).

Rugby match against Southmoor Saracens. It was a close fought contest where we won most of the fighting and they won most of the points. In one of the more brutal scraps one of their prop forwards lost two of his teeth which we later found in the back of Martin Padley's neck.

Monday April 2

Black Monday!! Executive Club Gold Card about to slip to Silver Card. Might as well announce you're a Junior Brand Manager over the tannoy. Asked Hayley to arrange immediate flight to Miami office before end of week to get points needed to avoid the drop. Sir Marcus going on holiday so no one need know. However, slight ointment in fly because before he left the building the Carcass (Sir Marcus) summoned me in for thermo-nuclear roasting over marketing department overspend. Accused marketing of being just a lot of overseas jollies and colour photocopying. I told him that he was way off the mark and what we were doing was actually customer-driven colour photocopying and overseas jollies. He demanded immediate 25 per cent cut in marketing cost burn rate and absolutely no more gratuitous Executive Clubbing this year. Lucky I spoke to Hayley before the meeting.

Tuesday April 3

Didn't sleep well. Gold Card expiry playing on mind. Woke up in a cold sweat after visions of me sitting in the back of the plane with a Blue card and everyone coming down from Club to laugh at me as I sat wedged between two economy style people. Got into orifice and Hayley pointed out that we didn't actually have a Miami office but had booked flight anyway. Smart cookie, Hayley.

Will have to risk wrath of the Carcass on flights but decided to go through department budget with fine tooth comb for superfluous expenditure that wasn't related to my lifestyle. Discovered we could save a few quid by changing our two Caribbean Holiday competition prize winners' flights to 84 hour Aeroflot flight via Murmansk and North Korea. (The judge's decision is final and I'm the judge.) Had long lunch with Bill Peters with just the one bottle of red each – economies have to start somewhere. He recommends outplacing (sacking) a junior marketing spod to save on salary and then have them work out their notice period by combing budget for further savings. Smart cookie, Bill Peters.

Wednesday April 4

Got in rather late because I ran over somebody on way to work leaving nasty dent in Porsche. Knocked him clean over a hedge. Threatened to sue him for leaving the scene of an accident which shut him up. Finally got to work and called in junior marketing spod – girl called Debbie – works in research or something incredibly low impact. Told her she had two major opportunities. Firstly, to analyse financial savings for the department and then to add financial analysis to her CV when she applies for her next job. Of course she burst into tears. Why do women always take being singled out and sacked so personally?

Left office early after giving Hayley year's worth of expenses to sort out before I get back from Miami (she'd only go shopping otherwise). On the way out Shirley on reception asked if I was going for a late lunch. I'll have to put her straight one day that if you work on reception you're supposed to receive sarcasm not dish it out. Met Howard at gym and did 70 lengths of the pool. Not bad I thought until I realised it was the hot tub.

Thursday April 5

Strode into Club Lounge at Heathrow, making straight for the FT and G&T and nearly walked straight into the Carcass togged up in Hawaiian shirt with bags packed for holiday on Miami beach. Managed to stifle burst of laughter and walked out backwards without being spotted. Marched straight up to desk, whacked down Gold Card and insisted on upgrade to First to avoid the Carcass, his Hawaiian shirt and mother of all bollockings for another gratuitous overseas jolly. The pitiful low-life slime behind the desk said the last seat had gone. Tried fear of flying routine, then corporate travel buyer with massive budget tack and finally abject grovelling. Nothing!! Waited until desk was clear and asked her in a whisper to be downgraded to economy. Possibly worst moment of my life. Spent seven hours wedged in Slum Clearance (economy) with baby on one side and Blue Card holder on the other. Didn't know which was more upsetting.

Friday April 6

After quick 'meeting' with G&T in Club Lounge in Miami, got the red-eye back with points safely on Gold Card. No one I knew in Club just the normal solid higher-rate tax payers quietly driving the world economy forward. Studied route map in in-flight magazine and started to plan marketing strategy for next year. Early long haul marketing push in New Zealand and Polynesia clearly required to avoid embarrassing last-minute flap with Gold Card again.

After landing went straight into office. Hayley was out shopping. Debbie (the sackee) had volunteered to do my expenses – alarm bells rang through the jet lag. Found report on my desk itemising my expenses and possible 25 per cent savings on them, all copied to Sir Marcus. Called Debbie in for quiet team meeting. Agreed she should stay on if both reports were in my hands by end of play. Smart cookie, young Debbie. Bit of a setback with her but I reckon I still ended the week ahead on points.

Saturday April 7

Picked up the ankle biters from Kate first thing. Not normally terribly keen on the soft side of maintenance as HR would no doubt call child visits. I should have argued harder in court for less access. If you're going to be an absentee father you should be allowed to do it properly. However, today I was quite pleased to have something to occupy me as I was in a bit of a quandary as to the Emma/Colin thing. I sat in the park for a couple of hours keeping a careful eye out for young single mothers and occasionally making sure the kids weren't juggling with dog shit or ripping their heads open on exposed scaffolding. Thought about perhaps having a man to man with Colin, pointing out that he really didn't amount to a man and that he should leave the field clear for the big boys.

Went and sat in McDonald's for a couple of hours. Emma for all her fine body had banged on about Colin's wonderful frailty and how attractive that was. If I give him a good punching it might leave him so frail and vulnerable, Emma would just have to go and nurse him for ever and ever. Handed back kids. Kate's mother gave me a look that would have contaminated soil for a thousand years.

Sunday April 8

Rugby match against Charney. We had one of the best matches of the season and only lost by a whisker. Martin Padley scored a last-minute try which brought us within 20 points of Charney. We all bundled on top of him to celebrate which left him with two slipped discs but otherwise pretty chuffed.

Arrived at Blue Boar just as Becky was opening up. She poured me a pint and then I watched her big arse circle the pub in pursuit of a mop. There was a message there if only I could see it. After three quick pints I was beginning to wonder whether a round of gratuitous sex with Becky would help put the Emma conundrum in perspective. Evan slunk through the back door. I said hello but held off from conversation until he'd downed his 'Beryl sorbet' – a quick pint that gets the taste of marriage out of his mouth.

A few minutes later The Terminator appeared round the bar closely followed by Barney. I told them about the Emma situation and after we'd all considered the various emotional complexities and ambiguities of the situation we thought it would probably be best if I punched his lights out. We then got down to some serious refreshment. After last orders I found myself round at Emma's. She was wearing a silk dressing gown with a floor to crotch slit that revealed one of the finest legs on God's earth. I was so moved I accidentally asked her to marry me. Then I think I must have passed out.

Monday April 9

Arrived late as I'd spent a good couple of hours trying to remember exactly what I'd said the night before. Spent the rest of the morning in the photocopier room running off 10,000 rugby club news letters. Amazing how long it takes. Might just as well take it to a printer. I heard two secretaries at the coffee machine talking about the top totty in the office. I thought how demeaning – can't women see that we're more than just sex objects. It was a little bit embarrassing listening to them but I didn't want to walk past them with a box full of rugby club newsletters.

After about half an hour's continual chit-chat they decided that Ross Fulbright (Sales Director) had highest shaggability factor. Then they went through just about every bloke in the phone book but didn't mention me. Which was pretty demeaning as I seemed to be the only person who wasn't a sex object. They went on talking for hours so I had to phone one of their desks from my mobile. Someone shouted that it was me on the phone and the other said what about Weaky. The only bit of her answer I caught was 'body'. Couldn't decide whether she'd said I had a great body or over my dead body. Gave myself the benefit of the doubt.

Tuesday April 10

Still can't remember what I said to Emma on Sunday. Her phone's been continually engaged so either I said something really good or really bad. My gut feeling is it's probably good for her bad for me. My other headache is the annual company conference on Friday and the fact that I haven't got a bloody thing to say. Marketing are supposed to be the stars at these things but we've done precisely sod all since last year and what we have done has been a disaster.

Old Shaggability Fulbright let it be known in the Board meeting that the sales figures are the best ever. Of course he's hit all his targets but then they were probably pathetically low in the first place. He should try marketing – building brands takes a lot more *cojones* than just tootling round the country picking up orders in your Mondeo. He then had the cheek to say that his team were really beginning to build awareness of the brand. As if a sales team could ever build awareness of anything other than their lack of taste in clothing. I saw Giles Renton-Willets after the meeting who said Fulbright was getting a good profile in the company. I didn't like the sound of that. Him and his bloody profile.

Wednesday April 11

I am worried about this profile thing. IT get all sorts of
Brownie points if they can keep our machines up and running
for two days on the trot. Accountants don't need to get a
high profile because they've got us all by the balls anyway.
Everyone has to be nice to HR because they do our salaries. I
need some kind of major coup to get some attention. Spoke
to our PR agency about raising marketing profile and more
specifically raising my profile within the organisation
(including shaggability factor if possible). They asked me out
for an immediate lunch which is their standard response. They
booked a top restaurant, wheeled out three of their top totty
and I felt better already.

Lunch was more of an event that I'd bargained for. We
were sitting at the table next to Posh Spice with lots of
photographers wheeling round her. I got a little bit over-
excited and knocked a bottle of wine over one of the PR
totty who let out a very choice expletive, especially from
someone with a triple-barrelled name who had no doubt
finished top of her finishing school.

Thursday April 12

Shirley congratulated me on my engagement on my way in
which solved the problem of what I'd said on Sunday and also
confirmed the fact that female gossip is the world's most
effective form of communication. Sat down to plan my
conference speech. Absolute disaster. A two minute silence
would be most appropriate for our performance so far this year.
Will just have to pad it out with mythical plans for the future.

Mobile started ringing mid-morning and carried on
continuously all day. Apparently there is a photo in the
evening paper of the wine spilling incident. They've cut out
the top totty getting soaked so it looks like me and Posh
Spice are sharing some kind of private joke. The PR agency
said that was their plan all along. I wasn't going to complain
although in an ideal world we would have had a couple of our

weaker brands also in shot. Went to the gym with Howard after work to see whether I could capitalise on my new found celebrity status. I couldn't so I ended up having to exercise which was a bit of a waste of time.

Friday April 13

PR and Advertising agencies reported in with the work I'd asked them to do overnight (if they wanted to keep my business). They've cut together a special interview with me and Posh Spice. I ask her a question about our brands and she says something completely unrelated. Very funny and a very good way of avoiding saying anything about our brands. Started my speech with, 'As I was saying to Posh ... ' and it was a rock concert from then on. They won't remember a thing about Shaggability Fulbright and his bloody sales figures that's for sure.

Profile is all about perception rather than reality and no one is further from reality than marketing. Then spent the evening at the hotel bar trying to find out whether my personal shaggability factor had gone up. A little bit of the Spice magic had rubbed off on me and I was determined to rub it off on someone else, preferably with a high shaggability factor of their own.

Saturday April 14

Flight to Malaga to meet Emma's parents and start reaping the grim harvest of my big mouth and its propensity to operate independently of my brain. My life could not have been transformed more if I'd actually had gender realignment. In fact it feels like I have had gender realignment because every spare waking moment I now have is spent planning for shopping, shopping or taking back shopping. Before I could say 'only joking' we now have a wedding list longer than the logistics requirements for the Normandy Landings. Emma wants to have the full monty Hello! style wedding which means Goodbye! to the contents of my bank account. I've seen it all before so I was rather hoping to skip the formalities and get down to the honeymoon stage. The only bright spot is that Colin has dropped off Emma's radar like Flight 316 to Bermuda. The main thing on my mind is how I'm going to explain to Evan in the Blue Boar how I managed to get married again when I'd already managed to wriggle under the wire once.

Sunday April 15

Emma's dad Maurice is a tomato grower. But he seems to have a very big house and very few tomatoes. I asked what he did before retirement and Emma said he was a businessman which I immediately took to mean a major league crook because no one in business ever refers to themselves as a businessman. He had a handshake that demanded money with menaces and the social graces of a randy pit bull – in that the more affection he showed me the more frightened I became.

Emma's mum Maureen looked like Emma with the lights out. She said virtually nothing and when she did open her mouth, immediately looked at Maurice for approval. If you've got to have a mother-in-law you might as well have one like her with the muzzle on. Not a bad looking woman either. She was still ahead in the race against gravity but gravity was gaining fast. The girls went off to talk about girls' things which left us men to have the world's most stilted conversation about the branding of tomatoes. Luckily he'd laid on some stiff ones and I relaxed. Told him about Snifters and he said if I ever wanted a business partner I was to look no further than him and some of his 'associates'. Wish I'd kept my mouth shut.

Monday April 16

Went on Diversity Training morning organised by the girlies from Human Remains. I am now gender and culturally aware and prepared to celebrate and encourage diversity (unlike some of the other bastards on the course). Which reminds me, there is a scorching new secretary in the building!! Apparently good old Bill Peters has got a new freshly minted one called Jane Edwards. The old one could type like the teleprinter but was aesthetically challenged as we politically correct directors like to say.

After work had a long session at the gym with Howard. Probably longer than it should have been as I accidentally fell asleep on one of the mats during a particularly long stretch. Howard thought it would be amusing to leave me sleeping for the entire evening while everyone worked out around me. Probably still sore about me getting Emma and him getting broken limb.

Tuesday April 17

Arrived so late I hardly had time to bin post, delete e-mails and cancel appointments before lunch. Over epic lunch at Mr Bojangles, Bill let slip after a third bottle of red that Sir Marcus had secretly let loose some management consultants in the company to see where improvements could be made. I suggested that a good start would be to get rid of the management consultants as they're just an extended sneer with an invoice attached.

Got back to the office and finally met the yummy Jane in the corridor. Absolute top drawer totty in an encouragingly diverse kind of way. Asked her how she was settling in, getting on with Bill etc. She admitted that she hadn't actually seen much of him. I said that if she wanted to see more of Bill she should get herself a job behind the bar at Mr Bojangles. She already knew who I was, so I asked her out for lunch for 'familiarisation'. She accepted like a shot so obviously haven't lost the old Weak pulling power.

Wednesday April 18

Had unsavoury meeting with Alec McIver a management consultant who sat in my office with brain humming like nuclear power station. I asked him whether he'd ever actually run a business. Of course he hadn't but he did have an MBA from Exeat or somewhere and spoke 17 languages – no doubt meaningless jargon in all of them. He wanted to talk to my team about delegation and empowerment but I told him firmly that when it came to empowerment and delegation the buck stopped with me.

Timothy Smallwood (Finance Director) stopped me in the corridor to warn me that the entertainment expenses on my credit card were now larger than marketing budget for some of our smaller products. I explained that brands were a complex matrix of emotional values that needed considerable amount of lunching to support. This didn't impress him and he skulked off to eat his smelly little cost-efficient sandwiches.

Thursday April 19

Arrived in the office late due to the wrong kind of woman on the road. Some old dear in a brightly coloured dress stepped out in front of me and went thumping over the top of the car like the swirling brushes of a carwash. Didn't clean as well as I'd hoped and I had to hang around for hours to make a statement. The statement naturally included strong recommendations about keeping that sort of idiot pedestrian locked in their homes during working hours when higher rate tax payers need to move rapidly from place to place adding value without being assaulted at every turn.

When I finally got in, Alec the consultant was sniffing around my department doing a little time and motion study. I said I thought it was time he was in motion. He smiled in an expensive kind of way and tapped something into his wafer-thin laptop. (Something is very wrong when consultants have thinner laptops than the people who pay their bills.) I told smart Alec that I ran a tight ship and that if he wanted economies he should be knocking on Operations door where the main operation seems to be pouring money down the drain. As he left I noticed he had my credit card statements in some sort of freezer bag as if they were forensic evidence. Where was he when the Gestapo needed him?

Friday April 20

Finally, lunch with the gorgeous Jane Edwards. Got a quiet table at Mr Bojangles (made sure Bill Peters was safely in Paris on business trip). Gave her some very high-octane chat, made sure my Porsche keys were not inconspicuous and told her the wide variety of corporate entertainment opportunities I had at my disposal. She seemed very interested in these, especially the travel options. Sadly Bill had bagged the freebie to Paris otherwise I would have had her on that plane before you could say 'chocks away'. Managed to get round to her love life and asked her what kind of man she was after. She got all coy and I teased her that it was probably someone like super-geek Alec. She laughed and said she wouldn't want to go out with her boss. Then she got the bill and I noticed her cheque book said Jane Richards and she had a very non-secretarial gold card. Pennies started dropping fairly heavily. On the way back to the office I tried to withdraw everything I'd said since I met her. She said that I'd helped her with lots of cost cutting improvements to recommend especially in the travel and entertainment area. Nasty piece of work. The sooner she gets gender sensitivity training the better.

Saturday April 21

Have decided to get consultants in to look at ongoing expenditure on wedding plans. Getting married to Emma is beginning to make getting divorced from Kate look cheap. In fact the thought had crossed my mind that if I divorced Emma now I'd probably be saving money in the long run. But that might take the shine off our relationship and we don't want that oily rag Colin Gilbey sniffing around again. Took Emma up to see my parents. Went up in the Porsche deliberately because there's very little room for shopping.

There's also the fact that my mother has a nasty habit of clearing every item of junk from the house, wrapping it in old newspaper and giving it to anyone getting married as a 'wedding present'. Don't know why she doesn't just hire a skip like the rest of us.

Sunday April 22

As usual my father spent the entire weekend in the armchair he grew up in with his eyes glued to Sky Sports, sipping his way through a litre bottle of sherry. He showed his usual level of sensitivity by asking how Kate and the children were and why they hadn't been to visit for so long. Mother kept herself busy in the kitchen. She's a bit off her chump these days and there's hardly an inch of her body which isn't covered by a hormone patch. Didn't stop her suddenly bursting into tears over some minor cooking glitch. She then howled like a bereaved wolf for half an hour. When the noise finally abated she said she just loved weddings. Didn't sound much like it. I could tell Emma was pleased to get out of there. Not half as pleased as I was. I'm thinking seriously of writing the wrong date on their wedding invitation.

Got back in time for evening rugby training. We threw a few balls around for a while and then retired to the bar. It was Martin Padley's birthday so we gave him the bumps. One half of us thought he was 31 rather than 32 so we let go of our end one bump early and he cracked his skull open on the floor. He was a little bit concussed but not so you'd notice after we'd all tucked into some serious refreshment.

Monday April 23

Innovation task force this week. I still think my idea for Snifters is world class so I'm going to put that in front of the group. We take innovation very seriously at Smokehouse. Well we talk about it very seriously which I'm sure is the same thing. During innovation week each day is spent with cross-functional teams examining a new idea for a product. Then we cross-examine its functional benefits. And then when we get to the last moment and find we've agreed on nothing, a tired and cross team go eeny-meeny-miny-mo and we pick one idea for development. Bill Peters is on the team as he has rightly identified it as a week's paid leave with the brain in neutral.

Idea for day one was a fragranced moisturiser for men. I kept a very low profile on this one as I don't want to get all enthusiastic about it and come across as a cantering homosexual. Besides which Bill Peters piped up and said that more and more men were exploring their feminine side and perhaps Smokehouse should take the opportunity to explore this market. Everyone looked at Bill to check he wasn't taking the piss, decided he wasn't and then nodded agreement.

Tuesday April 24

Got to the group just on time after an epic lock-in at Mr Bojangles with Peters the night before. Had beginnings of world's worst hangover so reacted badly when I heard the big idea for Tuesday – vegan fish fingers. Vegans shouldn't be given treats like fish fingers after they've made every one else's life a misery for years. They should just sit cross-legged in their squats and eat lentils and wood shavings as far as I'm concerned. I strongly objected to a good global capitalist company like Smokehouse wasting its valuable time cooking their dinner for them.

Clare O'Keefe laughed her headmistress laugh. Every time I make a serious business point she laughs like it's a joke and every time I make a joke she takes it as a serious business point. I've got a nasty feeling she's doing it deliberately. Bill Peters said that vegans were a growth market and we had an opportunity to get in at the ground floor. More sage nodding, especially from O'Keefe.

Wednesday April 25

Next idea was something that came out of years of research and millions pounds of R&D. It was a shampoo that straightens your hair. I made the obvious joke about making sure you didn't splash it on your pubes in case your John Thomas ended up looking like Adolf Hitler. O'Keefe took this very seriously and sent the product back to the lab rats to spend another three years and 50 million straightening out this issue (as it were).

We moved on to the product for the following day which was an anti-flatulence baked bean. It costs twice as much as normal beans but gas output is halved. I shuddered to think who had done the research on this one. If he's not on permanent sick leave with incapacity benefit, he should be. I made the serious point that a much better product would be a baked bean which doubled your flatulence. You could double the price and a certain carefully targeted section of the market (i.e. men) would lap it up. O'Keefe almost paralysed with laughter.

Thursday April 26

Thursday's big idea was a sanitary product for women with a new bio-allergenic lining. O'Keefe presented it in more detail than we really needed at that time of the morning. It was clearly her pet idea as she gave it a list of benefits ranging from the absorbency of a Dyson to the empowerment of a new generation of women in the workplace. Of course if she'd said anti-flatulence baked beans were empowering a new generation of women in the workplace we'd all have to vote them through as well. Bill raised the very serious point that there was still VAT on sanitary items for women and perhaps we could incorporate a PR campaign against this at the launch. There was almost a group hot flush at the thought. Thank God Bill didn't look at me at this point.

Went to the gym after work. Did a few laps of the pool following this very shapely young thing. She began to get away and pretty soon I had her behind me looking up my trunks. Got out at that point.

Friday April 27

As we'd managed to do two products on Wednesday, I suggested to the group that we could look at a new idea from the marketing department. I showed them all the Snifters concept boards and O'Keefe laughed like a drain as if it was the funniest thing she'd ever seen. She said we weren't in the spirits business but I pointed out that she should look at it like a pharmaceutical (the clear subtext being that she should look at it without being a silly tart). For some reason everyone looked at Bill Peters assuming that he would be the target market for Snifters. I knew if Bill went wide-eyed with enthusiasm and started frothing at the mouth, everyone would ditch the idea as being only for crazed alcoholics.

Fortunately, I'd pre-briefed and thoroughly rehearsed Bill on his behaviour all week. He'd got top marks so far for getting right behind all the lunatic ideas of the week. All he had to do now was say that there was a germ of an idea in Snifters, but the major resources should go behind O'Keefe's favourite idea (the suffragette tampon). Bill said exactly that, everyone nodded sagely, remembering how thoughtful he'd been all week and forgetting for a moment that he was a crazed alcoholic. Snifters snuck through with a small development budget and only Bill and I knew that he had just earned himself the entire first shipment of Snifters and an Oscar for Best Supporting Actor.

Saturday April 28

Spent most of the day sitting in a cramped church hall with a lot of love struck adolescents in a marriage guidance day that Emma insisted we went on. I pointed out that it would cut into valuable shopping time but she still wanted to go. They separated the men from the women and in our separate teams we had to go through what we thought might be the potential 'pinch points' of the marriage. The priest made the mistake of asking me first and I'd covered three flip charts worth without drawing breath when we were called back to consult with the girls. The energy of the room dipped slightly as I read out my list. It was all I could do not to say at the end 'My advice to you is pull out now'. Fortunately Emma wasn't listening as she had to take an urgent call on her mobile from one of her mindless friends, Tish, probably reporting the location of a new wedding shop in North East England that we haven't yet visited.

Spent the evening determined to get some decent sexual return for massive financial investment into wedding. Was doing rather well until Emma's mobile went at the vital moment. She then spent five hours talking through the seating plan with her friend Tish. Got to the Blue Boar before last orders and joined the boys in a frank and free-ranging discussion of why the Russians are such a funny lot.

Sunday April 29

Woken up my Emma's mobile ringing two inches from my ear. Before I could fling it through the window Emma was receiving that morning's hot news about bridesmaids' dresses from Tish's 24-hour news service. Got myself showered, shaved and shitted and then went to get the papers. Finished reading them and wondered whether Emma fancied a quickie before lunch. Non-starter as she was still on the phone to Tish. Waited for a while and wondered whether it was worth trying while she was still on the phone. She carried on talking til lunchtime. Probably be cheaper if we had Tish living with us. When she finally got off the phone she wanted me to go shopping. I put my foot down and said I'd be at the Blue Boar if she needed me. Spent next four hours in John Lewis looking at the bottoms of plates.

Missed most of rugby training. Spirits were a bit down as the team captain had hurt his finger trying to operate the industrial crusher behind the clubhouse. We found out what the problem was eventually and managed to get Martin Padley out of the crusher (or most of him). But it was a nasty moment for the captain. Managed finally to get to the Blue Boar. Evan had a black eye which we all studiously avoided asking about. Angela was wearing a Wonderbra which supported our entire conversation for a good hour or two until we discovered there was a little mousy American at one end of the bar. We then finished off the evening discussing in rather loud voices why the Yanks had turned up late in two World Wars and then taken all the credit.

Monday April 30

Arrived late after doing some vital paperwork at home. Shirley asked whether this was reading the *Racing Post* on the lavatory. Uncannily perceptive that woman. May have to get her sacked. This week Smokehouse are going to acquire Acidix, a small chemical factory somewhere up north big on grime. They only make one very nasty chemical but it's supposed to be the next big thing in floor cleaning. The point of buying them up is so we have them inside the tent pissing out rather than outside pissing in.

Sir Marcus has asked me to communicate good news to the City. Could use PR agency but let's face it, PR is like having a pee in a wetsuit – you get a nice feeling doing it but no-one else notices any difference. Far better to take the City boys out for traditional ten course lunch and crack open a case of something eye-wateringly expensive. It's the only language they understand. Phoned my own stockbroker last thing and bought Acidix shares. Told him to sell immediately after takeover announcement when the shares will go through the roof. I will then trouser the money and tap dance off to the Maldives for a six-month holiday.

MAY

Tuesday May 1

Took the train up to Acidix and was surprised how many northerners there were in First Class. Very large mobile phones though. I was forced to make a lot of unnecessary calls with my GSM WAP headgear just to show them the technology they can expect in the north a couple of years from now. Arrived at Acidix in time for coffee. Was going to ask for a tall latte but they probably would have brought me a long ladder. Their MD said he was just a simple man who knew nowt about owt. Saved me having to say it.

The MD warned me that tests weren't quite complete on their wonder chemical. It cleaned floors spectacularly well but tended to burn through to the foundations. That's my kind of chemical. We could work that up into some kind of children's toy. I reassured him that if we didn't take a few risks with technology we'd all still be travelling around the country staring up the backside of horse. Told him not to worry about the technical details and that the acquisition was on track as far as Smokehouse was concerned. I shook hands all round and said they could look forward to less grimness up north in the near future. Took them out for an evening meal to engender team spirit and to supplement their patchy northern diet.

Wednesday May 2

Stroke of luck!! On the train back to London, managed to sit opposite very tidy piece of totty with exceptionally pert mobile phone. Got chatting to her (after five false starts) and told her about me being a corporate raider pillaging the north. Gave her insider tip to buy Acidix shares pronto. Told her about the new wonder chemical and laid it on thick about how one mopping will burn you out a new cellar. I got her pretty stoked up and gave her my card telling her if she was interested in big tips I was her man. Shame she had to get off at the next stop. Although I could have sworn she said she was going all the way to London.

Had time for a good workout with Howard down at the gym. Wasn't feeling like too much strenuous activity so picked the lowest impact exercise machine and spent a happy half hour on that until one of the trainers asked me why I had been standing on the scales for so long.

Thursday May 3

City briefing day. Private room arranged at Savoy and have raided staff welfare budget to beef up expenses and provide an epic lunch. When I got in, Hayley told me all the City analysts had called and cancelled. Bit confusing but they're all probably too busy buying Smokehouse shares.

Couldn't let the staff welfare budget go to waste so I invited some key staff, namely Bill Peters, to have a quiet lunch for 15 with me and to see whether we could seriously damage the crate of Bollinger. After fourth bottle, I told Bill to re-mortgage his house and put the lot on Acidix shares before they went ballistic. Bill said he couldn't do that as all his money was going on his second divorce. Bit of a shocker as I didn't know that was on the cards. He said it wasn't yet he'd spent a lot of money on things that would lead inevitably to divorce.

Friday May 4

On my way to City press conference with Sir Marcus, I called the fox on the train to ask whether she'd taken my little tip on Acidix. She said she'd listened very carefully and had warned the pension funds she advises to sell Smokehouse shares pronto before we made a dodgy acquisition of a potentially lethal chemical. Bumped into Sir Marcus who told me our shares had nose-dived and gave me a thermo-nuclear bollocking before telling the City that the acquisition was off.

I had to break the good news to our friends in the north who told me they'd just bought 10 per cent of Smokehouse shares for virtually nothing and thanks to me had got considerably more than owt for nowt. How heartening. My Acidix shares have, like their sodding cleaning chemical, gone through the floor. Have cancelled Maldives holiday and am looking closely at Blackpool. I've always said the north has a lot to offer.

Saturday May 5

Went down to see my brother Matty in the country for which Emma had to buy a completely new country outfit with more wax in it than Madame Tussauds. Camilla the Anglo-Saxon immediately took her for a tour of the paddocks leaving me and Matt to have a couple of nostril cleaners in the living room. The girls seemed to be crippling themselves with laughter which was a bit worrying as they had only just met. Sneaky suspicion that I might be providing most of the punch lines.

Matt waited until the G&Ts had penetrated the wall of my stomach and then in his most diplomatic way said that Emma was a lovely girl but clearly not right for me. I didn't argue with him but said it was probably a bit late as I had transferred the contents of my bank account to Britain's retail sector. We then went out and watched a couple of pigs copulating. Made me feel a bit depressed as I was seriously beginning to wish that Emma was a little dirtier in the old porking department. She'll probably perk up after the marriage is over. I mean the wedding. I think.

Sunday May 6

Emma came down to breakfast late looking like a supermodel about to do a special farmyard fashion shoot. Matthew gave her a good country look that took in her breeding potential in one glance. Felix my sheep-like younger brother turned up for lunch to get a glimpse of Emma and was quite literally struck dumb by her beauty. He kept looking at me and shaking his head as if I'd won the lottery.

On the drive home Emma had a long and intimate conversation about all the details of her life which I'm sure Tish enjoyed. I dropped Emma at home to finish the conversation while I nipped round to the Blue Boar. Mike came in and told us that he'd just had to put down an old ewe that wasn't doing the business any more. Evan and I exchanged a look and then spent an hour reassuring Mike that there were plenty more sheep in the field. Barney arrived and we finished the evening on a high note agreeing what a rough old lot the Belgians were.

Monday May 7

Zut alors!! Smokehouse are introducing pan-European operations to cut costs in the value chain. (I've always thought the value chain sounded like a cheap bicycle – probably popular with the Dutch.) Doing business with the continentals is like the light bulb; we have a bayonet fitting in Britain and they have a screw fitting on the continent and the trick is to bayonet them before they screw us. The point of Europe is somewhere to go on holiday with good bread, not to do business with countries whose bank notes look like murals on a municipal subway.

Personally I love the Europeans; the French play great rugby (when they're not gouging your eyes out), the Italians make great cars (when they're not rusting to bits) and you can't beat the Dutch at drugs and prostitution. And then of course you've got the Germans. Normally I'd be the first on with the spiked helmet to crash test the Hun's legendary deficiency in the humour department but not when it comes to pan-European operations; when you're up against the Latin Mafia in these Euro-meetings, they're your only ally.

Tuesday May 8

Hayley has organised first Euro-meeting. Travel broadens the mind and I usually find the act of getting my passport out instantly makes me very broad minded indeed. There's nothing like clearing customs to get the old testosterone racing. That's the great thing about us Eurobusiness types; a lot of meetings in exotic capitals with uninhibited Eurotot. Had lunch with Bill Peters and we agreed that women are the ultimate marketing triumph: a unique combination of functional and emotional benefits in fantastic packaging. Normally I'm pretty good at being faithful (in the past have been faithful to three women at a time – that's multi-tasking for you!). Of course I'm happily engaged now but what she doesn't know won't hurt her. It's what we in business call Knowledge Management.

Managed to get down the gym for a quick session. One of the trainers kept trying to help me. His lycra was a little bit too tight and I had my suspicions that he may have been batting from the pavilion end. I cut short the session and worked out in the bar instead. Amazingly got talking to a very nice piece of Eurotot and I practised my French on her. Turned out she was Spanish but *vive la différence* I say.

Wednesday May 9

Flew to Charles de Gaulle for first Euro-meeting. Easy to spot the Euro types; the men wear brown shoes and sports jackets and the women look like models. The Italian guy used the No Smoking sign to light his cigarette. I told one of the French guys that this had a certain *Je ne sais quoi*. He didn't understand so I said *sang froid*, *élan*. Still nothing. His English obviously wasn't that good. Got chatting with Uwe the German and reassured him we were all on the same side now and for him the war was over. No need for the old spiked helmet. He took it all quite well considering the old sense of humour bypass.

Checked all the women for wedding rings as this is generally shorthand for 'I have the sex life of a dog blanket' (going by my ex-wife that is). Clocked a fantastic French girl and felt my mind broadening immediately. You know what they say about French women; they may be strangers to the old Philips Ladyshave but they go like a TGV, if you'll pardon my French.

Thursday May 10

Got up early and had a continental breakfast – when in Rome do as the Romans I say and when on the continent do as the continentals. All day meeting with the Europeans including the top French totty. She had an accent that made you want to wrap your head in the curtains and weep. Every time she spoke I just nodded soupily and agreed to everything she said (turned out afterwards I agreed to relocate major manufacturing plant to Grenoble). In a break I asked her to come for a drink *à deux chevaux* as we Eurobusiness types like to say but sadly *pas de joie*.

Just before end of meeting we decided on new Euro-strategy – we will meet four times a year in a major capital, agree high level pan-European strategy, do our shopping and then go home and do what we've always done in our own countries. That way the *grandes fromages* get their European matrix management and we get our fancy foreign shopping. *Voila!!*

Friday May 11

At the airport remembered to buy some Coco Chanel for Emma to show sensitivity etc. but can't remember if it's the one she loves or absolutely hates. Bumped into Uwe in lounge and we agreed what a fantastic piece of totty the French girl was. Asked him whether he had a problem being faithful with all his foreign travel and constant temptations of exotic natives. He said he didn't but then I imagine he's probably saddled with some Rhine-barge-towing Brunnhilde back at the old *Stalag Luft*.

Uwe then let slip he was actually married to the 'fantastic bit of French totty' in question. Typical bloody Germans – always first getting their towels on the bitches. Obviously a bit of a googly that one and I sensed that the spiked helmet might be about to go on. I made a joke about taking European integration a little bit too far and just to cover the old sense of humour black hole I then explained that totty was English for 'business woman' in case he took offence. Then he started laughing and told me I should see the funny side. He went for his flight otherwise I would have pointed out that we fought the war on the funny side.

Saturday May 12

My turn with the kids. Thought they'd like the London Eye so we slogged up to town only to find that the bloody thing was closed due to high winds. I put them on the Circle Line for a couple of hours explaining that it was exactly the same as the London Eye only underground. Took the kids to a film I've been wanting to see for ages. It had a frightening amount of explicit sex and violence in it but they seemed to lap it up. Emma would have come normally because she loves kids but she was preparing for her hen night.

I got to the Blue Boar early, determined to make a night of it. The divinely Wonderbra'd Angela was there providing emotional uplift left, right and centre and I gave her some raw Weak charm to see whether there was any mileage there. There wasn't. Becky smiled at me before knocking over a tray of glasses with her massive arse. Barney and Mike asked me what I was doing for my stag night. I told them that they were it and they lined me up a few straight ones. I described all the bizarre Euro-types I'd spent the week with and we agreed pretty rapidly that Europeans on the whole were a pretty rough lot. Then we all tucked into some serious refreshment.

Sunday May 13

Woke up with colossal hangover. But it was nowhere near as colossal as the arse that Emma had developed overnight. I suddenly realised that the arse did not belong to Emma. It was Becky lying there like a tranquillised hippo. It began to dawn on me what I must have done and horror filled my entire being. Barney and the boys would never, ever forgive me. They would never, ever let me forget it. I could already see their faces filled with glee. I suddenly had this daft plan that if I could get Becky into one of their beds before they woke up I could escape the pain. I ripped the bedclothes off Becky without looking too closely and told her to get moving. For once in my life I was glad to have a headache so I couldn't focus on her and felt too sick to think about much else. What would have happened if Emma had found her there? If it had been Angela lying there it wouldn't have been so bad.

Got Becky out of the house and drove her home. Then went to the café to get a cooked breakfast to soak up some of the alcohol before rugby training. It was the last match of the season so I had to be there. Martin Padley wasn't there because he was feeling a little bit under the weather. Wimp.

When I got back Emma was home leafing through a pile of catalogues and on the phone to Tish. I asked her how her hen night was and she let slip that Colin Gilbey had been on it. I was not well pleased but Emma said it was fine because to all intents and purposes he was just one of the girls. I told her I didn't mind a male stripper and that sort of thing but I drew the line at Gilbey. Told her that there wasn't room for that kind of thing in a marriage and how we had to have a relationship based on trust etc. Then rushed up stairs to make the bed and check that Becky hadn't left any of her enormous pants in it.

Monday May 14

I was just sitting in a small meeting room nursing a hangover and reading the paper when Sir Marcus popped in and sat down next to me. He asked me about how my job was going and warned me about the danger of our business falling asleep at the wheel and missing the turn off for the future. At least I think that's what he said because my head was beginning to droop. Suddenly Ken Carmichael put his head round the door to say he had the meeting room booked. Sir Marcus told him he could have it when we'd finished and that in the interim he would do well to piss off.

You have to admire the way Sir Marcus articulates our company culture so clearly i.e. if you're not part of the steamroller, you're part of the pavement. But let's face it, Ken is not one of life's radiators. He is the sort of man who comes into the room and makes the lights dim. He's our Research Director which means he spends money asking customers what we already know to produce fat reports to cover our arse in case anything we do flops. He's a lovely, lovely man but he should be taking money at a narrow boat museum not being buffeted around in the jet stream of international business.

Tuesday May 15

Arrived spectacularly late as I wanted to try a new route to work via various shops I also needed to try out. Spent half an hour plying Sam Whetstone with gratuitous flattery. Meeting rooms are booked through Sam Whetstone. I've had a good few drinks with her after work partly because she's got industry-leading charlies, but mostly because I want priority booking when I need a room and they've all been booked out by HR doing synchronised macramé.

Had long lunch with Bill Peters where he pointed out that he'd never had trouble getting a meeting room as long as you didn't mind having lunch at the same time. When I got back Hayley alerted me to the fact that mild mannered Ken had got onto the intranet and started a petition about lack of meeting rooms. For someone like Ken, this is the equivalent of going berserk. Tim Smallwood, Finance Director, is backing him up although why anybody from accounts needs to meet anybody outside accounts is beyond me. Intranet petition gaining a good few signatures but not from anyone likely to have the sort of meeting I'd want to be involved in. Looks like the pavement is fighting back.

Wednesday May 16

I got in bang on the dot of nine and Shirley wasn't there as she'd nipped away for a pee or something. When she got back

I told her that if she couldn't bother being at her desk then that was the last time I was going to be on time. She managed to get the last word in by saying that was actually the first time I'd been on time. Got to my desk, binned the post, deleted my e-mails and cancelled any meetings I didn't like the look of.

Sir Marcus can sniff mutiny in the air. He's instructed his PA to print out the entire intranet so he can see what's going on there. Called me and Ross Fulbright (Sales Director) in for emergency meeting (we had to clear some Sensitivity Training course out of the board room). Sir Marcus said we were supposed to be the ideas men, what were our ideas. That was a bit of a hospital pass. It's like asking the Managing Director what the Direction is and how he's going to Manage. Fulbright suggested we have meetings standing up as this would make them a lot quicker and wouldn't require big meeting rooms. Sir Marcus lolled back into his big leather armchair obviously impressed with this idea. I was a bit worried that I hadn't suggested anything and that shaggability Fulbright had got all the Brownie points.

Thursday May 17

Got into work rather latish and caught half of my team standing around in the corridors gossiping. I gave them a motivational bollocking and said if they didn't have any work to do, some could be provided. They informed me that they were actually in a meeting and that there had been a new directive from Sir Marcus that meetings should be held standing up.

Difficult to believe he'd actually taken up Fulbright's half-baked idea. In my opinion life is divided into what you do sitting down, standing up or lying down. Sex is the only thing that combines all three and meetings are definitely in the sitting down category. Meetings are the only place where you're safe from telephones, customers, and other bloody meetings, so you should be able to sit back and enjoy them. On my way home rather earlyish I noticed the other half of my department standing around gossiping. I assumed they were in another meeting but you don't often get that kind of excited tittering in a marketing meeting.

Friday May 18

When I got in (latish) the corridors looked like there was some kind of fire drill going on. I checked Sam Whetstone's room diary and there wasn't a single room booked. Even the board room was free all day. I almost suggested that we go in there and I use her to polish the table (I know this is every secretary's secret fantasy) but there's probably a hidden webcam in there, knowing our IT department.

I alerted Sir Marcus that thanks to Fulbright's half-baked idea all the meeting rooms were now empty and the corridors full. Instead I suggested a new rule that you can only have a meeting room if your meeting is important. And you can only judge if your meeting is important if you yourself are important. I explained this to Ken as I turfed some piddling meeting of his out of a room I required. Then got Sam to book the room for the whole afternoon for me and Bill Peters to watch a casting video for a new sanitary product ad featuring three hours of Britain's top totty leaping around for no reason. Meeting room crisis solved which just goes to prove that if you want to survive in business, you've got to be able to think on your feet.

Saturday May 19

Woke up alone with the sun on my face. For a moment I had that lovely warm bachelor feeling of a weekend of pleasure stretching away in front of me. Something was niggling at the back of my mind and then I remembered that I was getting married. Didn't really feel like it but I got up and got myself showered, shaved and shitted. Left in plenty of time and drove to the church slowly, feeling more and more like I was heading up a funeral cortège. Church seemed very quiet until it suddenly dawned on me that (out of sheer force of habit)

I'd gone to the church I'd married Kate in. Got back in the Porsche and booted it across town.

I arrived about quarter of an hour late. Emma was doing laps of the supermarket car park in her Roller and her dad looked as if he'd just taken out a contract on me. Anyway, I got up the aisle and took out the contract on myself. Emma looked so beautiful I couldn't quite believe she was real. Didn't like the way the Vicar was looking at her throughout the service. When it came to the question about anybody having any just cause or impediment, I nearly put my hand up but didn't want to take the edge off the moment.

After the service we went out on the lawn and the photographer and every other man with a camera concentrated on getting every conceivable angle of Emma. I think my right ear will probably feature in one of the shots so that's OK. Emma's mum Maureen was crying like a baby throughout. Maurice promised that he'd go and have a word with her which he did. Afterwards her crying was more like a suppressed scream. Another classic mother-in-law I've landed myself with. I noticed Evan standing on one side of the lawn looking like a small-time crook who had been allowed out on the condition that he was handcuffed to the ugliest prison warder in the service (Beryl). He mimed a throat slitting sign which cheered me up no end. Barney had brought The Terminator to the wedding on my express instructions and was employed to make sure Gilbey didn't get anywhere near any photos. I don't want his oily little face in any albums of mine thank you very much.

I hadn't had time to do much of a speech so I just printed out the one I'd used for Kate and updated it a bit. Unfortunately I'd forgotten to change the last Kate and accidentally read it out which rather queered my profession of undying love. Emma's dad, who'd had more than a couple by this point, then got up and made a fine three second speech which amounted to, 'Lay a finger on her and I'll kill you'. Howard did a best man's speech which started off as the usual hatchet job on my character, past girlfriends etc. which was absolutely fine but then he got out of hand and started going on about how much he'd wanted to marry Emma and if it hadn't been for his broken leg etc. I had to interrupt and tell him that as far as Emma was concerned, he didn't have a leg to stand on. In the laughter I told him to sit down and shut up.

Once everyone got tucked in to the free bar things passed off peacefully (Bill Peters was there when I got there and I had my suspicions that he'd been there throughout the service and the meal). Emma and Tish did a lot of giggling with the toerag Gilbey and I ended up in a corner with Barney and Evan giving marks to the waiting staff on their bras which were all clearly visible through their white blouses. Emma threw her bouquet over her shoulder and hit Evan full in the face with it just as he was passing with two pints of bitter which no doubt reinforced Evan's dim view of weddings and marriage in general.

Emma and I had the first dance and I suddenly remembered why I was marrying her. I wanted to leave there and then and get her tucked up but every man in the room wanted to dance with her so I had to work my way through all the other miserable tarted up hags she calls friends. Although to be honest Tish had scrubbed up rather well and if I hadn't been there on other business I wouldn't have minded a quick trip up her aisle.

I was getting a bit tired and emotional towards the end of the evening especially as Emma seemed to be spending half her time dancing with the vicious little worm Gilbey. Barney kept coming up to me and whispering 'chin the bastard' which didn't help my mood. Eventually I saw him plant a kiss on her cheek with his little goatee a millimetre away from her mouth. I started to go over to him ready to rip him a new arsehole when I suddenly found myself face to face with my sister Karen's boyfriend, Paul the trainee vicar. Before I could say 'stand aside Padre' he had me in some sort of death grip round the back of the neck. All I could feel was excruciating pain while he smiled at me and said it was probably time for me and Emma to begin our happy lives together. I was paralysed from the neck down while he just seemed to be fondling my neck. Next thing I knew I was in the back of the Roller with Emma on our way to the hotel.

By the time we got to our first night hotel I'd just about recovered the use of my muscles and was beginning to worry that the old purple helmeted warrior might be *hors de combat*. I needn't have worried because Emma spent half an hour folding her wedding dress up 'in case she needed it again'. I had just stripped down to my Calvins when Emma's mobile went. It was Tish. After she'd finished her brief 45 minute chat, I got down to the business of making love to one of the world's most beautiful women. I shocked myself by imagining I was actually on the job with big-arsed Becky. But it did the trick and we all went to sleep relatively happy.

Sunday May 20

Flew to the Maldives for honeymoon. Emma told me that Tish had always fancied me but she'd got in there first. Great.

Monday May 21

Woke up in our little villa and had a very nasty sensation that whole room was spinning. It gradually dawned on me that I was looking at the big fan on the ceiling slowly whopping round. Not a good start to the day. No sign of Emma just the slight whiff of sun cream. I looked through our French doors and saw her on the beach on her sunbed. My god I thought, I've married a German. My head wasn't quite ready for the tropical sun so I had a shower and read the remains of the Sunday papers.

By the time I got out on the beach Emma's sunbed was so hemmed in by other men's sunbeds that I could hardly get to her. I suddenly realised she had her jugs out!! No wonder every man in the Indian Ocean was getting a ringside seat. If it had been my wife I wouldn't have noticed but then I suddenly realised she was my wife. I thought the quickest way to clear the lot of them would be to slip my trunks off and then lie there with my chopper exposed. Then we'd look like naturists and there's nothing so unsexy as naturists who are basically ramblers who've forgotten their anoraks. Instead I plonked my bed down next to her and read my book in an aggressive manner. Emma then piped up that my book was putting her breasts in the shade. I assured her that nothing could put her breasts in the shade but she just sighed and moved her sunbed the other way so that she was practically breast feeding the man on the other side.

Tuesday May 22

Emma decided she wanted to lie in the sun all day and read the world's fattest book so I took myself off to do some watersports. I thought the water-skiing would give the right impression so I went out with this surly native in a speedboat that looked like a jet engine on floats. I sat back in the water and he fired up the boat which reared up out of the water like it had been stung in the arse. The rope straightened quicker than a rabbit's todger and I was ripped straight out of the water. I should have let go there and then because after I splashed down I went straight under and was dragged along underwater at about 90mph with my nads three inches from razor sharp coral. When I finally let go my arms had stretched to five times their natural length and I had swallowed an impressive range of tropical fish.

Johnny native came alongside and I asked him whether we could go a touch slower. He said the boat only had one speed but he would go and get the slower boat. I wasn't in much of a position to argue as my lungs were still pumping out a large part of the Indian Ocean. Half an hour later I found myself behind something that looked like a small tugboat which pulled me along slightly faster than a vigorous breast stroke. All the men sunbathing around Emma managed to tear their eyes away from her long enough for them to see me making a total arse of myself.

Wednesday May 23

Half way through the morning I was lying on the sunbed minding my own beeswax when I heard this blood-curdling screaming coming from our villa. As I rushed in from the beach I could only imagine that a great white shark had found its way in there. I found Emma standing on the bed with the sheets pulled up around her. When I got her to stop jibbering she finally managed to tell me there was a lizard on the floor. I walked round and saw this tiny little green thing sitting on the mat clearly wondering what all the screaming was about. I picked up one of Emma's five hundred shoes and smacked it on the head. Far from awarding me any sort of medal for bravery, Emma burst into tears again and started saying, 'I can't believe you killed it. It's just a poor animal, etc.' I promised her I'd only stunned it and threw the remains out of the bathroom window.

We then had our first major row in which she called me an insensitive bullying thug and I confirmed her in that view by pointing out in an insensitive bullying way that so far the honeymoon had been one mindless self-inflicted trauma after another from her and that she was a typical bloody woman. I told her that like all women she wanted to have her cake, eat it and not see it turn up on her thighs a week later. She had her revenge by spending the afternoon writing postcards to Colin Gilbey. I went down to the bar and got chatting with a Brit called Tommy who was from Huddersfield but not a bad bloke.

Thursday May 24

As a bit of a romantic gesture to patch up our marriage I booked us a trip to go to our own island for the day. We got in the same speedboat they'd used for my first bit of underwater water-skiing and it had the same grinning idiot driving it. As soon as we got on board he floored it and we were virtually airborne. We spent about 90 per cent of the time in the air punctuated by smacking down on the water so hard my nads were bounced up to my kidneys. I shouted to Emma that this was the life but she couldn't hear me because she was throwing up. We finally arrived at our little island and I had to carry Emma ashore because she was so ill.

The little seaborne Michael Schumacher loitered around in a 'Where's my tip' kind of way. Normally, I would have sent him away with a traditional English thick ear but he and I both knew that without him we would be castaways and he and I both also knew that the romance of being on your own island deteriorates swiftly around the time of your first major bowel movement. Emma was lying on the white sands of the beach moaning. She whispered to me to get her out of the sun so I dragged her under the one palm tree on the island and waited for her to recover. I spend time doing laps of the island thinking of all the love making in the breaking surf we could be doing. Knowing my luck at the moment we'd just be getting down to it and we'd be covered by raw sewage or I'd be hit by a piece of flotsam that had drifted six thousand miles across the ocean just to whack me in the back of the head. Eventually we were picked up by the pirate in his tugboat (he assumed rightly that the romance would have worn thin by this time). Emma went straight to bed and I went to the bar with Tommy to discuss how the Maldiviants were a funny lot.

Friday May 25

Emma stayed in bed. I stayed in the bar. Tommy and I were swapping notes about women and marriage and totty in general. He'd actually been here on honeymoon many years before and was now coming back to enjoy it. I sympathised. He'd also had a beautiful wife and we agreed (we'd had a few) that after a while you stop noticing how beautiful they are and instead start noticing things like how they take a long time in the bathroom and have the conversational prowess of a loofah. It struck me towards sundown that I ought to see how Emma was getting on. She was in the bathroom. We had dinner together and Emma talked about how this was a poxy kind of paradise that didn't give her a signal for her mobile phone. What she meant was she would really rather be on holiday with Tish. So would I.

Saturday May 26

Last full day of honeymoon thank God. Emma was on the beach before dawn to make sure she got every single second of sunshine. I wrote a couple of postcards to the kids and it struck me that they'd enjoy this place a lot more than Emma. Waited outside the beach bar until it opened and then began to relax with a couple of cocktails. Tommy joined me and we had a high old time until closing time which was sometime rather late. We both peed into the Indian Ocean together as a revenge for loss of Empire.

Sunday May 27

Flew back with world's worst hangover. And Emma. Forgot to post postcards for kids. Out of sheer force of habit bought perfume in duty free for Kate (first wife). Conversation limited on way home.

Monday May 28

Got into the office tired, jet-lagged, sunburnt and with a considerable amount of sand in my underpants. Not in my best mood. Will somebody please tell me what HR is actually for? Ninety per cent of their job seems to be just strolling around using your first name without you knowing who the hell they are. Now I've been told I have to have a personal development session with some tired old HR luvvy. How the hell is he supposed to plan the personal development of a heavy hitter like me when he's only got the personal development of a small cabbage.

Had long lunch with Bill to try and get the honeymoon

out of the system. Got back to my desk feeling much better and was just getting down to the serious business of reading the trade press when I noticed a gardener working outside my window planting shrubs. I slipped him a tenner to plant a couple of fast growing ones right outside the window of IT Director Gavin Smedley. IT people hate the light as it makes them start to photosynthesise and go all spotty.

Tuesday May 29

Arrived late due to prolonged agonising between the tie I usually wear and the tie I never wear. Plumped for the tie I never wear. Shirley on reception said she liked the tie. That's the last time I wear that one. HR have just dreamed up a new way of wasting time, money and effort. The whole company is to be profiled in some Myra-Biggs personality test. Can't help thinking they'd get the same effect cutting out a couple of quizzes from back issues of Cosmo. If they really want to know what kind of person I am why don't the nosy little parkers get out of their soft furnishings and come and ask me direct. I'd be more than happy to show them exactly what a ray of sunshine I can be.

Ross 'Shaggability' Fulbright (Sales Director) popped by to gloat over some massively over-inflated sales figures. We watched the bloke working outside and he said it was very Panglossian. I thought he meant a type of silk paint but apparently he was referring to something Voltaire had written about the secret of happiness being quiet work in the garden. That's the best the French can do on the philosophy front apparently.

Wednesday May 30

Human Remains are hassling me for my completed Myra-Biggs form. Seems they don't have anything to do until they get it. Had lunch with Bill and he said it was all just an excuse to sack people. They decide the types they don't want and then do all the dirty work by number. Admitted that he'd got his elderly mother to fill his forms out for years. Superb idea. You can see why Bill is still at the top of the tree even though he's out of his own personal tree most of the time.

Thinking of trees I got the gardener outside to fill out my form. He went through it like a dose of salts swearing under his breath. I made damn sure he got back into the flower beds pronto. Went to the gym after work. Howard's got these new prescription goggles that mean you can see all sorts of fascinating underwater life from a great distance. The great thing about women swimming is they never put their heads under water. Men do of course mostly because we want to have a good butcher's at all the other stuff women do put under water.

Thursday May 31

Received the results of 'my' Myra-Biggs. It said I was a JFDI – a Jaundiced Fossilised Demagogic Invertebrate. Well that was money well spent then. I asked Giles Renton-Willets what they were going to do now they had everyone completely pigeonholed. He said the results would help HR put people into jobs that suited them. I asked what that meant I was good for. He looked at his little chart and said Dictators of small countries, prison warders and TV evangelists. Which shocked me as it was pretty much spot on for Marketing Director.

Later I called a very low level PR girly and demanded to know what Renton-Willets's own results were under the Freedom of Information Act. She told me that he didn't have to do the test as he was sponsoring the whole initiative. I warned them that was exactly how Himmler slipped through the net.

JUNE

Friday June 1

Just for a laugh I put an ad on the intranet saying JFDI seeks GBYH for fun times. (I checked that GBYH were submissive private extroverts – i.e. quiet in public, go like a football rattle in private.) Then got talking to the gardener who was shovelling manure from a big pile around the base of all the saplings. Turns out he used to be a director of a big oil company, who had started drinking too much, lost his job, family etc. I said at least he'd found happiness working in the garden in a Panglossian kind of a way. Said he hated it, thought Voltaire didn't know his *derrière* from his *elbeau* and asked whether I would be happy shovelling shit from one place to another. I told him that we all did that and at least he got some fresh air doing it.

Got an e-mail response from my ad on the intranet from Clare O'Keefe Operations Director, telling me I was a pathetic, sex obsessed half-wit. I took it all very philosophically. I can't help behaving like that because I'm a JFDI and that's what we do. I'm not a free man; I'm only an alpha-numeric sequence.

Saturday June 2

Picked up the kids and gave them their presents which I'd brought back from the Maldives. Hula Barbie for Leah and Jungle Action Man for Kieran. They were actually from Toys "Я" Us but they're not going to know the difference. Anyway I'm sure as soon as they get them home the toys will be made wards of court and put up in the attic by Kate or her war crimes tribunal parents.

Took the kids to Epsom for the racing which they may well show an interest in later in life. When I finally got home Tish was on the sofa with Emma and they seemed to be making a list of all the things in my flat they could fit into a skip. Emma had clearly gone straight from stage one of marriage which is falling in love with a man because he's got something about him, to stage two which is change everything about him. I told her that nothing of mine was to be moved let alone thrown away without a written warrant signed by me and witnessed by two other responsible adults i.e. men.

Sunday June 3

Did not get my normal Sunday morning headboard hockey. Well I did but Emma didn't stop reading the Style section of the paper throughout. Not very satisfactory. If she'd been reading the Sports section at least I would have had the back page to read on the job. To honour a promise I'd made to the boys, I took Emma down to the Blue Boar for lunch. She dressed up like she was off to the Milan catwalks and everyone was suitably impressed. Even The Terminator started simpering like a big fur ball. Fortunately she developed a headache towards the end of the meal and went home (Emma that is).

I finished off the day with the boys who gave Emma marks out of ten which all hovered round the ten. Various jokes were made about her having to put a bag over my head in bed. I joked that personality was more important and accidentally caught Becky's eye at that moment. She blushed, poor girl.

Monday June 4

Organic is the big new thing in the food industry and it's time the big boys got stuck in. Generally I wouldn't give it the time of day. Organic food is like vegetarians – boring, sick looking and a pain in the arse to cater for. But Sir Marcus says we need to be organic by the end of the month or he'll have my guts for organic garters. Luckily I've found a little organic food business called Biolife run by a lot of sandal wearing do-gooders. Money talks and what our billion pound war chest says is get off our land you hippies. Oh yes, I love the smell of mergers and acquisitions in the morning.

Which reminds me. I must appoint someone to head up our new organic department. I've earmarked Celeste Nibelle who's about to return from two weeks away having major breast augmentation. I gave her two weeks training leave for it as it's all part of self-development. In her new role she'll need to work close to me or as close as she'll be able to get with her new chest.

Tuesday June 5

Surprise, surprise! Chief sandal wearer at Biolife is my very first boss back from the dead. When I was a young shaver I dreamed up a scheme where we gave away free flights for every washing machine we sold. The company went under, transatlantic air travel doubled but he took the heat and resigned like a gent. What a loser! Anyway he's now resurfaced at Biolife and I'm going to have the skin off his sausage again.

Marketing Department is on maximum excitement level. Celeste Nibelle's breasts have arrived back for work. We're expecting the rest of her tomorrow. Unfortunately Sir Marcus has suggested some woman called Ruth Parsons to head up our new organic department. She's got an accountancy background and to my mind that's where accountants should stay – in the background.

Wednesday June 6

Trouble down on the farm. Biolife have a whole load of poison pills to prevent takeover. Basically if we so much as look at a cabbage the whole company explodes in our face – not very organic if you ask me. But we'll get our legal boys on to them and we'll soon have the jam out of their doughnut.

This whole organic thing is pretty bizarre – we've been trying to get decent veg for years and now people want carrots that look like they've been grown in an infant school project. Why don't we just take all the veg we normally reject for looking too ugly, bag it up, double the price and label it organic. That'll teach the buggers.

Met Ruth Parsons to talk about the organic job but she's too aesthetically challenged for my team. That's the thing about ugly women; you don't want them working with you, you don't want them breeding: thank God for the public sector that's what I say. Anyway, it's difficult to see how I can't promote Celeste – those breasts are almost self-promoting.

Thursday June 7

Legal boys report back that Biolife are bombproof and we should back off pronto. Unfortunately, Sir Marcus has already promised shareholders we'll be as green as the arse of the Jolly Green Giant so it looks like I'm going to have my pants well and truly pulled down on this one. Took Celeste out for lunch to talk about possible new position (woof!). Spent most of first course with my eyes glued to Silicon Valley, as Bill Peters likes to call it. She ordered risotto and I suddenly realised she was a vegetarian. Disaster. You stop eating meat and the next thing you know you're demonstrating against the World Bank.

Went back to office very depressed about whole organic situation. If God had really wanted us not to eat animals he would have made them out of Brussels sprouts. Had one too many sherbets with Bill Peters after work and then mistakenly got a cab to the gym. Spent an hour drunk in charge of an exercise bike.

Friday June 8

Legal boys submitted bill for consultancy which would pay for breast implants for entire marketing department. Then found a report on my desk from the grizzly Ruth Parsons suggesting we fly organic food in from Asia. OK it's grown by five-year-olds in appalling conditions, it's the stuff the locusts won't touch and the planes transporting it rip a five mile hole in the ozone layer, but the food's organic, the customer wants organic and the customer is always right.

Told Sir Marcus that Biolife acquisition was off and that we were developing our own supplies because organic business growth is better than artificial acquisition. Told Celeste and her breasts that they couldn't have the job because organic growth is better than artificial acquisition. Gave the job to Ruth Parsons. Clearly, if you're going to have someone in an organic food job it stands to reason they should be a bean counter.

Saturday June 9

Had to take Kieran to hospital because he'd wedged Action Man's jungle machete up his nose. We spent about three hours sitting in the outpatients department watching various overpaid medical staff rushing around doing precisely bugger all while I ploughed through 85 back issues of *Woman's Realm*. A rather fit looking woman came in with a little girl and sat down opposite me. Sounds corny I know but I fell completely and utterly in love with her (the woman that is). My head started spinning, my heart was racing and for a moment I thought I was going to faint. In short it was the most pathetic display by myself I've ever witnessed and believe me I've witnessed a few.

I couldn't let this cracking piece of totty slip by so I managed to open my mouth to say something. What came out was a pathetic attempt at a joke; 'Are you a consultant?' She looked at me as if I was something she'd stepped in, said 'Yes' and then started talking to her little girl who also looked at me as if I was surgical waste. I sat there like an idiot with my mainframe computer for totty analysis and data capture completely seized. After a few more diabolical efforts from me I managed to find out that her name was Dr Madeleine Eccles and that she was a psychiatrist. I was just getting warmed up when someone called us and we had to go have Kieran's machete removed.

Sunday June 10

Woke up with a spring in my groin. The last thing I said to Madeleine was that I would call her and she kind of grimaced and said please don't. Fantastic!! That's the kind of woman for me. I spent all morning on the web tracking her down.

She had a private practice in town and had written all sorts of pointy-headed articles about Post Traumatic Stress Disorder. So she'll be well equipped with a date with me I thought. I thought long and hard about how to get a date with her. Clearly she was already playing hard to get with this don't call me business.

I sat and thought for a moment and suddenly had an absolute corker of an idea. I would book myself in for a course of therapy. In that way I'd be on the couch and it would only be a matter of getting her down there with me. I was so excited about everything I nearly rushed downstairs and told Emma. But a sixth sense I've developed from years of dealing with difficult and demented women warned me that she wouldn't be impressed. If there's one thing about marriage, it does heighten your appreciation of women (not including the ball and chain herself obviously). Had to go and collect Kieran from hospital as he'd been kept in overnight. Apparently he was also storing half of Hula Barbie's wardrobe up his nose. Bit worrying for a boy of that age to be sniffing women's clothing.

Monday June 11

Sir Marcus popped his famously fat head into my office and reminded me that e-commerce was the new way to market. And there was me thinking e-commerce is how we do business with Yorkshire. He demanded a demonstration of our website by the end of the week. (Luckily for me he can't operate a computer himself – he thinks a laptop is an optional extra from lap dancers.) Also reminded me how much he hates wheelbarrow management; i.e. unless he's hands on and pushing, nothing happens. What he really means by this is he prefers miracle management where you do nothing and things happen as if by magic.

Sadly we don't actually have a website because when Sir Marcus first asked me to explore the channel implications of internet all I heard was 'channel' and 'explore' and spent two weeks 'fact-finding' in some outstanding French hostelries. I realised I'd better think of something fast otherwise I'm FAQed, as we netheads like to say.

Tuesday June 12

Told Shirley I was late because of horrific pile up (of pants in laundry basket). Asked IT department if they could build a fully interactive commercial website with full CRM capability for a live demonstration on Friday. Of course they couldn't do anything but then they're probably all still working flat out to prepare us for the millennium bug. I've often thought that somewhere in the company there must a BULLSH department from which IT have been separated at birth.

Have decided that internet really isn't my thing: you can't have a drink with it, you can't take it to a box at Twickenham and you can't get its kit off and shunt it round the carpet – so how the hell are you expected to do business with it? The sort of people who spend time on-line are sad, socially challenged individuals whose idea of a night out is to move their chair further away from their computer. Who wants to do business with them? Not me. But then reminded myself of three-line whip from Sir Marcus and decided that I did indeed want to do business over the web.

Wednesday June 13

Interviewed web designers. Generally teams of two – one in anorak who's not allowed to speak and one in rectangular glasses who doesn't stop speaking. The one in glasses said there were three important things in e-commerce: magnetism, stickiness and community. I told him there was one important thing in doing business with me and that was not to talk bollocks. He said he could build an on-line interactive community for us for about half a million pounds and was I comfortable with that? I told him he could shove his website up his zip drive and was he comfortable with that?

Afterwards had a real-time off-line lunch with Bill Peters to discuss e-commerce. He gave me some website addresses which were not so much sticky as downright mucky. Very pleasant and informative afternoon on-line. Beginning to understand the attraction of the new economy.

Thursday June 14

Disaster!! Asked IT department to register Smokehouse name for website. They said it was already owned by a barbecued meat shop in Kansas. I e-mailed the owner and told him in no uncertain terms that we were a global industrial giant, they were a poxy redneck abattoir and we wanted our name back. Payton (the MD or the big smoke or whatever they have in Kansas) replied saying I could 'swivel'. Liked him immediately and we got chatting on-line. We crashed a couple of times when his brother Clyde plugged the coffee machine in their only socket but we were definitely on the same wavelength.

I suddenly had a brainwave and offered Payton a couple of grand if he would put up a big picture of Sir Marcus on his site on Friday. He said he was insulted and shocked and could we make that five big ones US. E-commerce strategy sorted, I packed in early and went to the gym. Found Howard standing stock still on one of these Nordic skiers with his bum sticking out. Said he was downhill skiing. Nutter.

Friday June 15

Gave Sir Marcus a live on-line demonstration of our 'barbecue meats site'. He said he was very impressed as he didn't even know we sold barbecue meats. He especially liked the local home-produced style of the site. I said that was the beauty of the internet – global reach, local feel. He wanted to see another page so I clicked on the photo of himself and suddenly the site was very sticky indeed. Then, just as Sir Marcus was getting ready to tear himself away from himself, Clyde in Kansas must have wanted a cup of coffee because the whole site crashed.

I explained to Sir Marcus that the IT department were having difficulty keeping it on-line and that they all required continual wheelbarrow management. Sir Marcus said I'd done a grand job and he would give the IT slackers a motivational roasting. Afterwards Hayley asked me what wheelbarrow management was. I told her it was an efficient way of moving piles of manure from one place to another. She said I must be a top wheelbarrow manager. Smart girl.

Saturday June 16

Got up early for industrial scale primping as this was first 'date' with the gorgeous Dr Eccles. I've persuaded HR that I needed some personal executive coaching as I wanted to sharpen up my soft skills (or blunt them down or whatever the hell you do with soft skills). They thought this was a fantastic idea and there was virtually a ripple of applause around the entire HR department when I asked. So I'm now getting my dates sponsored by Smokehouse – their concern for staff welfare really is admirable.

Arrived late at Dr Eccles's office because I had to drop Emma off at Tish's house. They're spending the day returning wedding gifts which apparently is like shopping in reverse and just as much fun. Knocked on the door half an hour late with a couple of absolutely choice lines ready for delivery, absolutely guaranteed to work directly on the knicker elastic. I'd hardly got through the door when Dr Eccles said 'You're late. Do you always treat people like this?' Wow!!! I thought if it makes you get all hot, cute and tempersome, I'm going to be even later next week. Unfortunately it also meant she threw me out after half an hour because some complete nutter was waiting. We hadn't got past me giving her my details. I probably gave her a little bit more detail than was required but as far as I'm concerned, having the keys to a Porsche in my pocket is a significant medical detail.

Sunday June 17

Emma invited her arty friends Octavius and Coriander for lunch. I volunteered to cook principally so I would have to spend less time talking about theatre and art and all that absolute bollocks. I remembered mid-morning that it was my turn with the kids so zoomed across town to pick them up from Kate. She asked me how my marriage was going which I thought was a bit snidey. I said the sex was great which I knew was also a little bit below the belt (as it were). Probably should have kept my mouth shut as all the way home Kieran and Leah were asking me what great sex was.

Got back in the kitchen and Emma reminded me that Octavius and Coriander were vegetarians. I thought I'd kill two birds with one cliché and make fish fingers and baked beans. I produced a whole plate full of fish fingers and bloody Octavius piped up that vegetarians don't eat fish. I was a bit cheesed off and said if you don't eat fish what do you bloody well eat. Emma got all huffy and did the kind of big sigh that I thought you only did after the first few years of marriage. She then took them out to a vegetarian restaurant. That left me and the kids with twelve fish fingers each which constituted a personal best for me. Dropped the kids off, popped down to the Blue Boar for a few straight ones and a quick discussion on why the Paraguayans were an odd lot.

Monday June 18

Looked in my diary to see what was in store for the week and saw that it was a continuous stream of meetings I don't need with people I don't like about subjects I don't give a monkey's about. I asked Hayley to clear my diary for the week. I don't often do this but she seems to be able to do it very easily and no one ever complains. Well, they might want to complain but as my diary is completely clear they don't really get the chance.

Instead I thought I would spend the week bringing the full force of my marketing brain to bear on Snifters. Something deep in my water tells me that there is an absolute gold mine there and I've learned that unless you listen to something deep in your water you inevitably end up in deep water if that's not mixing my metaphoricals. I've already got a little bit of research budget and I've got the green light from the innovation team so basically the full resources of Smokehouse are now at my disposal. Which seems like a good time to understand what the full resources of Smokehouse actually amount to.

Tuesday June 19

Got in late due to dental work (cleaning my teeth). Visited our R&D labs with Bill Peters. They're all part of his domain and he was happy to take me round because he said he'd never actually had a proper look round before. All the little boffins were working away happily. Am I odd or does everyone find something strangely alluring about women in safety goggles and white coats?

I stopped the first man I saw with a beard (you couldn't throw a test tube in the labs without hitting a man with a beard – or a woman with a beard for that matter). I asked him whether we had an expert on alcohol products. He pointed us in the direction of screen wash and mirror cleaners. Not sure whether to let Bill too close to this area in case he starts coming down here for lunchtime refreshment instead of Mr Bojangles. Dr Alcohol wasn't there that day (probably had a massive hangover) so we just mooched about the labs for a bit. I said to Bill that it must be quite fun having your own industrial sized chemistry set. Bill said that he'd never really liked chemistry and tried not to get involved. Very progressive manager, Bill.

Wednesday June 20

The resident beard in alcohol research demanded to see Bill's visitors pass. I pointed out that Bill was Director of Department and surely he must be a very new boy not to know that. In fact he'd been working in the labs for the best part of ten years but then Bill has never been one to hog the shop floor. Bill reassured him that his job was safe and then we sat him down with a cup of coffee or what could equally well have been the latest product from the lab. We asked him about the possibilities of delivering alcohol in pill form. He said there was no problem at all but that the higher life forms in marketing had decided that there wasn't a market for them. I told him that the higher life forms had now decided there was and would the lower life forms be able to run up a couple of test packs for yours truly. Bill chipped in and said that we should do a proper production run as research could be terribly wasteful of product.

Went to the gym with Howard after work and we concentrated long and hard on the upper body (always my favourite part of a woman). Howard was later yellow carded by the management for getting on the same running machine as a particularly pert little number and trying to chase her. She complained to the manager whereas if I'd been in her position I would have just hit the fast forward button and dumped Howard off the back.

Thursday June 21

Had a handwritten letter on my desk. Thought for a moment it was some young graduate totty asking for a full 360° appraisal but as it was spidery old writing in black ink I realised that was probably wishful thinking. I then considered it might be my Aunt Nell disinheriting me. She never liked me and is the only person to have called me to my face a cocky little sod. To put an end to this fruitless kind of speculation I opened it. Inside there was one yellowing paper with our original 1950s Smokehouse logo and a telephone number with three digits in total.

The letter writer introduced himself as our head of inorganic chemical research and understood we'd been enquiring about alcohol based products. He said he'd been waiting for a visit from somebody in marketing for the last 50 years. He knew all there was to know about alcohol and he said the marvellous thing about it was that it didn't actually give you a hangover in its pure form. He'd developed some capsules for his own use during a tricky phase in his marriage (1957–1998) and would they be of use? Finally there was a feeble signature that slumped down to the bottom of the page – Dr J. Cobb.

Friday June 22

Took the letter round to show Bill Peters. He was sitting at his desk in a chair that looked suspiciously like a hammock, swinging gently as he read some important figures in the *Racing Post*. If it was true that you could get absolutely leathered and not have a hangover it seemed like the product of the millennium to me. We agreed that Dr Cobb deserved a visit. Besides which Bill was getting quite a taste for management by walking about. He'd noticed that it put the fear of God into everyone especially if he didn't actually say anything to anybody.

We arrived at the lab just in time to see a stretcher being carried out to an ambulance. As the sheeted body on it turned out to be Dr Cobb himself we decided that our visit may have lost some of its urgency. In a show of respect to the old man, we rifled through his office and found his prototype alcopills. Then we adjourned to Mr Bojangles and congratulated ourselves on making sure that Dr Cobb died happy in the knowledge that we were going to profit from his lifetime's work.

Saturday June 23

Arrived for therapy ten minutes early with a song in my heart, love on my mind and a three pack in my pocket. Old Dr Eccles might not be keen yet but I was happy to have therapy for as long as it took to change her mind. Took us a bit of time to get going that morning as she kept asking me a lot of questions about myself. I could tell she was interested. Lots of intimate questions about past girlfriends, my mother, my car etc. Basically all the lines I usually fight to get out she was begging me for. I began to think this was going to be easier than expected.

Then suddenly she put her clipboard down and came out with, 'You have a defensive life positioning John, you don't have receptor sensibilities. Instead you project your wants and desires and concentrate on materialising them.' Couldn't agree more I told her. I had very powerful wants and desires and liked to materialise them as quickly as possible in whatever positioning she thought was most appropriate. There was a bit of a silence after this. I expect she was analysing her feelings and wrestling with the strength of the attraction. Before the end of the session she asked me to keep a journal of my dreams and other meaningful experiences. If I'd known therapy was such a hoot I would have done it years ago. Must get Bill Peters on to it.

Sunday June 24

I was happily on the job with Emma working off some of the excitement about seeing Madeleine for my 'therapy' when the bloody doorbell went. Outside there was a tiny little man in a black suit who looked like he was fresh from a school production of *Reservoir Dogs*. He said he was a friend of Emma's dad which immediately put me on my guard. Emma came down and gave 'Uncle Nathan' a kiss that had approximately twice the passion content of the ones I'd been extracting upstairs. Uncle Nathan gave Emma a bag full of presents from her parents which I assumed were a couple of tomatoes and several kilos of grade A skank. Uncle Nathan then invited me into my own garden for a smoke. I was on the point of making a joke about whether he was old enough but didn't.

Once we were out in the garden he said he had two messages from Maurice (Emma's Dad). Firstly, how was the marriage going. I told him that it was a match made in Heaven. I didn't add that it was assembled in Albania. The second question was Maurice wanted to know when he could expect his first grandchild. Normally I would have laughed out loud but there was something about Uncle Nathan's tone that suggested I owed Maurice something and he was demanding payment. I told Uncle Nathan to tell him I was trying as hard as I could. As soon as he'd got his answer, there was the patter of tiny feet and Uncle Nathan was gone. Emma was more rude to me than usual for the rest of the day as if she'd just had reinforcements. Migrated to Blue Boar as soon as I could as I felt the need to be with my own people.

Monday June 25

Arrived late due to genetic predisposition to lateness of which I am an unwitting victim. Bill Peters, the original technoplegic, has discovered text messaging. I know this because during a coma-inducing IT presentation he messaged me that Mrs Tooley (Office Manager) has an arse the size of Denmark. He also warned me about a vicious new decree from Tim Smallwood (Finance Director) that all purchases over 50k must be signed off by two directors. This would put the kibosh on the little 100K incentive event for my department in Barcelona I'm having organised by an absolute fox called Rebecca Clifton-Gould. Now there's a woman crying out for a bit of hands-on management. If I can avoid any form of communication with Smallwood to the end of the week I simply won't know about the new spending policy and I can sign the cheque and slip it to her (woof!).

Tuesday June 26

Working from gym today. Told Hayley I need to spend more time looking at the figures. Have arranged for all callers to be diverted to our Customer Careline where they will be patronised to death by a recording which says they're held in a queue but not to go away because we value their call so much. What we don't tell customers is we value their call because we're charging them £3 a minute for it and the queue they're held in is a circular one.

Three urgent e-mails from Smallwood and six phone messages, sadly none of which I received as I was too busy flicking through Barcelona brochures in the sauna. Left message for Rebecca Motivational-Totty asking her out for lunch to chat through Barcelona conference, rooming arrangements and how she can delight me as a customer. Howard popped by after work and we had a good long aerobic workout on the table football.

Wednesday June 27

Working from races with Bill Peters today. The good thing about pagers, WAP phones, laptops etc. is that you can be anywhere in the world, turn all the buggers off and be completely incommunicado. Thus avoided twelve phone calls and ten e-mails from Smallwood copied to all Directors. I have a golden rule that I never open CCed e-mail. I don't do copies. It's the original or nothing for me. I don't mind blind copies of course because they're often rich in unsubstantiated office dirt. In fact I often send messages as blind copies because that way they're guaranteed to get attention.

Had a light lunch and some serious refreshment and then put the entire staff welfare budget on a horse called Fast Return which crippled itself trying to get out of the starting gate. Fortunately Bill was so walloped by that stage that he'd spent half an hour trying to get the cloakroom attendant to take our bets, so no harm done. Nothing from Rebecca High-Totfactor about conference. Obviously playing hard to get but she'll come round eventually. Women can't resist a man with a big budget who knows what to do with it.

Thursday June 28

Working from Mr Bojangles wine bar today. It's amazing what you can do with a bit of peace and quiet away from all the noise and phones. I almost wished I'd brought some work with me. Bill turned up for an extended working lunch which got a little bit rowdy. On his third bottle of red Bill demanded a webcam on his barstool so he could see it when he was in the office and keep himself motivated. I told him it would be more useful for the taxi firm who could send a car round as soon as he fell off it.

Turned my phone on to call Rebecca Baying-Crumpet but Smallwood rang immediately. Let it ring for a good five minutes before he gave up. This reminded me of a game I used to play called 'hangman' where I timed how long I could keep people on hold. My record was 48 minutes – I believe that was the first wife towards the end of our time together. Twenty-five e-mails from He of The Small Wood all marked urgent, plus two from the Chairman. That'll be Smallwood getting the Chairman's secretary to send them. Smart but not smart enough. You've got to get out of bed pretty early to catch old Johnny Weak napping.

Friday June 29

Got to work bang on time principally because I decided to work from home today. Have instructed Hayley to tell anybody who calls that I'm at a meeting in a mobile phone dead spot. Wales or somewhere. Mid-way through Richard and Judy, postman delivered hand-written letter. Rebecca Posh-Tot finally caving in probably. Opened letter and discovered it was a handwritten note from Tim Smallwood telling me that Sir Marcus wanted me to urgently organise massive company-wide £1 million conference. Did I know anybody who could help?

My mobile went at that moment. Text message from Rebecca saying she couldn't do lunch as she had to organise last-minute conference in Barbados with a Mr Smallwood who's budget was a lot more impressive than mine. Felt sure I would understand. Buggeration!! Called the office to pick up the pieces and got put through to bloody Customer Careline.

Saturday June 30

I woke up to find Emma studying a book which was a bit of surprise because the closest she normally gets to books is some of the heftier catalogues the poor old postman has to bring us. She said she'd had a dream where she was running away from me screaming and was looking up in her Encyclopedia of Dreams what it meant. I suddenly remembered my therapy homework for Dr Eccles. As soon as Emma had gone off for her five-hour morning session in the bathroom, I got hold of her book and picked out a few choice dreams for Dr Eccles to get her teeth into – all of which indicated falling in love and consummating relationships.

Three hours later I was on the couch with my head only inches from the divine knees of Madeleine Eccles. We had to get through some dull stuff about my relationships with the various insignificant losers at work. She said that what I do to other people I'm really doing to myself. How does she know about my rich history of self-abuse I thought. Finally we got on to the love dreams but instead of asking me what they were she asked me how I felt about them when I'd woken. Bit of a tricky one so I just said I had no real feelings about them. She just smiled and did a big tick on a clipboard. Not sure she got the message I wanted to send.

JULY

Sunday July 1

Emma has invited all her ludicrous pretentious hippy friends round for a communal rebirthing or something which means I am going for a communal Blue Boaring with the boys. I went early to get out of the house and do my therapy homework. Dr Eccles says I've never recovered from having poor relationships with an absent critical father and a docile blocked mother and that I should write an imaginary letter to them exploring these feelings.

Becky asked me what I was writing and I said it was a long love letter to her. The letter to my mother and father wasn't easy to write as I've never been good at postcards and that kind of thing. But I managed to make up a whole load of stuff for Mad Dr Maddy to get stuck into. Needed another pint after I'd finished but Becky was nowhere to be seen. Turned out she was in the kitchen crying. She'd taken my love letter joke seriously which proves what an idiot she is. I took her out the back and tried to calm her down but then things went from bad to worse and she said she loved me. For one awful moment I thought she was going to say she was pregnant. She didn't, thank God, but I was so shook up that I accidentally posted the letter to my parents on the way home.

Monday July 2

I've got a week off this week. It's jury service or payback time as I call it. This is where the criminal establishment understand how important it is not to be responsible for my insurance premiums going up every year. Wore my twelve-piece suit just to scare the pants off the sponging, devious little weasels and for them to understand clearly that a higher rate tax payer is sitting in judgement on them, not one of their skanky council peers. Sat around with a whole load of other potential jurors most of whom looked as if they would have benefited from being locked up themselves. The only thing most of them were intent on was claiming all sorts of expenses. I bet there was enough fraud going on in those expense claims to get most of the claimants banged up for a hefty stretch.

Tuesday July 3

Finally got picked for action and was led into courtroom. Saw the defendant, some vicious-looking, conniving little scrote and gave him the Judge Dredd look that I'd been practising in the mirror. Sat down in the box and mentally totted up how long he should go down for. Before I could add it all up the barrister for the little lawbreaking dirtbag told the judge that his client claimed to know me. Naturally I wanted to grill him about his school, university and rugby club, but the judge had me dismissed from the jury as being potentially prejudiced by my association with the defendant. Went back to the cattle pens feeling as if I'd just been sentenced for crimes against the criminal underclass. Consoled myself with the thought that I'd just add a couple of years on to the next little villain.

Wednesday July 4

Didn't wear suit today. Instead I tried to look meek and liberal and soft on crime and the causes of crime. Slouched into the courtroom and shuffled to my seat in a depressed left-wing kind of way. Wished I hadn't bothered because there was a tidy little piece in the dock accused of handling stolen property. She could come round and handle my property any day of the week. Apparently the father of her three kids provided maintenance by stealing her a new credit card and cheque book each week. How could she explain this? She couldn't. Why was she pleading not guilty? She wasn't. Following this little exchange the judge gave the Crown Prosecution Service a world-class bollocking for bringing the case in the first place and wasting the jury members' time. Which was a bit rich because there wasn't one member of that jury who didn't want to be there for the interactive paid-for entertainment on expenses.

Thursday July 5

The next case was more like it. Attempted murder with nasty looking weapon caused by heated argument over money, women and business. Typical Board meeting really except the victim was stabbed in the front rather than the back. The person accused of doing the stabbing called on a number of character witnesses who were wearing baggy suits and loud ties that all said to me loud and clear, 'I am well dodgy and I am telling monster porkies'. I wanted to ask the judge whether any of the character witnesses had anything dodgy we could send them down for while we were there.

We got stuck in and heard the barristers tell their completely contrived sides of the story. It seemed the whole case revolved around why the defendant had a carving knife lying about in his living room. We went into the jury room. I had a quick smoke and then was half-way out of the room to tell the judge to start erecting the scaffold when some bespectacled wet-knickered librarian type suggested we examine the evidence for any reasonable doubt. I told the silly tart that there will always be reasonable doubt because life is a doubtful business. My view is there's no smoke without fire. If he was innocent he'd have been on the beach playing with his children not in the living room playing with an eight inch carving knife.

Friday July 6

The librarian, supported by a couple of women who thought the murderer 'didn't look the type', insisted we re-enact the stabbing to see whether it could have been in self-defence. I was picked as I was roughly the same size as the victim and some other bloke had to try and stab me. The man picked to stab me had breath like nuclear waste and insisted on getting

close enough to me to stick the knife in. After 20 minutes of struggling with him I wanted to stab him too.

We concluded that for it to be self-defence the defendant would have had to be double jointed or for the victim to have had exceptionally bad breath. I volunteered to be chairman so I could give him the good news. He took it all very badly and then the barrister asked for a lenient sentence as he would lose his top job in marketing. This put rather a different complexion on the whole thing. I just hope it goes to appeal.

Saturday July 7

Suddenly remembered it was my turn with the kids but there was no way I was going to miss my session with Dr Mad. I phoned ahead to the clinic and booked the kids in for a two-hour session with a child psychiatrist to check for potential problems. I said they were all right now but given their biological mother's family history of mental illness it was best to check. Turned out to be a lot cheaper than babysitters which is worth remembering for the future.

When I got to Madeleine's she had this big colour chart out and said she was going to do some body scanning energy mapping to find out where my blocked energy was. We finished with a picture of me with a lot of pastel shades and then a bright red groin area. Fantastic!! Couldn't have been clearer. She said this showed I had a disconnect between the adult self and inner child and my pubescent teenager was running the show. I thought knickers to that, I just need to get my snogs in. I thought it was time to bring things to a head (as it were) so I told her I fancied her and that I wanted me and her to be on the same side of the couch. She didn't bat an eyelid and said these feelings were common at this stage of the therapy as she represented my adult self. She then pointed at the clock and said my time was up. I was pondering whether this was a yes or a no when her phone went. It was someone called Colin on the other end who apparently had a lot of repressed anger.

Sunday July 8

Funeral of Aunty Nell. Emma managed to snatch the limelight from the corpse in her little black dress that had as much to do with mourning as a whoopee cushion. Vicar directed his entire address to Emma especially the bit about love being eternal. I half expected him to rip off his dog collar and go for it but he probably remembered just in time he had to get old Nell underground. At the graveside Emma's mobile went. As she tried to get it out of her bag she dropped it and it fell down onto Aunt Nell's coffin. The ringing tone was Wham's 'Wake me Up Before you Go Go' which added a surreal note to the proceedings.

Afterwards we all went round to my parents for tea and concrete cake. My father took me aside and thanked me for the letter. I thought there might be some sort of scene but he just took out his cheque book and asked me how much I needed as they associated any form of communication from me with a demand for money. I thought Madeleine would like that when I told her. I also took a grand from him as I'm unlikely to see any sort of return from Aunt Nell. She's more than likely to have given me a good slagging in the will which will then be read out to all interested parties and posted on the internet under johnweaksucks.

Monday July 9

Weirdo HR Director Giles Renton-Willets facilitated Board meeting. Sir Marcus occasionally allows this when there's nothing important on the agenda and we've all forgotten what an arse he makes of himself doing it. The first thing we had to do was share with other Board members something about ourselves they may not know. I thought about saying I had a nob the size of Norway just to show what a stupid exercise it was.

Ross 'shaggability' Fulbright (Sales Director) announced he'd just a bought a puppy but then really took the limelight by announcing another record set of sales figures. Obviously he wouldn't be getting half the results if it wasn't for our world class marketing but you've got to admire the man for his performance. The reason I'm not in sales is I can't be doing with targets. What's the point of meeting your targets one year just to have them put up the next. Marketing is all about self-expression. I've got a very big self which is why I have to spend so much time expressing it.

Tuesday July 10

Got in rather late as the car wouldn't start. (It wouldn't start because the ignition key was still in my trousers, my trousers were still in the wardrobe and I was still in bed but let's not get bogged down in detail.) *Smoke Signals*, our company Newsletter was on my desk, so that was my morning's work cut out for me. Fulbright was on the cover under the headline Close Relations With Customers Pays Off with a photo of him hugging some poor customer. OK he's got fantastic results but boy does he milk it. Do we shout about the quiet, unassuming, behind the scenes work we do day in day out in marketing? Well yes we do, but no one seems to listen.

Asked Fulbright out for lunch to congratulate him but he was too busy getting close to customers. Had to go with Bill instead. We got so excited by the sales figures we quite forgot the clock and got back to the office at around fourish. Managed to clear my desk by six (I put everything into a drawer at five to six) and went to the gym after work. All the machines were in use so I had a seaweed wrap instead and snored liked a drain for an hour while some heavily made-up fatty fiddled with my face.

Wednesday July 11

Normal day to start with. I got in late expecting a sarcastic comment from Shirley on reception but there was a temp there. She had a message for me which was a sarcastic comment from Shirley about being late. Deleted e-mails, wandered about a bit, long lunch with Peters, went home earlyish. That was when the day really hotted up. In the evening papers there was a picture of Ross Fulbright in a very tight t-shirt snogging the same customer he was hugging in *Smoke Signals*. The news item was about the customer coming out. He's a big backer of the Conservative Party so it's all a bit of a scandal.

Bloody, bloody hell!! Old Shaggability Fulbright's just been thrown out of the closet and we didn't even know he was in there. And I bloody work with him. What the hell am I going to do now? I should have seen the signs: when a woman gets a cat you know she's given up on men. When a man gets a puppy you know he's given up on women. If he's 70 that's fine, if he isn't it isn't. Went to the gym in a very loose fitting t-shirt.

Thursday July 12

I parked in a bright, well lit area of the car park and went in to assess the damage. I asked Shirley on reception if she knew that old Fulbright was a shirt lifter. She said she knew he was gay and had done for years. Yeah right. That hadn't stopped her and all the other women in the office wanting to get his kit off. Well good luck to them. I'm sure his shaggability factor has slipped now. Perhaps I'll move up the rankings now.

Sir Marcus has issued a red alert saying that we all have to treat Fulbright and his condition as if it were perfectly natural. He's called an emergency Board meeting to make sure that happens – Fulbright not invited obviously. Had lunch with Bill and we couldn't believe that Fulbright was an uphill gardener. Looking back of course we could well believe it. It's all taking getting closer to customers one step too far in my opinion.

Friday July 13

Bumped into Fulbright in the car park. He said he hoped our working relationship wouldn't be affected in any way. I said as long as we stuck to the work and left the relationship well alone we'd be fine. He then flounced off to reception and I moved my car just in case. Of course the whole building was alive with the news that we had a pillow biter on the Board.

Bill and I decided to have an emergency lunch to discuss the whole sordid business of unnatural relationships between men. Unnatural relationships between women we don't have a problem with as long as we can both have a ringside seat, but not men. As it was Friday the lunch went on a bit and we got a mite squiffy. I can remember both going to the gym for a seaweed wrap and then ending up round at Bill's place but then it all gets foggy. If it wasn't for Bill I don't know how I would cope with this whole Fulbright business.

Saturday July 14

Got home in time to meet sister Karen and Paul her trainee Vicar boyfriend for lunch. Karen and Emma got talking about those mindless trivialities that occupy 90 per cent of the female brain and Paul and I slipped out for a smoke. I found myself telling him all about Madeleine. He sucked his teeth and said I must be mad going to a therapist. He said they just made up problems that you didn't know you had and then charged you for solving them. I made it very clear that I didn't have any problems but I fancied the therapist. Probably shouldn't have done that as it will get back to Emma quicker than a small dog.

Paul has a way of getting you to confess things when you least expect it. He told me if I really wanted to get her interested then I should tell her I was finishing the sessions because her unresolved conflicts were clouding her analytical abilities. Apparently this puts the screaming abdabs up therapists because they're all barking nutters underneath. I asked Paul whether that meant that all vicars are the devil underneath. He winked and gave me a sly grin. He's not a bad bloke for a Vicar. I asked him whether he was going to marry my sister. He said marriage was a sacrament and not to

be taken lightly. Got the feeling that there might have been a
veiled message in there somewhere.

Sunday July 15

Woke up early and decided to work on my marriage. Brought
Emma breakfast in bed which she didn't eat because the
grapefruit didn't have the exact kind of microsurgery required
before it can pass her perfect lips. I got a bit huffy and said
she never appreciated all the little loving things I did for her.
Couldn't think of anything other than the grapefruit but
you've got to make hay while the sun shines. She then got on
the phone to her mother which is what she does instead of
arguing and I went out for a cooked breakfast and Sunday
papers.

Found myself in the Blue Boar. Miserable Mike was talking
to the divine Angela about marriage and how he'd managed
to avoid it. They were talking about how hard life was on the
farm which is a bit rich coming from Mike as he spends most of
his life filling out subsidy claim forms and setting aside his
fields. We had a few pints and got talking about how men and
women were from different planets and I had suggested that
they should only be allowed to meet in the dark and under the
influence of alcohol. Angela refused to serve me for the rest of
the evening which was annoying as she's delicious when she's
in a snit. Tony the intellectual served me instead. He must have
said two words to me in the last five years which consist of
'same again'. On the way home I kept thinking about Emma
and couldn't get the phrase 'same again' out of my head.
Think I may have ordered the wrong thing there. Again.

Monday July 16

I am writing this on a flight to Miami. Carlos, the Smokehouse
man in Guatemala, has gone native. He's using local voodoo
sun god as marketing tool for our 'fruit' drink Shiny Bright
and has apparently become a bit of a local deity himself. He's
getting great sales results but it's all a bit off-brand. I've been

ordered by Sir Marcus to go and sort it out and to keep it all very hush-hush. Shiny Bright is a global mega brand, so we can't have it tainted by voodoo marketing (all marketing is voodoo but no need for him to know that).

Interesting brand Shiny Bright – a cocktail of some of the nastier chemical agents we couldn't use in our oven cleaner. We put it in a yellow bottle with sunshine on the label and sell it to kids as a health drink. 'Health' in that what doesn't kill you makes you stronger. Put my seat back and fell asleep counting air miles.

Tuesday July 17

Landed in the dark heart of Central America – Miami airport in other words. Had a bit of time on my hands so downloaded my e-mails before going into the jungle. Bad news. It looks like Sir Marcus is using my absence to deal direct with Shiny Bright advertising agency. Apparently he's told them we need great creativity for a great brand. I shuddered. The last thing we need is a creative agency coming up with 30 seconds of art school rubbish with no sign of the product. If you want to sell things, you need a young mum with good teeth.

Arrived in Guatemala City airport and walked straight into some heavy looking local hoods, all in shades and all sipping Shiny Bright. They stuffed me in their limo and told me they would take me to Carlos somewhere in the jungle. Either a great promotional gimmick or I've been kidnapped.

Wednesday July 18

After long and uncomfortable journey, we finally arrived at Shiny Bright bottling plant deep in the jungle where I was met by the large shadowy figure of Carlos. I was very surprised when he gave me a Masonic handshake but then realised he had two fingers missing. A truck left the plant with the Shiny Bright logo on the side. Small children ran after it and Carlos explained that they were all 'repeat purchasers' of the brand. He laughed a cold, hollow Finance Director's laugh. The kids stuck their tongues out at each other (all the colour of a magnesium flare) to show they all worshipped the Shiny Bright sun god. Carlos mentioned this was particularly useful for the coroner when they overdosed.

Thursday July 19

Woke up with mother of all headaches after late night with Carlos talking about secrets of Shiny Bright marketing. He admitted that he made up his own recipe. I warned him that was against the rules but he said as long as the stuff came out yellow what did it matter if they added a little extract of coca leaf to every bottle. I didn't know whether he was mad or a genius. If we'd been in a film I would have to have shot him. Instead I told him he was being called in for IT training. That'll finish him off. Eventually I said my goodbyes and headed for the airport with a case of voodoo Shiny Bright for personal use. On my stop over in Miami I lay on one of the hotel sunbeds and marvelled at the grip the sun has on primitive cultures.

Friday July 20

Rushed straight from airport to agency to see their new incredibly creative work before Sir Marcus does. After a lot of needless build up about how excited they all were about the idea, they revealed their concept boards which said, 'Drink of the Sun God'. I told them it was the last idea on earth we wanted and they'd better come up with a young mum with good teeth idea pronto. As expected they threw an industrial size rattle out of their pram and started bleating on about change of brief, no time, artistic integrity etc. until I promised to do the selling for them and double their fee.

That afternoon Sir Marcus arrived at the agency to see the creative Shiny Bright work he'd ordered. I told him it was important to get into the product and poured him a large one fresh from Guatemala. Within seconds Sir Marcus's pupils dilated and he watched the young mum ad like it was the birth of his first-born. He then got all emotional and thanked the agency for the most creative work ever. While he spent 15 minutes trying to hug everyone from the agency, I just said a quiet thank you to Carlos and the sun god.

Saturday July 21

Woke up to find a strange man in my bedroom. I thought he was holding a knife. Before I could run through all the men it could possibly be who wanted to stab me, I realised it was a paintbrush in the hands of some sweaty decorator. Emma had clearly moved on to the change his décor, furnishings, wardrobe stage of the marriage. Had a letter in the post from my personal ad. No marks for speed of response but full marks for the photograph. Decided I would arrange to see her just to let her know that I was no longer on the market. She happened to be free on Sunday night so I booked a nice little restaurant with very subdued lighting.

Then sped off to my therapy with Madeleine. It's time I confronted her with the fact that her feminine energies are blocked and she needs me to earth them for her. When I arrived her receptionist told me she was running a bit late and would I mind sitting in the waiting room. I knew this was all part of her defensive construct so I played along. Bugger me!! Bloody Colin Gilbey was in the waiting room. It was him or *Woman's Realm* so we got chatting.

Gilbey turned out to be less of complete tosser than I thought, although still very much a tosser. He said he was there because he was in love with Emma and that I had derailed his life when I married her. I wanted to tell him that he could have Emma because I wanted to get Dr Eccles on the couch but in his frail and vulnerable condition I thought that might not have been constructive. We carried on chatting for an hour or so until we began to wonder what had happened to our appointments. The receptionist told us that we'd been booked in at the same time but Dr Eccles hadn't actually come in to work. We realised this was her little way of getting us to talk to each other. She may have solved Colin's problems but I still hadn't even got a smile out of her.

Sunday July 22

Woke up thinking of my chat with Colin and decided to give Emma a quick one just because I can and he can't. Emma pushed me away and said she didn't really like too much contact in the morning. Got up, got myself showered, shaved and shitted, bought the papers and had a massive cooked breakfast. Then went to Blue Boar for opening time. Chatted to Mike the Miserable about what a funny old lot the Sudanese are.

Arrived for my hot date and spotted Shirley from reception in restaurant. While I was waiting I got chatting to her and funnily enough she was waiting for her date too. I showed her the photo of the woman I was meeting and it suddenly dawned on us both that it was her. I took the piss mercilessly that she'd sent me her graduation photo when she was now older than I am. She asked me what I was doing going on dates when I was married and I told her that I'd only come to tell her that I was unavailable. I've never heard her laugh so hard.

She then said did that mean if she wanted a quick shag I wasn't available, which put me in a bit of a spot I can tell you. The lower half of my body suddenly became available, but before the top half could answer she'd put on her coat and left. Got home early and still a bit stoked up so I thought I'd give Emma a quick one. She pushed me away and said she didn't really like too much contact in the evening. Went to bed early and realised I now had the sex life of a peanut.

Monday July 23

Got into work very late so I wouldn't have too much of an audience for my encounter with Shirley on reception. She was very polite and asked me what I'd done over the weekend. I told her I'd had dinner with an exceptionally attractive lady and she agreed what a fine looking wife I had. She winked so I think my secret's safe with her although as soon as I got to my desk I checked the intranet just to make sure she hadn't taken out a full page announcement.

After I'd binned my post, had a cup of coffee and deleted all the e-mails from dull people, it was time for lunch. Called Bill Peters and we hot-footed it down to Mr Bojangles. Bill seemed in a very good mood indeed. Amazingly he refused to drink. I was about to phone for an ambulance when he passed a little pill across the table. I swallowed it and within seconds I had the sensation of a large glass of red wine settling into my stomach. It was one of Dr Cobb's prototype Snifters. I asked Bill for another but he said he'd had the rest that morning. We reverted to traditional liquid refreshment and toasted our impending success.

Tuesday July 24

I have decided to put the Snifters concept into consumer research. Obviously you don't listen to a word the public tell you about anything because generally they are as thick as the dung of a pig. If I wanted to know their opinion about anything I'd look at yesterday's tabloids. However, we are a customer driven company and as nothing moves without the customer having pronounced themselves delighted with it, we might as well waste a few grand on asking them some pointless questions.

Got a massive jiffy bag in the internal mail from Bill Peters. Inside there was a single snifter (red wine) and a post-it saying 'lunch'. I didn't have anything much on in the afternoon apart from annual appraisals for my team so we let lunch stretch out until it was time to go to the pub. We were both pretty happy as we knew we were onto an absolute winner with Snifters. Had a good chat with Shirley on the way out and wondered whether receptionists were generally receptive and whether I shouldn't try signing in to her visitors book as it were.

Wednesday July 25

Went into town for meeting with our Name Generation
Agency. They've had a week to think about what we should
call Snifters. First part of the meeting was replaying the brief
which I always think is spectacularly pointless as I gave them
the brief in the first place. The general rule with agency
presentations is the longer the build-up, the weaker the work.
They then gave me their 'sketchbook' presentation which is
basically a list of three thousand names which is supposed to
impress me with how much ground they've covered. I pointed
out that most of the words could have been generated by
computer because they were things like, 'Construct' and
'Tailgate' which they'd just stuck a capital letter on to make
them look like a name.

I gave them a preliminary bollocking half-way through
their presentation which I find is always a great way of
knocking their confidence before they unveil their 'solution'.
We got on to the short list to which I nodded slightly. They
then presented their final recommendation which I greeted
with absolute silence as if waiting for them to unveil their
proper final recommendation. Getting no reaction they then
went into an orgy of rationalisation and justification. I
promised to take their 'ideas' away and think about them. I
also insisted we take away their 'sketchbook' list as this will
save us name generating for our next ten products.

Thursday July 26

Sifted through the name recommendations with Bill. Their
short list was: Quenchers, Snorters, Swiggs, Sinkers, PitStops,
Dog Hair, Alcopoppers, High Balls, Coasters, Bushwhackers,
Zippers, Oggies, Tiny Tots, Drams, Vipers and Slammers.
Having gone through them all and decided for various
reasons that we didn't like any of them (mostly because we
hadn't thought of them) we decided to go for Snifters but
register all their suggestions so that competitors couldn't
have them.

I got the designers to do up tasteful illustrations of the little pills in their blister packs so that the customers would know what the hell we were talking about when they went into research. Finished early and chatted up Shirley on reception. Turns out she is divorced which is always a good sign as you have rock bottom expectations of relationships but you're desperate for good sex to make up for the wasted years. She said she knew sex wasn't going to be good with her husband when he brought a one-man sleeping bag on the honeymoon. I found myself saying that I had a double sleeping bag if she was interested. She told me to get home to my wife but did lean forward when she was saying it so I could see that gravity had not yet significantly impacted in the breast department.

Friday July 27

Spent day in research lab listening to a bunch of badly dressed, half-witted customers talk absolute bollocks. No one liked Snifters at all and thought of all sorts of reasons why they wouldn't work. Normally we would send them on their way with a big smile, 30 quid expenses and never think about them again in our lives. However, O'Keefe the Operations Director and Smallwood the Finance Director were waiting to hear the tapes and we needed to make sure they were onside to get the big cheques signed. As neither of them would recognise a breakthrough product if it sat opposite them on a train we needed to have customers saying the right thing.

I had an emergency meeting with Bill and we got the visualisers to draw up a four litre bottle that was half the price of a normal bottle, had twice the alcohol content and had a free lottery ticket strapped to the side. We did a quick research session with this and of course the consumers went into raptures about what a great idea it was, great value for money, perfect way of getting their alcohol etc. Bill and I retired to the edit suite and came out with some customers sounding very, very positive about Snifters. Not long after we got an email from O'Keefe saying consumer feedback was very positive, it was time to start Snifter production and get them into a test market. Bill and I retired to our little test market (Mr Bojangles) and had a few quick ones.

Saturday July 28

Sat in the park for a couple of hours with Kieran and Leah watching them screaming about in the playground. For a moment I was grateful I'd had them in my first marriage so they wouldn't have to clog up any of my subsequent marriages. That said, you can never be sure with women, because even when they're your sixth wife they can still get it into their head that rather than wanting their body what you really want is more children. Linking sex to having children is one of the main points of evidence that God has a sense of humour.

Emma was away for the day with Tish no doubt swapping all the innermost secrets of all the boyfriends they've ever had like football cards. Waited till the kids were exhausted, took them for a quick balanced, nutritious box of nuggets and dropped them back with their biological mother. She was looking suspiciously glam (if a komodo dragon can look glamorous). She said she was going shopping but then her mother-in-law swooped in and boasted that she had a date with 'a really nice man'. I could already picture his grey shoes and 1.4 engine. Went down to the Blue Boar to drown my sorrows. Inexplicably none of the boys were there and only Tony the intellectual was behind the bar. Having exhausted his witty repartee with 'same again' he retired to the other end of the bar leaving me to drink alone.

Sunday July 29

Woke up next to Emma and was once again shocked by just how beautiful she was. Wanted to climb on top but suddenly came over all virtuous and tried a little bit of gentle foreplay with little nuzzling little kisses, teasing butterfly caresses, sensitive stroking etc. After about two minutes of this by the bedside clock I finally got a response which was a loud double-action fart from my beloved. I thought if that's what you get from foreplay, you can keep it.

Cooked an epic breakfast for myself and then took the papers down to the Blue Boar. All the boys were there and we soon made ourselves comfortable. Becky was also there and looking at me like a little lost lamb. I may have to put her out of her misery again if only I can find a way of doing it with her arse out of sight.

A couple of ramblers came in with their big boots and woolly socks. After they'd ordered their half-pints of shandy we all had a whale of a time making up interesting local sights that they simply must see while they were in the area. The Terminator was all over the little bearded one who kept muttering good boy. Barney said, she's a bitch, and the little rambler was virtually in tears. We finally sent him on his way which sadly for him was completely the wrong way. When I got home I mistakenly let slip to Emma that Colin was in therapy. I thought I was going to be rumbled for my dates with Dr Eccles but instead she was on the phone in a shot and talked to him for so long I had to go into the spare room.

Monday July 30

The week started with a bit of bad news. I suppose it had to happen sooner or later but Sir Marcus has gone and read a business book. Marketing is too important to be left to the marketing department he now says. Or rather some slap-head guru with the business experience of a pair of tights says. He's probably only read the back cover but now he wants to axe the whole marketing department to cut costs and improve marketing. Brilliant.

Sir Marcus has also decided now he's a big business gnu to give each director a fixed amount from which to pay their department's salary increases so that we have to make the decision about who's worth what. This will be a bit tricky for me because two of my team want the full monty – Emily Reimbold (Pammy Anderson with brain implant) and Nigel Henwood (grey shoe with brain implant) – which would mean less fat for this cat. I smell the influence of Timothy Smallwood, Finance Director, who's so mean he dilutes his water. Worked off frustration on gym running machine doing power ramble.

Tuesday July 31

Red Alert! Sir Marcus has read Chapter 2 of business book. He's discovered KPIs which up to now he'd assumed was some kind of smart peanut. He wants to measure Marketing on Key Performance Indicators. Of course what gets measured gets done (that's why women have vital statistics) but you can't measure marketing, it's an art for God's sake. If a product does well it's great marketing, if it doesn't then something's wrong with distribution. We marketing types are freewheeling, creative spirits who can't be tied down by budgets, targets, KPIs or any other nasty little accountancy tricks.

However, Board meeting has been called for Friday to agree new KPIs, so I quickly arranged emergency lunch with Bill Peters to discuss marketing peril. As we were internalising our second bottle of red, Smallwood walked past window. We wondered whether he'd ever been inside a restaurant. Apparently he cuts his company credit card in half as soon as he gets it. What a pale value-brand little life he must lead.

AUGUST

Wednesday August 1

Got to work late because of roadworks. I had to stop and watch for a while because there's something about the sight of someone digging themselves into a hole which I find fascinating. Just to keep one step ahead of the game I asked Sir Marcus's secretary what Chapter 3 of his business book was called. It was called 'Leadership through Engagement' apparently. I didn't ask what the book was called – probably *Business through Bollocks*. I then tackled the thorny issue of salary increases: checked through team's KPIs and noticed I'd included teamwork, probably because I couldn't think of anything else to put in.

Called Emily into my office and gave her a quick 360° appraisal (if her skirt was any shorter it would be a collar). Told her she'd done well and would she like to have dinner to discuss a more involved management style. She did a good job of looking flattered and said it was her second invitation as Henwood had asked her earlier (fat chance). Gave her maximum rise and reminded her that my door was always open (the one marked 'Bedroom'). Finally, rang Smallwood and asked him out for lunch to chat through department KPIs. He checked his diary (total whiteout obviously) and said yes.

Thursday August 2

Called in Henwood for his 3° appraisal where I give him the third degree. Started by telling him that a salary increase was out of question because he'd slipped up on his teamworking KPI: he looked puzzled until I said 'Emily Reimbold'. He then blushed redder than my gas bill, started muttering all sorts of excuses and apologies and I trousered his salary increase.

After appraisal, me and Bill Peters took Smallwood out for a prolonged death by lunching. After half a shandy Smallwood can't do his two-times table so after our second bottle of red he was well out of it and started blubbing about Financial KPIs and how he had nothing left to axe. I told him there were three fat areas of overspend he could easily cut in marketing: new product launches, media spend and agency work. He was pathetically grateful. We kept him drinking until he admitted he really wanted to be a choreographer and had the leotard to prove it. No surprise there.

Friday August 3

KPI Board meeting. Massively hung-over Smallwood slunk in late looking like a rotting courgette. I crisply unveiled Marketing KPIs focusing on massively increased spend on product launches, media spend and agency work. Then got top agency totty in to show selection of gratuitously dirty marketing concepts followed by personal plea to Sir Marcus for more active 'engagement of leadership'. Engagement obviously wasn't going to be a problem for Sir Marcus as his eyes were practically married to her shockingly ergonomic top.

Smallwood then presented his KPIs, just managing to say massive cuts in product launches, media spend and agency work before chundering into a yucca. Sir Marcus visibly underwhelmed at Smallwood's attempt to undermine his engagement with top agency totty. I declared that financial direction was too important to be left to Financial Directors and we should make our spending decisions without him. I emerged with my budgets secure and everyone seemed very impressed. I may have to write a book about it.

Saturday August 4

Woke up and said something like good morning, Emma. This somehow developed into a full-blown row where I was accused of not respecting her as a person. After a titanic effort I managed to calm her down and then blew it by asking her whether it was her time of the month. Fortunately, we had to leave shortly afterwards to go round to my sister Karen's for lunch.

Went out into the garden with the Reverend Paul for a smoke. He had just come from a funeral which was also pretty much how I felt. I asked him when he was going to make an honest woman of my sister. He said she was already far too honest for his liking and winked. He does a lot of winking for a vicar.

Before I knew what I was doing I was talking about my marriage being a sham. I told him that I was deeply hurt from the divorce and had probably married in haste on the rebound. Paul turned to me and said 'my arse'. Which didn't strike me as the standard response one would expect from a minister although with today's Church of England nothing would surprise me. He then handed me another fag and added, 'She's a great looking girl and you were thinking with your dick.' That just about summed it up really. I told him the only good thing about being married is that it stopped you marrying anyone else. He winked.

Sunday August 5

Have decided to have one more go at cracking Emma. I thought long and hard about what she's really like as a person and what she wants in life. I've concluded that what it all seems to boil down to is shopping for herself, sensitivity in her men and furry ears in her animals. I've therefore booked a holiday for two in the Rockies to look at bears, moose, chipmunks and a whole selection of animals with furry ears. This also has the benefit of showing how sensitive I am. There are also a couple of fringe benefits; national parks don't have shops and I've always fancied getting my leg over on a deep fur in front of a fire (making sure it doesn't still have the ears attached obviously).

I thought this was guaranteed to bring us closer so I phoned her on her mobile to find out where she was (shopping) and told her I had some good news for her. She said she also had good news. I imagined for a moment she'd decided to enter a religious order but I thought that would be too good to be true. We had supper together which felt a bit weird as I knew the Blue Boar boys would be worrying

themselves sick thinking that something had gone disastrously right at home. She told me that Tish was now seeing Colin. Difficult to believe really as Tish is a tidy looking piece. Sounded suspiciously like charity work to me. I announced the holiday to her and she was absolutely over the proverbial. She jumped around the room saying we could make it a foursome. She got on the phone to Tish and I got myself down to the Blue Boar to share the bad news.

Monday August 6

As a marketing-led, customer-focused company we continually update our brochure. Well, every time some Johnny no-stars at BT changes our telephone numbers we do. Organising the corporate brochure is like organising a wedding; everyone wants to be included and you're bound to upset someone somewhere however hard you try not to. Gavin Smedley the IT Director asked why we needed a brochure at all when we've got a million-quid website. I told him it's because 95 per cent of the hits on our website ask for a brochure (subtext: IT know precisely FA about marketing or anything else for that matter).

Human Remains have called me in for a quiet word which probably means some girlie's weeping into her fruit tea over some constructive feedback I gave her. But in fact it was something completely different. They told me in very serious tones that they had noticed Bill Peters's binge drinking and they thought it might be a cry for help. I immediately volunteered to help, managing to keep my face straight and my tone serious.

Tuesday August 7

Time to ruin someone's life by giving them the corporate brochure monkey. I asked Hayley if I was supposed to be mentoring anyone and if so to send them up to my office. Someone called Vanessa Cowley showed up; low tot factor and nasty pencil-case mind. Told her about the fantastic corporate brochure opportunity she'd been hand-picked for and that she should start by getting a good photo of Chairman. Without batting an eyelid she said that on the contrary we should start by talking to customers and added for good measure that she had majored in internal communications at Business School. She'll be the expert then.

Bill Peters rang and I heard his cry for help. Had lunch and even after three bottles of red we still couldn't see what the drink problem was. We committed to exploring it further especially if we could put it on HR staff welfare budget. Sir Marcus rang later to say brochure should start with a fantastic quote he'd heard but couldn't quite remember. Felt sure we would know it. They must be called Chairmen because a chair is the closest thing to an arse.

Managed to get down to the gym where there was a bit of a panic because a new member had got a portion of his genitalia caught in a machine. Two paramedics carried someone out on a stretcher who turned out to be none other than Martin Padley. Surprised he had anything left to get caught up.

Wednesday August 8

Photo shoot with Sir Marcus and Board which I know from bitter experience is by far the trickiest part of the whole corporate brochure operation. I told Vanessa that her job was to swoon over photos of Sir Marcus even if he came out looking like Goofy's dad. She got herself into an instant snit and told me that her Business School said the contents of a corporate brochure should be consistent with company mission statement. If that meant one long cliché from beginning to end then they're spot on.

After another session helping Bill with his drink problem, I got photos back and went through them. Board all looked relatively human except Bill who looked like an oversised scrotum with a seventies hairstyle. Sir Marcus loved the photo of himself and asked Vanessa if she'd like a copy.

Before she said anything stupid from Business School, I jumped in and said she already had one blown up on her desk. Interestingly, Bill Peters got very upset about his photo and wants us to use one taken 30 years ago when he had one chin instead of five.

Thursday August 9

Got in late thanks to a misapprehension regarding the speed of light being a constant. Well that's what I told Shirley which managed to shut her up for once. Sir Marcus rang to ask whether we'd found his quotation. Said it had word 'retail' in it or 'detail' possibly. I promised it would come to me in time (but not in time for brochure). Went for lunch with Bill Peters and spent almost four hours listening to him cry for help. Bill said his real drink problem was the fact that he had two arms and only one mouth.

When I got back from helping Bill, Vanessa told me that while I had been wasting my time at lunch she'd organised everything and was circulating final text for approval. I warned her that it wasn't over until the spatially challenged totty sings. What she really needed to worry about was the Chairman's completely gratuitous last-minute changes designed to show everyone who was boss. She ignored me and went off in one of her arsy Business School snits.

Friday August 10

Got in late and found Vanessa in tears. Chairman wants type size of entire brochure half a point smaller, his quotation is 40 lines of Kipling, everyone's butchered her copy and the printers need everything by end of play. What would the Business School recommend I asked her. I could see a big girly blub coming on so I told her to increase the size of the Chairman's photo so there was no room for his quote, paste in last year's copy in new typeface and then reduce brochure on copier by 4 per cent to show 'new point size' to Sir Marcus. Vanessa perked up but then remembered the problem with Bill Peters and his photo. I told her he'd signed off the chinless scrotum version yesterday sometime after I'd helped him to a fourth bottle of red. Vanessa said I was a one-man business school. I'll drink to that.

Saturday August 11

Picked up the kids from Kate and asked her how her hot date went. The mother-in-law shot out of a cupboard at precisely this moment and said that he was a charming sensitive man with lovely manners. That meant he was probably a screaming homosexual I told them. Probably shouldn't have done as I spent the morning in the park trying to persuade Kieran and Leah not to go round calling all their little friends screaming homosexuals. Dumped them back at their mother's for tea and roared round to the Blue Boar.

When I arrived the boys were discussing what a funny lot the Mexicans were but we soon got on to Disaster in the Rockies. Barney had all sorts of great ideas about picking them all off one by one in the wilderness and feeding their bodies to the bears. We agreed it would be a waste of a couple of great bodies so only Colin got fed to the bears. For the girls I was going to continually promise that there was one more shop just ahead until they were in the Arctic circle and then leave them to survive on their credit cards.

Got home rather late but Emma and Tish were still up planning our relaxing carefree holiday in minute detail. They were on the web and seemed to have discovered satellite photography of every retail outlet in the Rockies. Tish was in her dressing gown and actually looked quite promising. She said how excited she was about the holiday and for the first time I began to get a little bit excited too. Just a shame Emma's coming really.

Sunday August 12

Took breakfast in bed to the girls but Tish was well covered up. Was just settling into the papers when I got a call from

Kate who gave me a thermo-nuclear bollocking about teaching Kieran and Leah bad language. They had spent the entire evening calling my father-in-law a screaming homosexual. I apologised profusely and promised it would never happen again. That particular phrase won't happen again but now I've realised the ankle biters are such a good messaging service I'll be teaching them all sorts of choice little phrases.

Colin came round to join in the grand holiday planning and was soon laughing and joking with the girls. They kept touching him as they spoke to him which made me want to knee him in his vulnerabilities. I should have killed him when I had the chance. Thought it would probably be best if I went down to the Blue Boar to let off steam. Tony the intellectual asked me whether I wanted 'the same again' which he always does even when I've just arrived in the bar. Kind of gives the impression that I never stop drinking. Funny that. Becky wasn't on duty and I found myself pining for her big friendly arse knocking over bar stools, customers etc. Got home late found them all still tittering about mooses and furry ears. It's going to be a long, long holiday.

Monday August 13

Sir Marcus's meaningless management platitude of the week is 'the bottom line is the bottom line' and he's got a plan to improve it. It's a breathtakingly audacious idea called customer focus. He thinks customers are always right. I think that's a load of bollocks. These are customers who have trouble opening the front door of your shop and when they're inside they're suddenly supposed to be infallible. Do me a favour. Sir Marcus chuntered on about customers and I slid my brain into neutral until I suddenly thought I heard something about Vauxhall Vectras. I would not be delighted as a customer if anyone swapped my Porsche for a Vauxhall Vectra. Fortunately what he said was he wanted to revector the company to a customer service space and wanted to have a Board session every day this week where we all show how we're so focused on the customers we're virtually cross-eyed. Whoopee.

Tuesday August 14

Got in at crack of dawn in my sheer enthusiasm to get in touch with the customer. Or I would have done were not the roads clogged up with bloody customers doing what they do best. Getting in the way and obstructing business. First meeting of customer focus started with Renton-Willets suggesting we kick off by doing warm fuzzies: this is where we go round the room telling each other what we really like about our fellow directors. I started by telling Renton-Willets that I would really like him if he stopped being such a big girl's blouse and doing bloody stupid party games in business meetings.

While he picked up on my negative energy we got on with the serious business of customers and how they can be well and truly rogered – I beg your pardon, how their expectations can be exceeded. Ken Carmichael – Research Director and by unanimous acclaim lowest man on the corporate totem pole – dared to suggest he knew about customers because he was always talking to them. I told him that the Research Department was basically a glorified tape recorder and that the serious analysis happened a lot higher up the food chain. He didn't say much for the rest of the meeting so he must have taken my point.

Wednesday August 15

Ross 'ex-shaggability' Fulbright flounced in radiating industrial strength bonhomie and immediately claimed ownership of the customer as it was his sales team who met their needs. Which is true if you think our customers have a pressing need to be smarmed to death by grinning wide boys. Our Legal Director then spoke which is a bit of a rarity because generally he prefers not to implicate himself. He said his department provided the constitutional framework for customer service. I presumed he was referring to the Smokehouse lifetime guarantee for our products – as soon as we've installed them we guarantee you won't see us again in your lifetime.

When we'd all finished laughing at the Legal Director, Giles Renton-Willets piped up and claimed that customer service was a state of mind and HR were doing a fantastic job developing training to help people discover that space. I suggested this might actually be a complete waste of space along with the rest of HR. After work managed to get down to the gym and sat in the sauna for an hour trying to sweat out all the customer service bullshit.

Thursday August 16

Got in on time for the fourth day running. Shirley on reception asked whether I'd been on a time management course. I told her I didn't have time for that kind of thing. Also suggested she went on a basic human pleasantry course. In the meeting Clare O'Keefe had the audacity to claim Operations had responsibility for the customer as it was her responsibility to get the products in their grubby little mitts. I told her the only contact Operations have with customers is when they run one over with their trucks.

Bill Peters then strenuously denied any responsibility for customers. He said that if they messed with his chemicals they tended to die or get badly burnt which kept them in their place. Bill's attitude absolutely cock on, obviously, but I could see by Sir Marcus's facial hernia that it wasn't exactly flavour of the week. I then talked long and loud about how Marketing were already so close to the customer we were currently being sued by some of them for invading their body space. Once I was into my stride I started getting quite flowery about how Marketing was the heartbeat of the customer within the company. I was really only playing for time as I could hear Geraldine outside clinking the coffee cups. The chocolate Hobnobs came in and everyone forgot about the customer in their rush to get at them.

Towards the end of the session Ken Carmichael piped up again saying that perhaps some internal research or something was required. I cut him short because most of what he says really isn't mission critical data. I'm sure his work is very important and old Ken is a lovely man but he's definitely not first XV material. I must get round to sacking him soon.

Friday August 17

Arrived on time again. I'll have to watch I don't get into the habit otherwise work will start pouring in to fill the time available. In the last customer focus meeting Gavin Smedley claimed IT had responsibility for the customer as his Customer Relationship Management system owned the integrated customer interface. One day he'll say something we all understand. The only reason the IT department has got the rest of us by the scruff of our Y-fronts is because in the land of the witless, the half-wit is king.

Sir Marcus stopped us and said a thought had crossed his mind. I thought that it must have been a long and lonely journey. He said we couldn't focus on the customer until we'd all learnt to treat each other as internal customers. Which was the cue for everyone in the room to gang up on me and accuse me of being the nightmare customer from hell. I told them they'd all forgotten one thing. I was their internal customer and therefore I was always right. I think that left them in a fragile space.

Saturday August 18

We moved house to Canada or that's what it looked like anyway. Emma had packed everything that wasn't plumbed in. She said she'd done her normal packing and then had some extra stuff for travelling light. Colin and Tish came over before breakfast. Tish had her own seventeen tons of luggage and Colin had this manky looking knapsack thing with biroed doodles all over. I can't believe my luggage is going to be sharing a carousel with that. The taxi arrived which was just big enough to fit inside one of Emma's mid-size suitcases. The driver had one look at the luggage and his face took on the expression of one of the defenders of Rorke's Drift when confronted with 5000 oncoming Zulus. Half an hour later we were all in the back of a mini-bus with another driver. The first had attempted to help with the luggage and was now in some kind of specialist unit for spinal injuries.

When we got to the airport I naturally gravitated towards the Club check-in only to remember that I had Colin and his manky knapsack in tow. I swallowed hard and joined the endless line of unwashed council types queuing up for cattle class. The girls then left us to inch forward with their 24 tons of luggage while they went for some last-minute shopping to make up the extra weight. Colin and I chatted about where he'd been (nowhere) and what he'd done (nothing) and who we knew in common (nobody). Finally got to check-in and they naturally volunteered to upgrade me and my partner when their computer told them I had more gold cards than King Midas's birthday party. They couldn't upgrade us all so I told Colin he'd have to stay in the back with Tish while me and the missus resumed our natural place in the order of things.

Needless to say Tish and Emma went up the front and I found myself in the back with Colin and the rest of the slum dwellers. This was a deeply depressing experience and we were a good way out into the Atlantic before I could shift the elbow of the fat woman next to me off the arm rest. There was a baby in the seat in front of me who periodically stood up and looked over the seat back and threatened to vomit on my *Economist*. After 11 hours of this I felt so vulnerable and fragile I could almost feel affinity with Colin except he slept through the whole bloody flight. Probably luxury conditions for him compared to the filthy student squat he no doubt lives in.

Landed in Calgary airport. I looked with pain at all the people from Business Class filing quickly off just as some cretin lifted an anvil from the overhead lockers straight on to my head. I looked up and down the aircraft and everyone was standing with their heads bent under the bins like idiots. It looked as if the flight was in-bound to the World Congress of Village Idiots. Thought I could just whip through the airport like a dose of salts but then remembered that Emma had five hundred tons of luggage. We stood by the carousel and some eight-foot balding idiot from economy stood right in front of me. When I finally got a glimpse of Emma's half-ton bright orange suitcase, I accidentally pulled it off into his shins. Finally loaded up enough luggage to evacuate a small city and pushed it through into arrivals. Went straight to car rental, showed them my gold card and demanded the top of the range vehicle. Could have had something rather svelte and convertible but because of the luggage situation we ended up in some sort of truck. Drove to hotel went to bed. No todging.

Sunday August 19

We had about two hundred miles of driving to do to get to Lake Louise when Colin announced he couldn't drive. Emma was impressed with his commitment to the environment, I couldn't believe what a spineless gimp he was. I had to do all the driving which at least meant I had some excuse for not being part of their pathetic girly chit-chat. I had the foot on the floor and the van was managing to do 90mph but Emma insisted we slow down in case we hit a bear. I told her if we actually saw a bear she'd want us to be doing a lot more than 90 – in the opposite direction.

I wanted to crack on to the hotel to get in some moosing time but Emma insisted on stopping at every historical marker. I told her that Americans had historical markers for anything that's past its sell-by date but she wanted to stop and read them all. After a long drive during which the phrase 'bear with furry ears' was mentioned 346 times, we arrived in Lake Louise. Very nice log cabin kind of arrangement. Young lad shot out of reception and asked whether we had any luggage he could help with. Everyone has a major learning experience in life; that was his.

Beautiful room with open log fire and deep rug in front of it. Told Emma I would get the fire on and she could get her kit off. I struggled with getting the fire going and had to rip up some of Emma's five hundred magazines that she needed for the flight but didn't actually look at. Heard excited noises coming from the bedroom and thought I was in for a five-star moosing but discovered she'd found a picture of a bear with furry ears. How exciting!!

Monday August 20

Beginning to realise that going on a touring holiday with Emma and Tish was a mistake of epic proportions. With their combined luggage, it's like organising a UN relief effort every morning. By the time we've had breakfast, they've chosen what to wear and then repacked their 101 suitcases, it's time for lunch.

Finally got going at about 11.30 and drove up through Glacier Park. Obviously great scenery but otherwise really boring drive as I couldn't get any decent stations on the radio except for Moose FM which seemed to play home-made tapes of people singing their own suicide notes. Stopped seven hundred times to take the same photo of mountains and trees with Colin, Tish and Emma blocking the view. Every time we got out of the car Colin said, 'Wow, I just can't take it all in'. My thought was if you can't take it all in, why don't you just sit in the car and shut up.

Tuesday August 21

Stopped at historical marker which pointed up a trail to a viewpoint where some trapper had once stopped for a slash. Before I could say 'Let's press on', Emma and Tish were already walking up the snow-covered trail in search of furry ears. I had to follow in my brogues slipping around like an idiot. After about a hundred yards we met a group coming down who looked as if they'd just come off the North col of Everest. They gave me funny looks as I slithered past. Emma was still forging ahead like a snowplough. That's the trouble with second wives, they don't know the limits. My limits that is.

Finally got to the viewpoint by which time I had altitude sickness, snow blindness and hypothermia. The view was exactly the same as it was in the car park – i.e. mountains, trees and snow – only a mile higher. Just to capture the moment Colin said, 'Wow, I just can't take it all in'. Emma gave me a little hug and said it was the best holiday she'd ever had. Totally ruined the effect by then hugging Colin for at least one and a half seconds longer.

Tish threw a little snowball at me to prove how much fun she was having and then Emma followed it up with an unethically large one. It all developed into a bit of a mêlée during which I accidentally shoved Colin down a little bank which turned into a slightly steeper slope. After he'd edged his way back for an hour or so up what was probably in strict geological terms a cliff, he saw the funny side. Emma and Tish treated him like Scott of the Antarctic and started rubbing bits of his body that were in no danger from frostbite whatsoever.

Wednesday August 22

Mountains, trees, road, historical markers, no bears. That evening I suggested we find the best steakhouse in town and eat half a cow each. Americans cock most things up but one thing they can do is a good steak. Emma sighed and said that Colin was vegetarian and we'd have to make sure there were options suitable for vegetarians. I thought that is the bloody limit. Not only does the spineless gimp not drive but he doesn't even eat meat. Can't they bloody well see that my company is not suitable for vegetarians.

I had to go for a little walk to clear my head. Found myself in a nice little bar built of logs and had a couple of beers. I looked round at all the frontier types in the bar and tried to work out why women found little piss-arse scrotes like Colin attractive. He seemed to be made of some kind of anti-matter in that the more pathetic and girly he was, the more the girlies were attracted to him.

I wondered whether the bloody great lumberjack who'd just sat down next to me had trouble with women because he wasn't vulnerable enough. Or whether the Mountie in the tight fitting boots in the corner was complaining to his mate with the hard hat about how perverse women were. It then struck me that there wasn't actually a woman in the whole bar. A split second before the lumberjack next to me opened his mouth I realised I was in the frontier branch of the YMCA and got out of there quicker than a turbocharged woodchuck. Talk about out of the frying pan into the fire.

Thursday August 23

On another incredibly long drive from one tree to another remarkably similar tree, the girls were all talking about their respective mothers so I had shut down all my vital signs and gone into a kinder, quieter world of famous sporting/totty replays. While I was in this state I saw a big brown bear loping through the woods alongside the van. Emma was still batting on about her mother so I didn't interrupt. She doesn't like me interrupting as she says I'm trying to oppress her. I thought I wouldn't mind oppressing her on a bear rug and giving her a damn good moosing just once on this sodding holiday. The bear got tired of running alongside us after a while and loped back into the woods, no doubt to have a proverbial shit.

Over dinner I eventually got a decent amount of wine into Emma and finally thought I'd get some rug time. Once we got to our room I mentioned the fact that I'd seen a bear. Suddenly everything went glacial. Moosing was off the menu and Emma put on her special chastity pyjamas with armoured gusset. All because I didn't tell her about the sodding bear. I said I hadn't wanted to interrupt her because she was talking about her mother. Somehow she managed to put the words in my mouth that I thought her mother was a grizzly. I spent the whole night on the rug by myself contemplating the fact that the marriage was going nowhere fast (unless I sprouted furry ears).

Friday August 24

Emma and Colin went off early to an exhibition of Native American art. The combination of native and American and art summed up just about everything I take care to avoid in life so I decided to have a close look at the exhibition of native American bourbons in the hotel bar. Tish turned up after I'd already had one too many and I found myself getting rather chatty with her. She was looking quite fit but I kept reminding myself that I was a married man, she was going out with Colin, I had my self-respect etc.

Then for some reason I will never be able to fully explain in a divorce court, I attempted to snog Tish. She immediately gave me the world's hardest slap which hurt so much I seriously thought she'd dislocated my jaw. It even crossed my mind to phone the police and have her charged for assault and battery but I really couldn't face the prospect of a squad of Mounties mincing round the hotel. Tish immediately went to the exhibition of Native American art to report the incident and I knew that I would then become the subject of major extinct male dodo exhibition for the girls for the rest of the trip.

Saturday August 25

Long day's driving with a high level of tittering from the girls in the back. I noticed Gilbey was beginning to get slightly out of order with me. I can take that from any woman, even when I'm married to them but I can't take it from some stinking, goateed, fragile, vegetarian, non-driving, sock-sucking hippy with a manky knapsack. To be honest I worked myself into a bit of a state.

When we got out for our 'next' comfort break I waited for the women to go behind a bush and introduce their beavers to their Canadian cousins. Then just as Gilbey was going to say his, 'Wow, I just can't take it all in' line I grabbed him by his vulnerable collarless shirt and told him in a free and frank discussion that if he ever took the piss out of me again I would realign his gender on the spot. Judging by his exemplary behaviour afterwards I think he finally managed to take it all in.

Sunday August 26

Arrived at the airport with seven hundred tons of luggage and five hundred tons of shopping. For me the holiday was already well and truly over so I went straight to the check-in, flashed my gold card and said that if they wanted to keep my business they'd have to get me so close to the pilot I could count the hairs on the back of his neck. Had a very comfortable flight back in Business. Colin flew back wedged between Tish and Emma in economy so we were all happy.

Monday August 27

Got in relatively early (after nine but before ten) simply because I'd got into the habit of getting up early to begin the process of moving five hundred tons of luggage. Looked through all the rubbish that had piled up while I was away. Utter disaster!!! While I've been away furry ear spotting Tim Smallwood has introduced timesheets to improve efficiency and save costs. Normally I make a point of principle to ignore any kind of initiative from the Finance Department as they're not paid to take initiatives they're paid to stop initiatives.

Had an extended lunch with Bill and agreed with him that time sheets were an underhand Stalinist tool of oppression that reduced people to the status of worker ants. Bill was outraged that he was being asked by Finance to account for his movements in 1999. We agreed this was an unwarranted intrusion into his working life. Of course the main reason behind all this cost cutting is because last year Smallwood bankrolled an internet enterprise called Blackhole.com and he's now trying to recoup some of the millions that disappeared into it.

Tuesday August 28

Got in late due to slightly delayed onset of jet lag. Shirley made some joke about local time being 10.09. If she was keeping my timesheet I would be well and truly stuffed. Arrived at my desk after quick detour through totty-rich zones just to get me back into office mode. Discovered that the Finance Department have now decided that our global competitiveness will be enhanced if we charge staff 2p for vending machine coffee. I have called this visionary new policy change management because it now means that everybody has to start carrying around four tons of loose change.

At the afternoon Board meeting I fiercely resisted this vending machine daylight robbery but Tim Smallwood looked all pious and said look after the pennies and the pounds will look after themselves. I told him in no uncertain terms that if you spend the whole time looking after the pennies, what you will end up with is a sack full of coppers and someone else will be waltzing off with the high denomination notes. After work went to the gym with Howard. Got on the step machine, switched it to escalator mode and ascended the equivalent of Everest while my eyes were glued to the tidy little package in front of me doing it the hard way.

Wednesday August 29

Arrived late for work as I had to search back of sofa for coffee money before leaving. Shirley on reception had world's largest Thermos sitting on her desk as a big two fingers up to Finance Department. I like Shirley. She's got balls and I like that in a woman. Tim Smallwood is on a roll. He has now instituted a new policy of double-sided photocopying which he believes will impress the city analysts. Notices about the new policy have gone up round the building. They are a bit difficult to read because they've been printed on both sides.

Had crisis meeting with Bill Peters over lunch at Mr Bojangles. We agreed that Smallwood wouldn't be happy until we were a cost free company producing profits from thin air (a consultancy in other words). Our suspicions were confirmed when we discovered that Smallwood had cut Smokehouse expenditure on biscuits for staff. This was a bit rich considering he insists on chocolate Hobnobs at all Board meetings which he then consumes single-handed.

Thursday August 30

Got in late due to appalling traffic congestion. I blame the Third World. If they kept up with their debt payments we'd have enough money to build a few more decent motorways. Shirley on reception is selling Jammie Dodgers at 10p a shot. She should be stopped except it's probably the most profitable part of our business currently. I spent the morning filling in my timesheet. It was divided between 'filling in timesheet' and 'finding change for coffee machine' and 'turning over photocopies'.

Smallwood circulated in advance the paper he'd prepared for the Board meeting itemising the cutbacks he's implemented without any mention of the Blackhole.com fiasco. I think he's hoping we'll forget he's pissed away ten years' profits. Faced with that kind of corporate shenanigans especially from a little tit like Smallwood, Bill and I decided a little 'pushback' was required. Over lunch we agreed the strategy and before going home we put together a plate of chocolate Hobnobs and glued them all together.

Friday August 31

Board meeting to discuss mid-year results. Smallwood started in about slashing costs and circulated his report. At that point I sent a text message to Hayley who brought in the coffee and chocolate Hobnobs exactly as ordered. Bill emptied a little bag of coppers onto the table and started working out what 2p times twelve was. I asked whether there was a discount for volume. Hayley then asked me to fill in her timesheet. I filled in hers and then got mine out to write 'filled in Hayley's timesheet'. Sir Marcus moved from simmering to boiling to volcanic in the space of a few seconds but he got the drift.

Smallwood called the meeting back to order in his fussy mother hen voice. He then reached for a Hobnob, lifted the entire plate off the table and, would you believe it, some bastard had left a Post-it note underneath which said 'Blackhole?' Sir Marcus stopped stirring his coffee, remembered why there was a black hole in his profit and loss and asked for an explanation. I then asked everyone to turn their reports over. Someone concerned with cost saving had photocopied a summary of the Blackhole losses onto the reverse side of Smallwood's cheeseparing report. We then got down to the business of slashing things such as Smallwood's salary, reputation, department, bonus, future etc.

SEPTEMBER

Saturday September 1

Woke up with a slight feeling of fear and then realised that Emma's parents were visiting for the weekend. We went to pick them up at the airport. What I hadn't expected was Uncle Nathan to be one of the family. He was carrying their luggage, all fifteen tons of it. Big luggage seems to run in the family. We all went out for lunch in the Blue Boar principally so the boys got a chance to look at Emma's parents and decide for themselves whether Maurice was a major league criminal.

On reflection this was probably a bad idea because when I went up to the bar Barney warned me that they were going to play a game where they held up score cards to show how many years Maurice should be in prison for. This got underway during starters when Evan held up a large eight on a piece of paper. Maurice and Emma had their back to the bar but Maureen saw what was going on. I told her they always gave marks out of ten for the ladies. Maureen seemed quite chuffed especially when Mike held up a 15 a few minutes later. I was on the point of telling the boys to cool it when Maurice banged his fist on the table to add emphasis to some psycho point he was making. Barney held up a picture of a noose shortly afterwards and Maureen burst into tears. Maurice completely ignored her and we carried on as normal with the boys pissing themselves at the bar.

Sunday September 2

Maurice woke me up at six o'clock and asked me to go for a walk with him. It felt disturbingly like I was going to be shot at dawn. As we shivered round the block he told me they all got up early in Malaga every morning (and Wormwood Scrubs probably). He asked me about the grandchildren and their current whereabouts. I reassured him that everything possible was being done in that direction and that no I wasn't shooting blanks how kind of him to ask.

We eventually took them back to the airport and Maurice left with his usual loving words about if anything happened to Emma he would kill me. Emma spent the drive back on her mobile to Tish making plans to go through the fifteen thousand photographs of mountains and trees we're now the proud owners of. Colin looks very sweet in some of them apparently. And fragile and vulnerable in others no doubt.

Got down to the Blue Boar sharpish to replay the high points of last night. The boys all agreed that Maurice was an animal and should be locked up. Congratulated me on my choice of in-laws and an absolute piss-taking festival got under way. Mike admitted that he wouldn't mind giving Maureen one, which took some of the pressure off me for a while. Tony the Intellectual admitted that he knew Maurice from a past life which was the surprise of the evening, the surprise being that he'd said something rather than he had a shady past which we'd all kind of assumed anyway.

Monday September 3

As I arrived in the car park I saw Shirley the receptionist getting out of her car. She was obviously late so I roared round to my Director's reserved spot right next to the front door. I shot inside, turfed Len from security out of Shirley's seat and installed myself just before she came through the door. I then managed to get an epic amount of piss taking out about her being late before she told me she'd just had a family bereavement.

I got to my desk and noticed the smell of corporate restructuring is in the air. All the Directors are doctoring their budgets, dusting down their CVs and eyeing up smaller departments. The rumour is that Smokehouse is either going to reorganise its functions into horizontally integrated client groups or reorganise its client groups into vertically integrated functions. Either way it's just an excuse to get rid of some dead wood and show the City boys we're awake. Sir

Marcus wants voluntary redundancies and not the Bill Peters variety either, where you declare yourself voluntarily redundant and keep your job for 20 years.

Tuesday September 4

Got in late and was ignored by Shirley. I've got to do my appraisals this week. This is when the team get to have an exchange of opinion with me. It's called an exchange of opinion because they come in with their opinion and leave with my opinion. Smokehouse has 360° appraisals – which means everyone gets a chance to stab you in the back. One I'm not looking forward to is Trevor Keene, a senior brand manager who's an ambitious little snake and doesn't mind who knows it. Saying you're very ambitious in business is like going on a date and saying you're very randy. It may be true but it won't get you what you want any faster.

Still a bit concerned about restructuring rumours so after work took Clare Bridport, Sir Marcus's secretary, out for a drink (you should always pretend to fancy Chairman's secretary even if she's an absolute swamp donkey). It took me three Bacardi and Cokes, a bag of pork scratchings and some outrageous lies about her general attractiveness to find out that Sir Marcus is thinking of promoting internally for a joint Sales and Marketing Director. Which means I'm either getting the job or Ross 'Sailor' Fulbright is and I'm getting the push.

Wednesday September 5

Red Alert!! Sir Marcus asked me what I thought about Trevor Keene. Sir Marcus never asks people what they think unless he's had a thought. I think Keene is a cocky, Oxbridge tosser with ideas well above his station, which translates for Sir Marcus as 'He's an interesting young man we should keep an eye on'. Apparently they met on a flight from Frankfurt where Keene was telling him all his fantastic bright-eyed ideas for my department. Sir Marcus said we need to promote young talent. The only young talent I want promoted in my department has long hair and short skirts. Looks like it's time I applied some crushing pain to Keene's low hanging fruit.

Had lunch with Bill Peters who is dead wood above the neck (and below if we're honest). He said that the deadest wood is in the handle of the axe. I wanted to clarify what he meant by this but after his third bottle of red he suddenly became horizontally integrated with the floor. Popped back into the office to delete my e-mails, got my kit and then motored down to the gym where I found Howard doing a lot of stretch exercises on the mat. He said it was a form of yoga which gave him a better outlook on life. It certainly gave a better outlook on the totty sweating on the machines, so I got down and gave myself a good stretching (as it were).

Thursday September 6

Got in fairly early and apologised to Shirley about my jokes about lateness especially when one of her close relatives was now probably one of her late close relatives. Realised I was getting into deep water, so mumbled something and got out. Got to my desk and checked my diary. Show time. Appraisal for Trevor Keene.

I started the 360° appraisal by giving Keene a good length of rope: I asked him to give me my appraisal first. He struggled for a moment and then managed to say that I was fun to work with but that I didn't listen to people's ideas. Wasn't really listening so had to get him to repeat it. I asked him what the ideas were he shared with Sir Marcus. He said he couldn't remember so I asked him point blank whether I had his 100 per cent loyalty. If he said yes I won, if he said no, he lost. I could feel his wood dying. He said no his loyalty wasn't quite 100 per cent and to save him having to give his reasoning I sacked him. We can't run an effective team with disloyalty. I'm sure he'd understand that being the bright young Oxbridge graduate he is (was). Went home happy and dreamt of axe handles.

Friday September 7

Arse safely covered, concentrated on getting myself joint
Sales and Marketing job. Decided to get Keene to prepare
case but then remembered I'd sacked him. Never mind. I
used his salary to get in marketing consultants. Told them the
conclusion I wanted so they could merge print some tired old
rubbish to get there. Went for lunch with Bill Peters and
discussed the art of business survival. He said you had to be a
sod to people on the way up because it was a massive
incentive not to come down again.

Got the report two minutes before my own appraisal
with Sir Marcus. He flicked through report and then asked
whether the consultant who wrote it was the same Trevor
Keene that was in my department. I said probably and
wasn't it a shame we couldn't retain talent like that. He
gave me a look that converts alligators into handbags. He
said the problem with voluntary redundancy programmes
was their effect tended to be dead wood retention. No
idea what he was getting at. Sir Marcus finished the
meeting by saying that Directors weren't to be reshuffled,
so was safe. Touch wood.

Saturday September 8

Emma up and away early to go to Tish's for the Festival of
Mountain Photography. Tish not so keen on coming round
here anymore for some reason. I'm not complaining because
at least it gets rid of Emma for a while and there's no chance
of that little shit Gilbey clogging up the place. I lay in bed
nursing a healthy looking erection and worried about its
current underemployment. At my time of life, with the keys of
a Porsche in my pocket, it should be engaged in almost
continuous undercover operations. It's important to respect
your body and that particular part was simply not getting
enough respect from anybody (apart from me).

I was going through a list of potential beneficiaries when
the phone rang. It was my ex-beneficiary wondering why I

hadn't turned up to take the rugrats off her hands. An hour later I found myself using 250bhp of Porsche to ferry around two grubby little squealers. Supermarkets are a great place to pick up women, I've heard, so I took them shopping. I threw the kids in the trolley and found that if I wedged them in with enough cases of beer they couldn't move around that much. Kept my eye out for desperate young mothers but just seemed to see a lot of desperate dads pushing around trolleys full of beer. Got to the checkout and discovered Leah had a slight case of frostbite as I'd covered her lower half with frozen oven-ready chips.

Sunday September 9

Woke up alone. Emma was obviously still engaged in day two of Festival of Mountain Photography. Really could have done with a good moosing and the thought did cross my mind to give Becky a call. The only reason I didn't was to be sure she was behind the bar at opening time. When I got to the Blue Boar Evan was outside waiting for starter's orders. Beryl was holding a Tupperware party at home and he'd been told to make himself scarce. We got talking and after agreeing that Malaysians were a funny lot, I managed to get out of him that by Tupperware he actually meant rubberware and other assorted bedroom aids.

Becky turned up at that point and I thought about encouraging her to get down to one of Beryl's parties. She might look rather tasty in a one-piece PVC number as long as you could keep the bottom half well out of sight. Becky kept giving me sly little looks which generally meant taking her eye off something else which she then knocked over. Barney and The Terminator came in and he asked how my lovely wife was. I was opening a packet of crisps at the time and said without thinking that she was still in the packet. We all agreed it was a lovely packet and then moved on to more important things like why the Italians were so rubbish in the Second World War.

Monday September 10

Snifters are now rolling off the production lines. HR told me that this was by far and away the happiest production line they'd ever set up and they couldn't explain it until they discovered that the 'workers' were sampling product quality more than was strictly necessary. To my mind it's always a vote of confidence that your own staff are nicking your product. All we have to do now is to get them out into the test market so that the general public can start nicking them. Went to the gym on the way home and discovered they'd put table football in the bar. Played all night with Howard which was probably the hardest workout I've ever had at the gym. Also best possible workout for wrist muscles (barring the obvious one obviously).

Tuesday September 11

Got into work late. Shirley shook her watch and checked it was still working which was a bit of a relief. I was beginning to miss my daily dose of sarcasm. Our legal boys have played an absolute blinder. We were worried that we wouldn't be able to sell Snifters anywhere except pubs, but the legal boys have got them registered as a medicine. Quite right too! As long as we put 'contains alcohol and can make you drowsy' we're fine. I wanted to put 'contains pure alcohol and can make you completely bladdered' but I was advised to quit while I was ahead. All we need now is an advertising campaign.

Fortunately I've already come up with a brilliant campaign. It's about a man who has to go through a series of increasingly unpleasant things at work, at home and at a party but perversely gets happier and happier. The secret is 'Snifters – the pub in your pocket'. I've always had a gift for advertising. I've got a feeling the Agency will be impressed by my creativity.

Wednesday September 12

Up to town for advertising agency presentation. They always have about 17 people in the room, mostly cracking totty to distract from the mindless rubbish they come up with on the creative front. Before they started they told me that the Creative Director was right behind their idea which usually means they bumped into him in the lift on the way to the presentation. After a long preliminary analysis of the marketplace during which I completed my preliminary analysis of the agency totty, they got on to the concepts.

The first was a post-modern ironic reworking of the classic anytime, anyplace, anywhere Martini ad. They got terribly excited about this until I asked them if they had anything in the way of fresh thinking. As expected they all went into sales overdrive about how they knew this was going to be an award-winning, mould-breaking, target-hitting, client-promoting campaign. I could see they were short of ideas so I told them my pub in the pocket idea and they were impressed into total silence. Clearly they didn't expect award-winning, mould-breaking, target-hitting campaigns to come from their clients. I told them to use this as a springboard for more thinking and just to keep them focused, reminded them Smokehouse had a media spend of about £3 million to put behind the campaign.

Thursday September 13

Back to agency to do further totty analysis and pick up well-worked-up version of my pub in the pocket idea. First thing I noticed was that totty count was well down. Instead they had a couple of hard-faced short-haired todger dodgers in and some heavy hitting account men. They told me how they'd incorporated my excellent work and reworked their own concept. They then showed me a concept which was identical to the one they'd shown me the day before except with a few new camera angles 'derived from my inspirational input'.

At this point I 'accidentally' snapped one their agency pens in half. Psychologically this always works wonders because they think I'm expressing deep inner anger. I told them if we couldn't work collaboratively on a win-win basis (i.e. do the creative work I tell them to do) then I'd have to look for somewhere else to put my media spend. Worked out frustration in gym with Howard. I did a few weights and then spent some time in front of the mirror waiting for the benefit to show up.

Friday September 14

Arrived late due to head being wedged under headboard. Got to my desk and deleted all my e-mails. Work done for the day, I got my feet up on the desk and started reading the trade mags to see if anyone I knew had lost their jobs. This always makes the day seem brighter for some reason. Hayley put a call through from the agency Managing Director who wanted to talk about Snifters campaign. I kept him waiting for a few minutes to establish his position in the food chain and then picked up the phone. There's nothing like having the top dog grovelling. He had called to check that what I really wanted was them to make my pub in the pocket idea. Finally the penny drops!! I've always said if you want things done, go straight to the top. Having got this clear he then told me that they were a world class agency not ProntoPrint and that I could stick my campaign and my media budget up my arse. He put the phone down and for the first time I really wanted to do business with them.

Went for lunch with Bill to talk him through the advertising impasse. Much though we admired their new business culture we agreed we'd have to go elsewhere if I wanted my work done properly. Bill knew a man who ran a small agency from a converted barn in Oxfordshire who was completely untroubled by artistic integrity and would do precisely what we told him. With that out of the way we got down to untroubling ourselves with some serious reds. I got back at about four and realised I'd missed a disciplinary proceeding for one of my staff for persistent absenteeism.

Saturday September 15

Got up late and found Emma was already gone. Emma hasn't been speaking to me much lately, which is a relief in one way as she is about as interesting conversationally as an extractor fan. On the other hand it makes getting her to agree to a bit of conjugal rights a bit problematic. Maybe Tish told her about my abortive snog. Maybe definitely. They've told each other everything else so they're not likely to keep that a big secret. Went to a big industry environmental awards bash in town in the evening. Emma took 15 hours to get ready but looked absolutely breathtaking. I jumped on her and tried to have a quick one but she doesn't like anything to be touched let alone removed once it's on.

We had Ross 'chase me, chase me' Fulbright and Bill Peters on our table so we all got leathered in short order to overcome any social tension due to his condition. Fulbright was on the other side of Emma and she was laughing and giggling as if everything he said was incredibly funny. Incredibly dodgy yes. Funny no. As the drinks were on the company Bill and I decided to see whether we could dent the bottom line and went for it big style. Amazingly Smokehouse won an award for Most Improvement in Environmental Performance. Bill Peters told me that it was because our effluent discharge pipe was pumping so much stuff out that it had blocked itself up. Bill insisted on making a thank-you speech where he staggered up to the podium, pushed the guest speaker out of the way and announced Smokehouse was as green as Kermit's foreskin. Then in a brilliant piece of timing he also turned green and threw up on the podium. Classic Bill Peters moment. Made me proud to work for Smokehouse. Don't remember much after that.

Sunday September 16

Woke up surrounded by an incredible number of sheets and couldn't work out how I'd got myself in such a tangle. It slowly dawned on me that I was in a big bin in the hotel laundry room. I could see Bill Peters's feet sticking out of the top of another bin. We got ourselves sorted, had a big breakfast in the hotel and went home, Bill Peter still clutching his award. Emma was at home with Tish and Ross Fulbright which was a bit of a shock. Apparently he'd brought Emma home last night after I'd disappeared with Bill. I was going to ask whether he'd shunted her round the carpet as well but Emma added that he'd slept on the sofa. Fulbright left shortly afterwards and for the rest of the day the girls banged on about how one man could be so sensitive and so good looking and so single. I wondered whether I should tell them about his condition but then I didn't want them to know that I spent a lot of my working life with a Queen's Park Ranger. Decided it would be better all round if I had a work out at the Blue Boar.

When I got there Barney and Mike were discussing where the Canadians had gone wrong in the personality department. I was about to join them when I noticed Uncle Nathan in the corner. He beckoned me over and asked me straight out whether Emma was pregnant yet. I said that after last night there was now a very good chance. He said that was good because Maurice was beginning to lose patience. That was all I needed. I joined the boys at the bar and was feeling so low I decided that I would have to shag Becky despite the wide arse situation. Luckily for me she wasn't on duty.

Monday September 17

Arrived at work in good time. Good time for me that is, which is approximately an hour after everyone else. It's roll-out week. This is where Gavin Smedley tries to justify the millions of pounds that disappear into the IT Department swamp every year. They've just spent five million smacker on a new Realtime Inventory Processing system (RIP). Theoretically this means that as soon as granny takes one tin of ointment off the shelf, one of our genetically modified warehouse staff pops another one in a lorry which rushes it off to the shop before granny has finished her shoplifting. And if you believe that you probably believe pigs are frequent flyers. Had long angst-laden lunch with Bill Peters where we digested the shocking news of a moratorium on new company cars from end of week probably to pay for RIP financial haemorrhaging.

Tuesday September 18

Shirley clearly well on the way to recovery having been outstandingly rude to me when I arrived shortly before ten. I explained to her that I didn't want to get into the Japanese situation where all the workers had to get in at the crack of dawn to be at their desks before their boss arrived. I would love to start work early if it wasn't for the welfare of my people.

I got to my desk for a leisurely coffee and Gavin Smedley came in to explain to me in great detail why RIP is technically superior. I told him to keep talking as I always yawn when I'm interested. I don't really trust Smedley because he's one of those grinning born-again Christians and if there's one thing that puts the fear of God into me, it's born-again Christians. Let's have some born-again lions in born-again amphitheatres to balance things up, I say. RIP Consultants fired up system, sent a test order and then left the building with half our annual profits. On drive home my Porsche was overtaken by latest model Porsche. Pretty humbling experience I can tell you. Diverted to the gym to work out my frustration. Spent three minutes on the weights and warmed down with three hours on the table football with Howard.

Wednesday September 19

Board visit to warehouse to see the horny-handed sons of toil coping with white-hot RIP technology. Mick the warehouse manager was surprised to see us as he hadn't been told about our visit and said they hadn't touched the system because they hadn't been trained. Collective sigh from the Board. Having IT department in Smokehouse is like those twilight years in evolution when Homo Sapiens and Neanderthals shared the earth together before the latter became extinct through their own crass stupidity.

Warehouse IT nerd desperately searched for test order on the system. Nothing. RIP Consultants long gone of course. Only one person in the whole of Smokehouse knows how RIP works and naturally he's on leave. RIP consultants are happy to come back and sort things out as long as we don't mind diverting our entire cash flow to their accounts department. Smedley almost in tears. The trouble with born-again Christians is they have too much faith in things.

Thursday September 20

Sir Marcus came down the mountain to give Smedley a thermo-nuclear bollocking. He wanted to know why the warehouse hadn't been RIP trained. Smedley managed to sputter that training was unnecessary because the system was idiot proof. I shook my head at the profound stupidity of IT – never has so little been achieved by so many with so much money. Had lunch with Bill Peters and we congratulated ourselves long and large on not having anything to do with IT.

Our RIP expert has been found. Apparently he's moonlighting for consultancy company installing RIP system into some other poor bugger's company. That afternoon I saw Smedley in his office praying. Instead of being born again why don't they just grow up. Returned to office and turned on the computer. Got Hayley to access the system and then sat down and ordered myself one underarm deodorant for delivery to me at the office. Completed order in under a minute and sent it 14 times just to be sure. Called Smedley to ask if I could upgrade car before tomorrow. He said it would take a miracle.

Friday September 21

Got in early enough to get an extra ten minutes of Shirley's sarcasm. It suddenly struck me that where there's badinage there's bonkage. I'll have to keep an eye out to see whether all this energy invested in sarcasm might not be better employed in a stationery cupboard for a quick Boris Becker.

Smedley burst into my office all excited saying he'd got good news and bad news. The good news was that there were 14 delivery lorries in the car park with my order. I was a bit confused as he was behaving like he'd just witnessed the feeding of the five thousand. He then told me that word had spread round the company that this was my order, so not only did RIP work but it must be idiot proof. Great.

The bad news was that one of the lorries had accidentally written off my Porsche while manoeuvring, but Smedley was now happy to sign for a new one. My gob was well and truly smacked I can tell you. I bring back RIP from the dead and I'm rewarded with a new Porsche. How do things work out like that? God only knows.

Saturday September 22

Emma away for the weekend with Tish. I've got a sneaky feeling that Colin's involved somewhere but they're all welcome to each other as far as I'm concerned. It was my turn for the kids so I popped round to Kate's. She had her new man there. He was called Malcolm and looked relatively normal except for the fact that he was ten foot tall. My immediate thought was that sex with Kate (who's a short arse) would mean that she would be face-to-face with his navel.

He drives a Rover 75 which means they probably don't have sex in the first place. Or if they do he probably wears leather driving gloves and does it under a picnic blanket. Kate seemed very proud of him and the kids seemed to like him. I gave them the option of staying to play with Malcolm but Kate insisted I take them because they wanted to go for a picnic (I knew it, the dirty sod). Kieran had got it into his mind that he wanted to see the country because his granddad said it was disappearing fast.

I drove them to a field somewhere and let them run around until they were caked head to foot in cow dung. They loved it and it will give Kate something to wash along with the picnic blanket when she gets back. Spent evening at the Blue Boar. Evan was very down. He'd applied for planning permission for massive shed in his garden with central heating, satellite telly etc. but Beryl had found out and lodged a formal objection with the council. Later on I shagged Becky without looking down. She was pathetically grateful.

Sunday September 23

Woke up alone in my own bed. I hadn't stayed the night with Becky as the thought of waking up in the shadow of that arse was too much for someone in my current fragile space. Colin called round later for Emma so he obviously wasn't with her. We had a bit of stilted conversation until I gave him a couple of Snifters to try. We relaxed and I asked him what he saw in Emma apart from her stunning good looks and fantastic body. He said she had cute energy and they shared the same powerpoints in life. He had to leave shortly afterwards partly because I told him he should stop talking bollocks and get the hell out of my house.

Got down to the Blue Boar sharpish and joined the general discussion about why Bolivia had never really made it as a world power. Becky was behind the bar and kept giving me coy little conspiratorial glances so I had to spend the whole evening trying to avoid the bartender's eye which was bit of a novelty for me. I weakened towards the end of the evening and gave her a quick one in the cold store. Nearly froze my arse off doing it though. How Eskimos keep their numbers up I'll never know.

Monday September 24

Nasty little Vauxhall Nova parked in the spot for my Porsche. Might just as well have put a sticker in their window saying 'abort my career'. Binned my post, deleted my e-mails and then spent the morning reading *The Art of War* by Sun Tzu. We've got a major competitive struggle on our hands and I need all the help I can get. It's quiz night on Thursday and if marketing lose again my office credibility will slip to HR Director level.

Sun Tzu says know your strengths. Have analysed marketing and realise we have too much beauty and too little brain. The most intelligent person in the building is Len, the night security man, who's read a book a night since the Blitz. Have therefore seconded him into marketing as close partnership between marketing and night security is vital in the new economy (at least until Thursday night).

Tuesday September 25

Sun Tzu says know your enemy. The IT team have a junior nerd who knows all the science questions so have arranged for him to look at my computer on Thursday afternoon. Sales team are hot on all subjects so I've ordered a crate of champagne for them to be delivered lunchtime Thursday. Tim Smallwood (Finance Director) says Jenny in accounts is their secret weapon as she has a brain the size of Cardiff. Could be a threat but it's impossible to nobble people in accounts unless you surgically remove the spreadsheets from their souls.

On the way home was cut up in car park by the same ruddy Vauxhall Nova who nicked my parking spot. Had to calm myself by accelerating past it at 150mph on the way out of the car park. Met Howard at the gym and we shed a good few pounds at the bar. He had a free kick in the table football which he managed to get right out of the table and into the mineral water of some stick-thin old biddy. She didn't see it go in so was highly unamused when we went and asked her for our ball back.

Wednesday September 26

Got in late and had a good long chat with Shirley which made me even later. No sooner had I got to my desk when the bloody fire alarm went off and everyone hotfooted it to the car park. Sun Tzu says seize opportunity. Slipped into Clare Bridport's office – Chairman's PA, major league swamp donkey and Quizmaster. Riffled through her papers, found the list of questions and ran it through the copier.

On the way out I looked out of the window – great to see all the non-smokers shivering outside. Lit four cigarettes on my way down and breathed smoke over everyone's desks. Noticed Jenny from accounts getting into the Vauxhall Nova (if accounts are so worried about costs, why aren't they using public transport?). Finally got back to the office and discovered I'd accidentally photocopied agenda for Friday Board meeting with surprise questions from Sir Marcus to keep us on our toes. Gave questions to my department to answer by end of tomorrow as 'teambuilding exercise'.

Thursday September 27

Arrived late to torrent of Shirley sarcasm. I suggested that if she was so concerned that I get up on time perhaps she wouldn't mind being my personal alarm clock. She said she'd think about it. Spent day rehearsing answers to Board questions. Junior IT spod came round and pronounced my computer dead (not surprising as someone else from IT 'fixed' it yesterday). I told him to work through the night or I'd wipe his personal career hard drive.

Got to pub for Quiz and found the entire Sales team completely cabbaged. Apparently they'd been drinking champagne since lunchtime and were now in the loos taking turns to drive the porcelain bus. IT team couldn't answer anything because their star nerd was working through the night. Marketing were doing better than ever, the only fly in the ointment being Jenny from accounts was still answering like the talking clock. Sun Tzu says be aggressive. Made a quick call on my mobile and got the barman to ask anybody owning a Vauxhall Nova to move it as it was blocking other cars. Jenny disappeared and this gave our night marketing man Len time to list the members of Boyzone and secure us total victory. Old Sun Tzu would have been proud.

Friday September 28

Telephone rang at 6.30 in the morning. It was Shirley pretending to be my wake-up call. When I got in four hours later I told her I was late because I had woken up with a terrible ringing in my ears. Went into Board meeting and immediately noticed other directors looking suspiciously jolly. They told me they'd all bet on Marketing winning quiz night because they knew my ego couldn't stand losing. I was more than slightly miffed but kept my rattle in the pram as I knew what was coming up.

Sir Marcus breezed in and started asking questions about the business, really underhand stuff like 'what is our mission?' I answered everything without batting an eyelid while Bill Peters looked at me with an expression like he'd walked straight into a plate glass window. I said this stuff was all in *The Art of War*. Sir Marcus asked whether it mentioned anything about not leaving your original on the photocopier. Made a mental note to check what Sun Tzu says about having your pants well and truly pulled down. Let air out of Nova's tyres on way home.

Saturday September 29

This is going to be a very good weekend indeed. Emma is going to the Opera in Paris with an old friend. So that's three things that I find deeply unpleasant successfully avoided: opera, the French and Emma. All of which leaves me free to get my bat out, get the batting average up and generally have a stonking time of it. But then got a call from my mother saying that my father had gone off his chump and could I come and have a look at him. I said give him a scotch and phone the doctor but she phoned another six times so I promised to whiz up there. Turned out she was the one off her chump and the doctor had already seen her. I suggested she go straight into a home which probably wasn't the right thing to say.

Put my foot down on the way back because I could see my weekend disappearing. Disaster!! My beautiful Porsche was smashed by some hit and run idiot in an old Lada. Had to be towed to a local garage where the local mechanics' idea of a performance car was one that could overtake a running pig. They looked at it for half an hour before they realised its engine was in the back. It was pretty clear that between them they didn't have enough forks in their family tree and I made them aware of their general personal and professional inadequacy. I called a tow truck but they said they wouldn't be able to get to me until the morning. Which meant I had to go to a local pub to stay the night. The bar was chock full of the mechanics and their first cousins so I had to beat a hasty retreat to my room and lock the door. The next five hours I spent by myself without women, TV, my car or the Blue Boar. I thought this is what it must be like to be an accountant.

Sunday September 30

No sign of the tow truck. I decided to look around the town. The town was shut. Eventually, I decided to walk up a hill and see if I could see anything by way of civilisation. At the top I bumped into a couple of ramblers. There was no way of escaping and to their minds the only conceivable reason I would be on top of the hill was that I too was a rambler. I wondered whether I could get away with killing them and burying them in their cagoules. I decided conversation was the marginally better option. They followed me back into town talking merrily about the kind of mud they had on their boots. I wanted to tell them about the kind of rambler I usually had on the bumper of my Porsche but remembered that I no longer had a working Porsche.

The ramblers invited me to the pub for lunch. I couldn't think of a single excuse not to other than a burning desire to stand in the street alone with my hands in my pockets. Two minutes later I was back in the pub while they scanned the menu for vegetarian options. The mechanics and their mutant family were still on the other side of the pub with a couple of motor parts on the table which looked suspiciously like Porsche spark plugs to me. In the fascinating conversation with the ramblers I had while they ate their UVO (unidentified vegetarian options) we discovered that we were near neighbours. Oh Joy!!

As the tow truck didn't appear I found myself cadging a lift in the back of their car, which surprise, surprise turned out to be a knackered old Lada with bits of my Porsche's paintwork on the bumper. I gripped on for dear life as we hurtled along at well over 40mph. I arrived at the Blue Boar just in time to hear the news that Mike the Miserable and Becky were engaged. Becky gave me a little triumphant look and Mike patted her arse as if he was steering a large Friesian into a milking shed. What a good weekend that was.

OCTOBER

Monday October 1

Bad start to the week. I put up a very tasteful impressionistic nude study in my office and seconds later the office manager, Mrs Tooley, stormed in and told me to take my pornography down. I said it was perfectly natural and helped my creative juices flow. She looked closely at the picture and said she'd be surprised if the lady in question was perfectly natural. More importantly it was against the company policy of providing a non-threatening work environment. I decided not to threaten her there and then and instead asked what company policy did allow me in the way of decoration. She said I should have pictures of my family like every other normal decent person. She then stormed out of the room and it was all I could do to stop myself wolf whistling.

Tuesday October 2

Things are getting worse. I ordered a few bottles of wine for the Board meeting to liven up proceedings. When I arrived (late) there was nothing but mineral water. I asked Geraldine the catering woman what had happened and she said Mr Smedley has said water would be fine. He'd filled out the correct green catering form so he got what he wanted. Besides which Mr Smedley was a man of high Christian principle. I thought Christians were in favour of turning water into wine not the other way round.

Spent the meeting entirely sober looking at all the shampoo samples on the table and wondering whether they annoyed Smedley who is a raving slaphead. Was so upset that I had to go to Mr Bojangles with Bill Peters after work to get myself completely toasted.

Wednesday October 3

I feel the company is sliding into the abyss of a new dark age. Sir Marcus who is violently anti-smoking (he used to be a 40-a-day man) has banned smoking throughout the building and even outside the front door as this is bad for the corporate image. How this sits with us having some of the world's filthiest factories he didn't make clear and as the company name is Smokehouse I would have thought a few smokers around the place would reinforce the company image. If I wanted to live a life of high moral principles I would have become a vicar not joined a multinational.

Got myself so worked up I decided I needed a breath of fresh air and a fag (they tend to come as a package these days). Got into the lift and bumped into Kim, a secretary from Operations, also going for a smoke. Rather surprisingly the lift went up rather than down and she admitted she always smoked on the roof of the building which is strictly illegal. She's not a bad looking piece so I went up with her.

Thursday October 4

Brought in a picture of Emma (wife) in her swimsuit where she is displaying rather a lot of the qualities that attracted me to her in the first place. Got the design studio to blow it up to poster size and then I put it up in my office. Found myself on the roof having a smoke with Kim again. It occurred to me that if we're going to smoke together, we might as well have a bit of pre-cigarette sex while we're at it. That would give planes coming into Heathrow something to look at.

While we were chatting we suddenly heard Sir Marcus's voice coming from somewhere. I thought at first he was broadcasting on the tannoy telling everyone to work harder or die. We peeked over the railing and saw him barking into his mobile phone on his private balcony. After he'd gone in, we dropped our stubs right onto his balcony. Possibly one of the high points of my life. We both smoked another and dropped them as well. Kim missed but she's a girl and they can't throw for toffee. Got back to my desk and filled out a blue form for 'product research samples' for tomorrow's Board meeting.

Friday October 5

Imperial edict from Sir Marcus. Would the person who has been smoking on his private balcony own up and receive his P45 like a man. I sent Sir Marcus an anonymous e-mail from someone else's computer saying it was Smedley up there smoking.

Later that morning Mrs Tooley walked past my office, saw the poster of Emma and looked as if she'd stood on a landmine. She barged into my office to give me a bollocking but I pretended I was on the phone to a journalist talking about how supportive I was of equal rights for women. When I rang off, Mrs T did her nut and accused me of creating a climate of fear and oppression. Silly tart. I told her it was my wife and did she have a problem with stable loving family relationships.

Slid into Board meeting just in time to see crate of red arrive. Smedley started waving his green form around. I waved my blue form back, told him they were all product samples and would the Board like to help in some research. Bill Peters had the cork out of the bottle before you could say Mouton Rothschild 74 and I felt the forces of darkness in full retreat.

Saturday October 6

Went round to Kate first thing to pick up the horrors. Malcolm the skyscraper's Rover was parked in the drive in a neat safe way. He's probably one of those annoying people who gets up at dawn and does useful profitable things for three hours before breakfast. That or he's been shagging Kate rigid on his picnic blanket all night. I found him in the kitchen talking to my ex-mother-in-law. For a moment my heart went out to him.

Picked up the kids and took them to the supermarket for a few bits and pieces. I was just putting a case of Old Speckled Hen in the trolley when I bumped into Kim from the office loading up with Bombay Sapphire. She said she was staying in that night to get ratted. I said I wouldn't mind joining her and she said why not. Half an hour later the kids were back with Malcolm and I was in the shower giving the nether regions a wax and polish and making sure they were combat ready. Went round to Kim's nasty little basement flat, got through a bottle of gin like it was mineral water and then we went to bed for what was without doubt the best shag I've ever had in my life. Correction. We went to bed for what was without doubt the three best shags I've ever had in my life.

Sunday October 7

More of the same with Kim. Much more of the same. I was fantastic. I was an all-powerful, all-conquering, awe-inspiring, ever lasting, magnificent, throbbing beast of sex. There wasn't a single bit of her I didn't chew up, spit out and mangle into orgasmic oblivion. We tried every position I've ever done, ever heard of, ever wanted to try but was too afraid to ask. I burnt more calories, stretched more muscles, poured more sweat, did more reps than I've done in a year at the gym.

Kim is without doubt the dirtiest, cleverest, evilest, filthiest, hardest, softest, sickest, sweetest, hungriest, nastiest, loveliest, vicious feral little demon I've ever, ever had the supreme pleasure of shoving up against a headboard. I've finally found a woman who can read the smuttiest parts of my dirty mind like an instruction manual. The sex was so epically good the whole street had a cigarette afterwards. At nine o'clock that evening I staggered home and fell into bed. Emma wasn't there. Thank God. My gonads felt as if they'd just been on selection for the SAS. The only thought on my mind was when and where I was going to get my hands on her again. I don't know what I've been doing before, but it wasn't sex.

Monday October 8

Board meeting to talk about Change Management. Sir Marcus said that I was good at reacting quickly and gave me company-wide responsibility for Change Management. Obviously didn't react quickly enough because I got lumbered with it. Being put in charge of Change Management is a bit like being asked to make love to the Queen Mother – obviously a great honour but not something you're very keen to do. Sir Marcus said change needed to start with the individual and the Board needed to be Champions of Change. All I could think about was Champion the Wonder Dog. Then I started thinking about the sweaty flanks of the woman who brought the tea in and missed the rest of the meeting. On the way out bumped into Polly Trip (junior research spod) who immediately burst into tears for no reason. Told her to stop blubbing and get herself some hormone patches pronto.

Tuesday October 9

Got in relatively early. Shirley's away for the week so some of the incentive for being late has gone. Should have stayed at home really because Sir Marcus gave me a premier league bollocking about insensitive treatment of Polly Trip and rest of my team. He then banged on about how business was all about building strong relationships. He said I was in charge of Change Management so I'd better start by changing my management style to be more sensitive and coaching in my business relationships. He added that I'd better buy into a sensitive management style or he'd rip my head off.

Bit depressed afterwards. How do you coach someone like Polly Trip who is lard from the neck up and obviously not on the success curve: as far as I'm concerned she's careering down it on a bobsleigh called oblivion. And if you ask me, coaching is for Saga holidays. Directors direct that's why we're called Directors and not Suggestors.

Wednesday October 10

Got in early to crack Change Management. If it means changing our clock watching rabble into managers, we're doomed. Of course all this should be a Human Remains job but the last HR Director was so keen on change he went off to become a woman. Pretty typical of HR if you ask me. Have yet to be told the difference between Change Management and a colossal kick up the pants. Maybe managing change is the same as the feminised workplace with everyone changing their minds all the time.

Got Hayley to arrange in-depth coaching session with Polly Trip that afternoon where I can listen empathetically to her concerns and develop a strong win-win mentoring relationship with her. Shortly afterwards Howard called me to see whether I was on for a marathon table football session that evening starting early. Cancelled Polly Trip coaching session.

Thursday October 11

No progress with Change Management. Maybe it just means changing your figures, changing your story and changing your job before the dung hits the fan. Better get some consultants in, they're bound to have some fancy ideas and if they charge enough they may even put Sir Marcus off the idea for good.

Polly Trip was hanging round my office so I told her that my door was open anytime if she wanted a chat. Got a confidential call from Sir Marcus halfway through chatting to her and had to close my door. When I opened it an hour later she was outside crying. I asked Hayley to give her some coaching while I went for lunch with Bill Peters. Found Bill in Bojangles wine bar 'continuously improving' with two bottles of red. I told him about the Change Management nightmare. He downed his drink in one, shouted, 'For God's sake, it's not Bosnia!' and then fell on his face. I left him to his 'tour of the factory floor' as he likes to call it. Some things never change.

Friday October 12

Much better day today; three big wins. Firstly, got Hayley to arrange flowers for Polly Trip to rebuild our strong nurturing relationship. Secondly, applied some top marketing thinking to Change Management problem: i.e. when in doubt, repackage. As I see it we lurch from one disastrous cock-up to another so we're already continually managing change. I therefore identified those responsible for most of the cock-ups in each department and made them Champions of Change. This gives them an incentive to report their disasters earlier as Champions of Change and gives me an opportunity to sack them for not Changing fast enough. I win, the business wins and they win in their next jobs. Final win was the fact that by some miracle I managed to remember Emma's birthday. Diverted Polly Trip flowers at last moment.

Saturday October 13

Woke up with one thing on my mind. Well two things, the first being how to get rid of Emma so I could give Kim my undivided attention. I went for a shower, shave, shit to think it over and when I got back she was packing. She said she was off for a hen night of her old friend Siobhan in Dublin, which she said she'd told me about three months ago. I couldn't believe my luck and volunteered to help her pack.

As soon as she'd got herself and her 58 tons of luggage out of the door I was on the phone to Kim. I arranged to pick her up later and gave myself enough time to get down to the Blue Boar for a bit of carbo-loading. I was in such a good mood that I was even nice to Becky. She said there was still time to call off her engagement to Mike if I wanted. I bit back the tears and said she should go ahead (after all it would be physically impossible for Mike to get any more miserable). Had a fairly rushed discussion with the lads about why the Bulgarians were a funny old lot and then motored round to Kim in a state of high excitement.

She was dressed in that smart but obviously cheap way secretaries specialise in. I couldn't contain myself and had to give her a quick one in the hall while she hung onto a cupboard door for support. Then drove her to a nice little pub I know in the country which is perfect for a filthy weekend. Over dinner we described in Technicolor detail what we were going to do to each other. I wanted to pack in the eating there and then and get her lashed to the headboard. But I forgot for a moment that she was a woman and that she couldn't function emotionally without a look at the dessert menu. Finally got her into the bedroom and then we tucked into a five course gourmet jabfest of cosmic proportions. All modesty aside I was a towering inferno of raging hot sex. Oh yes indeedy.

Sunday October 14

Went to church. Only kidding. We had breakfast in bed and then got stuck into another mammoth session interrupted only by a quick flick through the results in the sports section of the Sunday papers. Amazingly there was a story about Mrs Tooley, our office manager, being arrested for Grievous Bodily Harm. Apparently, she'd assaulted some poor man who'd taken too long choosing a cake in his local bakery.

We had a long leisurely bath together which inevitably degenerated into more acts of unspeakable depravity. After we checked out I drove her home keeping one hand on the wheel and the other on various bits of her trim little bod. By the time we got to her flat I was ready for another carpet burner but she said she wanted to call it a day as she was a bit tired. That's the trouble with these modern girls, they just can't last the pace when an experienced rider gets in the saddle.

Drove back to the Blue Boar and had to remind myself not to tell the boys about my extra-curricular activities. Barney came in shortly afterward with The Terminator who shot over to me and started sniffing my groin. Barney said I'd clearly got my leg over because The Terminator was trained to smell fish at a hundred yards. I told him that Emma had suddenly come over all romantic. He asked me whether this Emma knew the Emma I was married to. I promised the drinks were on me for the evening and he dropped the subject. My mobile phone went at that point. It was a text message from Uncle Nathan which just said Grndchdrn? I didn't reply. When a man has had 48 hours of almost continuous sex the last thing on his mind is children.

Monday October 15

Whoa! I'm going to Barbados. Whoa! To the sunny Caribbean sea. I'm not taking old wifey, so there's an island full of totty for me. It's the annual advertising shoot where we go to a tropical island, film 40 seconds of soft porn and stick our Coconuts bar at the end. Sophisticated marketing at its very best. This is the perkiest perk of my entire job and, let's face it, my job is a perk-rich environment.

I'm clubbing it out to Barbados with Bill Peters. As he works in chemicals he shouldn't really be going but the Coconuts Brand Manager suddenly got ill and it would be a shame to waste a ticket. How Bill made him ill like that I'll never know, but he does work in chemicals.

Read the evening paper and saw a photo of Mrs Tooley's victim who had virtually every part of his body bandaged. He was identified as a Mr M. Padley.

Tuesday October 16

On the flight out I tried the famous Weak charm on the trolley dolly. Asked her if there was anyone interesting on the flight apart from me. She checked the list and I noticed the initials SCO against a couple of names. She said it meant Spill Coffee Over. We had a laugh and then she had to cross-check and put doors to automatic. I wouldn't mind cross-checking her and putting her doors to automatic I can tell you. Bill Peters and me then tucked into some serious refreshment and were both feeling extremely tropical by the time we crossed over the coast of Ireland.

We finally got to our hotel and met Tibet, the 'actress' for the shoot. It's important that actors reflect the core values of the brand and as the core value of Coconuts is moist sensuality I had insisted on being closely involved in the casting. At the casting session I had suggested some subtle casting exercises such as asking the totty to jump up and down and seeing what moved. This was dismissed by the Director, some hatchet-faced woman in trousers. Probably a todger dodger.

Wednesday October 17

Arrived late for our hard day's work in paradise due to inability of liver to handle local rum in the quantities presented to it. Tibet's role was to walk out of the sea and up the beach. She wanted to know what her motivation was. I shouted that twenty grand for a week's holiday was all the motivation she needed. The Director told me to shut up. I reminded her that I was the client and that she was dangerously close to shooting carpet ads in Swindon for the rest of her career.

After she'd mastered walking out of the sea, Tibet announced she didn't actually like Coconuts and would only work with rice cakes. Brilliant. After we'd sorted that one out, she decided she was allergic to sand. Bill and I decided it was time for us to adjourn to the Bamboo Club, famous for 'native culture'. We soon got rather squiffy and gave some of the exotic dancers a few bars of Coconuts to get creative with. Believe you me, there's nothing I could teach those girls about product positioning. We got drinking with some other Brits and had a high old time.

Thursday October 18

Woken by call from Sir Marcus (CEO) from London who started a thermo-nuclear bollocking before I could remember where or who I was. Apparently all the tabloids were carrying a shot of an exotic dancer doing unspeakable things with a Coconuts bar. Bill Peters was in the background draped around a pole in his Y-fronts. Apparently every single paparazzi was in the club waiting for a rumoured guest appearance by Prince Edward. I recovered slightly and said it was excellent PR for Coconuts and all consistent with brand values.

Sir Marcus responded with a variety of expressions popular with our Anglo-Saxon forebears and told us to be on the next flight home to collect our P45s. I managed to find Bill Peters who was still drinking rum with the local witch doctor. Bill didn't want to leave as he was being shown how to stick pins into a voodoo doll. Useful though this would have been for dealing with HR, I had to drag him away to start the trip back.

Friday October 19

We called the office from the plane. Probably cost more than the flight itself but Hayley told me that Coconuts sales had shot up since the splash in the tabloids and Sir Marcus was now claiming ownership of the new PR initiative. Bill and I celebrated with a drink or two. Bill then pulled out a massive cigar and within seconds was surrounded by trolley dollies acting as if he'd pulled out a hand grenade. For a moment I thought we were going to be diverted to Newfoundland to be met by the FBI. We had a few more stiff ones, pulled on our eye shades and went out like lights. I was woken by a crashing sound as Bill tried to get to the toilet with his eye shades still on. Landed after successful week (except for getting a massive amount of coffee spilt over us for some reason).

Saturday October 20

Woke up at crack of dawn. All I could think of was getting round to Kim's and carrying on where we left off. I left a message on her answer machine and then went to get the papers. Emma was still lying in bed looking stunning even though she'd just woken up. It crossed my mind to try and give her a quick one but then I thought it really wouldn't be fair on Kim. Had shower, shave, shit and then called Kim again. Answer machine. Went to get the papers, cooked breakfast, called Kim. Nothing.

Emma said she was going out for the day with a friend I'd never heard of and didn't know when she'd be back. I was one microsecond away from accidentally calling her Kim. You have to be bloody careful when you're playing away. Just one little slip could give the whole game away. Emma spent an hour in the bathroom getting ready and then finally she was off. I gave Kim another call, got nowhere and decided to drive round to her house. She wasn't there. No note, no nothing. She must have known I would call her as soon as I got back. Went back to the Blue Boar. Angela was on duty looking annoyingly pert. The more I looked at her the more I wanted to get back on the job with Kim. I called her again. Nothing. Spent all afternoon drinking with Mike the Miserable who banged on about how he'd found true love with Becky and tried to persuade me that there was so much more to her than a big arse. The more I drunk the more annoyed I got with Kim. Called her about another five hundred times but still nothing.

Sunday October 21

Called Kim first thing. Still not there. Got Sunday papers read them all then called Kim again. Nothing. Read interesting story about top surgeon going berserk in hospital and stabbing patient. Picture of Martin Padley with final unbandaged part of his body now covered with new bandages. Waited until ten then drove round to Kim's house. Not there. Waited in my car for an hour. Nothing. Drove back home. Called. Nothing.

Went to Blue Boar for lunch in a bit of a state. Barney and Evan were there having an intimate discussion at a private table. I knew immediately something was up. Mike whispered to me that Barney has been sleeping with Beryl for the last five years. I wasn't really that interested. Went out into the car park and called Kim. She picked up the phone. I asked her where she'd been all weekend. She said out. I said I was going to come over but she said not to because it was all over. I couldn't believe what I was hearing. She then said I was sweet but it was just a fling. It all seemed surreal. She couldn't be saying all this. She was ten years younger than me for a start and these were all my lines. I said what about the volcanic sex. She said I was very sweet but she'd moved on. *Very sweet!!!* That wasn't very sweet, that was the best sex ever perpetrated by a human being. I started to complain but she told me not to get bourgeois on her and put the phone down.

I wandered round the Blue Boar car park in a daze. I simply couldn't believe what was happening to me. I felt like a 14 year old. I barged back into the pub. Barney and Evan were hugging in the bar. Mike was tearful and even The Terminator looked pretty choked up. The whole world had gone mad. Mike started to talk to me about Becky and what a wonderful human being she was which was the final straw. I went round to Becky's flat and gave her a damn good seeing to. That'll show Kim what's what.

Monday October 22

Almost relieved to get back to work until I discovered that Sir Marcus has joined a cult. He shocked everyone at the Board meeting by saying he was deeply concerned with vision and values. Then without warning introduced aging Elvis lookalike in some kind of one-piece suit who revealed to us that our people are our brand. Let's start selling them then, I suggested, because that's what you do with brands. Sir Marcus gave me his P45 look so I communicated internally for a while.

Rasputin and his agency Breakout (they're called Breakout because by rights they should still be in prison for fraud) have proposed a total integrated programme with vision and values, team building workshops, and a colourful, easy to use, jargon-free binder all nicely branded *Vision 2010*. Sir Marcus then announced how much it all cost and while I was choking he added that as it was internal marketing it should come out of my marketing budget. Over my dead body!! All surplus budget is earmarked for Board team building at Japanese Grand Prix. That's a non-negotiable.

Tuesday October 23

St Marcus patron saint of values (as Bill Peters now calls him) summoned me into his office again. There was a big poster on his wall with Breakout Values on it: CREATIVITY, EFFICIENCY, INTEGRITY, COURAGE, LEARNING. Rasputin appeared from nowhere and intoned that the people have to live the brand and its values and everyone must be involved. Then he said something like 'Tell me and I forget, Show me and I understand, Involve me and I remember.' I told him with my team it's 'Tell them and they forget; show them and they forget; involve them and they forget.'

Rasputin is obviously a world class fraudster but seems to have got Sir Marcus by the scruff of his cheque book. Got back to office and began wide-ranging staff focus groups to involve them in creation of Smokehouse vision and values i.e. asked Hayley when she brought in my coffee what the team wanted. She said more money, less work. Smart girl. Must get off with her at some point.

Wednesday October 24

Got in rather late for no particularly good reason other than the underside of my duvet is a better space to be in than my office. Shirley had a poster of the Breakout Values up in Reception. She pretended to tick them off when I came in. I got a tick for creativity and a cross for the others. Smart woman. I must get off with her at some point. Sat down at my desk and cleared the decks for lunch.

Had long lunch with Bill Peters who knows all about internal marketing as he supplies half the company with cheap cigarettes. Told him about Rasputin situation and he volunteered to take him outside and have his balls for cufflinks. I thought a more subtle approach might be required and as Bill puts subtlety in the same category as needlepoint, I dropped the subject. Sat in office in despair with the Japanese Grand Prix rapidly disappearing over the horizon with its arse on fire. Glanced up wistfully at last year's team photo taken at Brazilian Grand Prix with Bill Peters's face down in gutter. I noticed that the far end of the shelf was being held up by fat ring binder of Vision and Values from ten years ago. I took it down and blew the dust off. *Vision 2000 – These values aren't just words, they will become our way of life.* Signed by the then Chief Exec who's now serving life for corporate manslaughter. Binder could be just what I need. Seize the Carp!!

Thursday October 25

Called Timothy Smallwood, Finance Director, to talk about the vision thing. Naturally being Finance Director his vision for the company is to put an immediate stop to every form of expenditure. He is the chewing gum on the bottom of the corporate shoe, making continual irritating efforts to impede forward progress. Normally I would phone him only in dire emergencies, for example when my expenses are being held up. But this time I actually invited him out for very cheap lunch at very authentic Mexican restaurant (so authentic they bring you a glass of water and warn you not to drink it).

Over lunch I told him about Breakout and their Values which all translated into massive expenditure. Smallwood visibly shrunk as a person when I detailed the costs. I then delivered the *coup de grâce* by adding 'plus expenses' and then, when I sensed he was at his weakest, I showed him my old *Vision 2000* binder. He said it looked expensive. I said it was already completely paid for. He liked it.

Friday October 26

Arranged a meeting with Sir Marcus and told him that I would welcome Rasputin's presence. He would have been there anyway as he seems to have Sir Marcus completely on a leash.

Told Sir Marcus that in the interests of EFFICIENCY I had found another agency called Internal Organs who had proposed a much more CREATIVE approach to Smokehouse Vision and Values. They weren't here to present it themselves because they believed external agencies shouldn't be involved in internal company issues because, unlike some (Breakout), they had INTEGRITY. This approach was more in keeping with our own vision and values and I wondered whether we (Sir Marcus) had the COURAGE to accept this important LEARNING?

I could see Rasputin getting hot under the habit but I didn't let him interrupt. Timmy Smallwood then pointed out that our approach was 90 per cent cheaper and Breakout's bill would mean cancelling other team building activities. Saw scales fall from Sir Marcus's eyes and Rasputin's suddenly looked like the shoddy little am-dram queen he really was. Returned to office and prepared to live out brand values at Japanese Grand Prix.

Saturday October 27

Woke up in bed with a strange woman. It was Emma my wife. It was so long since I'd seen her that it came as quite a shock to find her in my bed. Got up and made her breakfast including correct microsurgery on grapefruit. She was unusually thankful and as I watched her scoop the fleshy, pink pieces into her fleshy, pink mouth, I remembered that I had married a supermodel. Why was I messing around with the likes of Kim and Becky and Madeleine and some others whose names escape me? Emma announced she wanted to go shopping all day and I suddenly remembered why. We went to 40 different shoe shops, tried on four thousand pairs, bought two hundred. I remembered to like every single one that she tried on so I got through it relatively unscathed.

Was allowed to go down to the Blue Boar early as a special treat. Not sure what to expect after last week. Luckily Barney and The Terminator came in first and I asked him how things were with Evan. He said they were absolutely fine and then told me in a whisper that Beryl was the hottest woman he'd ever slept with and went on in great detail just how good the sex was. The Terminator was drooling buckets by the end of it. Evan came in shortly afterwards looking perfectly normal i.e. miserable. I nearly asked him how Beryl was but stopped myself in case Barney answered that she was red hot. Mike came in at that point, we got the beers in and after a few quick rounds things got back to normal.

Becky was wearing a new outfit. She came round the bar and asked us whether we thought her bum looked big in it. There was total silence from the boys. At some point I'm really going to have to explain to Becky and to all womankind for that matter, that if you've got a big arse in the first place, it's going to stay big whatever you put it in. Instead I said she looked like a Peach (as in James and the Giant Peach) and then rapidly changed the subject by asking Mike about the wedding plans.

Sunday October 28

Tried to climb on Emma first thing to get rid of a persistent erection but she swatted me off saying it was Sunday in a voice which implied she had been strictly observing the Sabbath since childhood. Later we had to go up and see my mother who is getting further and further off her chump. She seemed perfectly normal to me but when we sat down to lunch she started telling Emma what a lovely girl she was and how she should steer clear of me because basically I was a shit. It wouldn't have been so bad if she hadn't referred to me as Kevin throughout. I thought at one point that she knew something I didn't and that Emma had another man called Kevin. But Emma looked as confused as I was.

After lunch, my father took me aside and told me that he wanted to get his financial affairs sorted out in case things turned nasty. I agreed that was a good idea and started eyeing up the furniture. He then presented me with a list of all the money he'd lent me since I was 18 and asked for it back. I told him the cheque was in the post and we left shortly afterwards. Couldn't decide which one of them was the loopier. On the drive back Emma said she wanted to have a dinner party for a few friends the following weekend. The list included most of the usual tossers but she also wanted to invite Ross 'Close to the Customer' Fulbright for some reason. I thought it was probably a good time to tell her that he was a Tail-end Charlie. She vehemently insisted he wasn't so I didn't press the point. I suggested that we allow him to bring a partner and see what he turned up with. Emma thought this was a stupid idea. I was quite relieved as the last thing I want is two men with their tongues down each other's throat while I'm trying to eat a sausage.

Monday October 29

Got in on time. Shirley was speechless. Sat at my desk and did nothing. To be honest I'm a bit off the job at the moment. You work your teats off for 20 years and then a bunch of snot-nosed kids with laptops become millionaires overnight. Hayley asked if she could go on self-assertion course. I said no.

Later that day I found suspicious looking criminal type lurking on Directors' floor – grungy teenager with more studs in his ear than a Welsh prop forward. Called security who told me his name was Neil and he was on work experience from the Prince's Trust. If the Prince is trusting little scrotes like that, then God help the monarchy. Got him started on changing photocopier toner. It's work and he should experience it. After work cheered myself up at the gym with Howard, checking whether no-bounce sports bras contravened Trades Description Act.

Tuesday October 30

Ross Fulbright dropped in to thank me for dinner invitation. He looked a bit sheepish (I wouldn't mind if he fancied sheep at least that's normal) so he changed the subject and told me our fruit yoghurt sales were going pear-shaped and what was I doing about it. Reassured him we had a major advertising campaign planned. He said that was great but what about sales? Told him that was his job and to get his Mondeo back on the road. Those sales boys are a menace in the office – they should stick to their Little Chefs.

Told Neil to clear out cigarette butts from my desk drawers. It's all good experience and he can put 'environmental management' on his CV. Surreptitiously counted his studs – a couple more perforations and you could rip parts of his head off like a postage stamp. Hayley asked me nicely about self-assertion course. I said no. Why do secretaries need to assert themselves? That's my job.

Wednesday October 31

Supply Chain Management meeting (lunch) with Bill Peters to talk about fruit yoghurts sales drive. He said they already had every chemical known to man (and some still hush-hush); half the chemicals kill the live yoghurt and the other half embalm it. Apparently they use children's yoghurt to mop up after acid spillages in the factory. Over a very acceptable bottle or two of red he asked why I was bringing my love-child into the office i.e. Neil. I explained about work experience and suggested it was never too late for him to try it. Bill said he was too old to start complicating his job with work. When you've accumulated enough experience you shouldn't need to work at all.

Got back from lunch and Hayley asked about assertiveness course again. I said read my lips: no. Neil gave me dirty look. I gave him bin bag and told him to clean the car park – 'logistics streamlining' on CV. Left early so I could get a good long game of table football in with Howard. When I arrived there were two women playing. I'd had quite enough unnatural practices for one day so I went home (after a few health drinks).

NOVEMBER

Thursday November 1

Friendly motivational chat from Sir Marcus i.e. yoghurt JFDI
or P45. If I had a monkey I certainly wouldn't give it for
yoghurt – let's face it, if you can't drink it, chew it or smoke it,
you shouldn't put it in your mouth (slightly different for
women obviously). Applied first rule of marketing: when in
doubt, brainstorm – you either get an idea and take the
credit or you get nothing and blame the agency. Either way
your arse is well and truly camouflaged.

Agency said they'd be happy to organise brainstorm (I'd
be pretty happy if I charged what they do) and could we
bring along a couple of free thinkers from Smokehouse.
Considered Bill Peters but wasn't sure whether agency could
cope with that kind of lateral thinking (lateral because he
does most of it lying horizontally in the gutter). Said no to
Hayley before she opened her mouth again about bloody
assertiveness and got Neil busy straightening files
–'horizontal integration' for CV.

Friday November 2

Up at the agency all day for piss poor brainstorm. The
facilitator had us role playing Babylonian slaves at one
moment, dancing with the spirit of the elf the next. Naturally
I asked what the hell all this fooling around had to do with
yoghurts but I was taken aside and told to align my energy
with the rest of the group. Disaster all round really. Took Neil
along as token free thinker (real thinkers don't have time for
brainstorms) but he said nothing and just played with the
stud in his tongue.

I asked Neil afterwards if he had metal fatigue. He
grunted and passed me a grubby piece of paper with ten
absolute corking ideas for selling yoghurt to the youth
market. Amazing stuff. We could absolutely dominate the
market, I could get massive brownie points and Fulbright
would be well and truly shown up. Offered Neil immediate
job as youth 'consultant'. He said he was already setting up a

net-based agency for the youth market called large.com. Immediately visualised my dot.com retirement package taking shape and suggested he might want some heavyweight business experience on the Board. He said read my lips: no. Clearly learnt a lot from his work experience.

Saturday November 3

Went round to Kate's first thing to pick up the kids. Malcolm the Tall and Kate were going off for a dirty weekend in the Isle of Wight. That ferry ride really is so romantic. Still, as long as they've got the picnic blanket in the back of the Rover they'll be fine. The ex-mother-in-law was there in attack mode and started dropping in gratuitous comments about just how superbly happy everyone was now (that I was no longer a feature of the domestic landscape). Then Mr mother-in-law floated in and made a big show of just how well bonded he was with Malcolm by making a lot of little in-jokes with him which I can guarantee weren't funny in or out.

From nowhere I suddenly announced I was taking the kids to Eurodisney in Paris for the weekend. That certainly shut them all up except for the kids who went berserk. I stuffed them into the Porsche and was half-way to Waterloo when I remembered the sodding dinner party Emma had arranged. Diverted to Legoland and told the kids that you had to go there before you were allowed to go to Eurodisney – it's like junior school and infant school. Arrived home late for the dinner party which was great because all my least favourite people were there. It's a bit of a shame Fulbright is a left footer because he was the only interesting person there. He looked as embarrassed as I did about Emma's arty, vegetarian, new age friends. I went up to check on the children at 11.00 and accidentally forgot to come down again.

Sunday November 4

It was my sister Karen's birthday so we piled round there for lunch. Matty and Camilla showed up and all the girls were gossiping like this was the last opportunity ever to dish the dirt. For the first ten minutes they all seemed to be talking at once. Frightening. All the men were left in the kitchen and we winced at the sight of all our innermost secrets being gaily tossed around like salad.

We got talking and I said Emma was fine, Matt said Camilla's pregnancy was going fine and the Reverend Paul said his training was going fine. He then announced that as soon as he was ordained he was going into the City because Vicars earn sod all. We agreed that would be an interesting and vital ministry but he said he wasn't going to be ministering he was going to be making a fat load of wonga. Interesting character Paul. Matt said he'd found God but had returned him to the lost property department. Was just trying to make sense of the conversation when all the girls swept in and we had to feed them.

After one too many sherries, Camilla started having a go at men in general and said she had more complex emotional relations with horses, chocolate and shoes in that order. Matt mimed having a pregnant bump and then tapped his head. We all knew exactly what he meant.

Managed to get down to the Blue Boar in reasonable time. Evan and Barney were chatting away in a friendly enough manner and we all got talking about how the Syrians were a funny old lot. The Terminator was harassing a couple of young lads who clearly smelt funny, Becky knocked over a tray full of glasses with her arse and all in all things seemed pleasantly normal.

Monday November 5

Had to get in early (nine) for strategic planning Board meeting. Sir Marcus is a bit worried about the competition and says that if we want to run with the big dogs we've got to get off the porch. With that kind of leadership, strategic planning is virtually unnecessary. Normally I would reprint the last five-year strategy but the person who wrote that was sacked and later killed himself. Not much of a strategy if you ask me.

On the way back to my office, walked straight into a door that wouldn't open. After I'd silenced the outburst of secretarial tittering, I discovered that you now need a swipe card for the door. Tried another route and found myself stuck in internal audit. The grim little accountette I asked couldn't let me out because I wasn't authorised to be there in the first place. I'm going to find out who's responsible for this rank stupidity and swipe his card.

Tuesday November 6

Meeting with Tim Smallwood (Finance Director) to talk through his rank stupidity and the world's most fatheaded security system. He said because of fears of industrial espionage the whole building was being divided into sectors with restricted access. I asked him about the free flow of people and ideas. He said that would continue to happen but within restricted areas. Finance Director probably not the best person to talk to about the free flow of anything. I pointed out that people like Bill Peters had special technological needs and that the system would make him a prisoner in his own office. Smallwood suggested this might be healthy for the business. It won't be healthy for Smallwood when I tell Bill. Must get this door thing sorted as no day is complete without a quick stroll through the company's totty-rich zones.

Wednesday November 7

In the morning went to Luton to see a small supplier that's absolutely dependent on Smokehouse. Didn't really have anything to discuss, just a nice feudal day out seeing people grovel. Decided to have a crack at the strategy on the train on the way back. Strategic planning is where we think about the business and decide what we're going to do with it. This is obviously where 90 per cent of damage to the business is done. I say why have consultants and think for yourself?

Bloke opposite me was working on some business papers so I postponed strategic thinking in case he saw the budgets I'm playing with and felt inadequate. He got off forgetting his papers so I had a quick flick though them. Realised with a bit of jolt that it was the strategic plan of our direct competitor and he'd made a lot more progress than I had. Very useful. Rushed into the office and nearly broke my wrist on another bloody locked door. I used bad language out loud.

Thursday November 8

Got in late due to invisible but painful swelling in the wrist area. Shirley took lack of sympathy to a level commonly reserved for people married to me. Bill came round to my office later on and I told him about Smallwood's little comment. Bill went storming out saying he was going to grab Smallwood by his assets and make them sweat big time. He was back in two minutes saying he couldn't get through any doors.

I then spent all day writing top strategic plan which would have the competition in intensive care taking food through the nose. Then tackled security system: humans are always the weakest link in any high-tech system and our weakest link is that we've given the master key to a vegetable i.e. George on security. Spent a good hour getting to know George and simulating life-time interest in pre-war football programmes. Left office with headache, friend for life and master key. Met Howard at the gym just in time for aqua-aerobics which we watched from the hot tub giving marks for swimsuit design and content.

Friday November 9

Presented my strategic plan at Board meeting and announced that our big dogs would be well and truly off the porch. Sir Marcus looked underwhelmed and said my plan was more of a pup. He said if that was the quality of our thinking, the competition would eat our lunch. Couldn't really say where I'd got the thinking from so I blamed someone in our department whom I had foolishly over-empowered.

Had to work late rewriting the strategic plan by copying great chunks out of the *Mammoth Book of Business Clichés*. Left the building at midnight and used my master key to leave every single door of the office open. With a bit of luck the competition will steal all our strategic planning. That'll really mess them up.

Saturday November 10

Had just got my feet up with the papers when Emma announced she had a migraine and could I go to the supermarket to get a few things. She then gave me a list which included every item in the supermarket. I had to leave the Porsche behind as its boot only holds a face flannel and a packet of three featherlites. Instead had to tank across town in her hairdressers' Suzuki jeep. The only reason Emma needs permanent four-wheel drive is so she can get up the kerbs easily when she's parking.

Arrived at the supermarket and was manoeuvring into a space for toddlers and children only, when some bastard in a Mercedes CLK nabbed my place. That kind of behaviour really sickens me. Got stuck into the shopping and noticed a tidy little piece on till 14. At first I was a bit narked that I had to find the exact kind of olive oil that Emma has to have, but then I realised that it was quite a good way of segmenting out the well-clipped professional totty from the flyblown council types clustering around the value white bread.

Spent a happy five minutes following a very tidy little arse around the pet food section. When she hung a right at the custard tarts I got the frontal view. She had a face which could have opened bottles so that was the end of that little detour. Suddenly Merc man swerved across my path. I just caught sight of his bachelor trolley full of beer and ready meals before he parked at till 14. I got in the queue behind him and accidentally dropped a jumbo pack of Tampax in his trolley which slightly took the edge off his sporty single image.

When I got home to Emma she said that her headache had miraculously cleared up and that she was going out with Tish. I got down to the Blue Boar pronto just in time to contribute to a fairly detailed discussion on why the Finns were a funny old lot. Evan and Barney seemed to be bosom buddies now that Barney had taken Beryl off his hands (not that she was ever on his hands).

Sunday November 11

Woke up with no Emma but a cracking hangover. One was as good as the other, I thought. Really fancied a Sunday morning nut loosener but was a bit stumped at who to call. Becky would drop her knickers faster than a tray of glasses but I thought I really couldn't keep doing that kind of thing to a mate. I gave Kim a call. She answered but then told me she didn't want to see me because I was a sad fat old bastard. A real morale booster there. For a very, very split second I nearly thought about calling Kate but then I remembered Malcolm would probably be busy shunting her round the picnic blanket in his leather driving gloves.

I suddenly felt very low and decided what I needed was a hair of the dog. I had a couple of Snifters that I kept by the bed for just such an emergency. I then decided out of the blue that I would call Bill and see if he was on for a drink. I called him at home and his wife, who had the telephone manner of the speaking clock, said he was at his Alcoholics Anonymous group. I said they must miss him at his local. She said that the Hind's Head had taken quite enough of their money already. Half an hour later I found Bill down at the Hind's Head. We then got stuck in together and tried to work out why women were bent on denying men all the good things in life like beer, sport and everything below their neck.

We finished at about midnight and Bill suddenly looked at his watch with horror. He insisted I take him home and take the blame. When we got there all the doors were locked and the lights out. I suggested to Bill that we used his key but apparently he wasn't allowed one. Bill then said we'd have to revert to Plan B. We spent the rest of the night in the Wendy house where Bill had very cleverly secreted a six-pack of Tennant's Extra.

Monday November 12

Got in first thing. Well, the first thing I did was get in which is the same thing only three hours later. Miracle I got in at all after the weekend session with Bill Peters. Shortly before he went completely comatose, Bill admitted he hadn't done any meaningful work for the company for the last five years. We made a bet that I couldn't get through an entire week without working and that he couldn't work for a full week. We'd call it quits Friday lunchtime and celebrate. I therefore instructed Hayley to hold all my calls and cancel all meetings. She was a little bit confused as there weren't any major sporting events on.

Tuesday November 13

Read in the papers that competition have launched new miracle toothpaste. Obviously requires immediate reaction from me and Smokehouse marketing department but I'm not about to lose a bet with Bill Peters for the sake of some piddling multi-million global market. Caught Bill Peters carrying some papers through office. Said it was his job description and he was just checking up what he actually did before he attempted to do it.

Sat in my silent office and listened to the sound of my calls being held. Got bored after five minutes so decided to walk around the department to boost morale etc. Got Hayley to write down the names of who worked where first so I'd know who the hell they were. Picked someone at random (totty with cracking bag of clementines) and chatted to her for a couple of hours about some impossibly urgent deadline she was trying desperately to meet.

Wednesday November 14

Got in a little bit later than normal but missed Shirley because she was on her coffee break. Did nothing all morning which was much more difficult than pretending to work. Called Bill Peters for lunch and he told me he was having a sandwich at his desk. Things must be getting serious if he's found his desk. Instead went to the canteen with Giles Renton-Willets (weirdo HR Director). Well, I had lunch, he just had some low-impact yoghurt and sucked the protein from his napkin.

Renton-Willets said he'd been trying to call me all morning but understood in a nurturing supportive way that I was probably in emergency mode responding to competitor's miracle toothpaste. Assured him that nothing was occupying more of my time. Canteen alive with news that Bill Peters had called status meeting for team and announced back to basics policy (i.e. him finding out what the hell's been going on for the last five years).

Thursday November 15

Spent entire morning playing solitaire on computer (useful insight into IT department) and all afternoon lying on the sofa constructing complex tottometer of women on internal phone list. Interrupted by phone call which surprised me as I'd specifically instructed Hayley not to put any through. Sir Marcus was on the other end. He had heard that Bill Peters had organised a breakfast meeting and did I think he was off his chump. I said that was most unlikely (Bill doesn't have a chump to be off). Sir Marcus had also read about launch of new toothpaste and was sure I was working flat out on counter-attack. I assured him I was indeed flat out.

Later on, I saw Bill Peters on my way out of the office. He said he was working late so I winked at him assuming he meant after hours stationery cupboard activity with some bright-eyed graduate. He tapped the papers he was carrying, winked back and said he was really enjoying working but wouldn't want to do it for a living. Couldn't smell alcohol on his breath either. Worrying. If Bill got sucked into this work thing it would be a very great loss to the company.

Friday November 16

Went to lunch with Bill to settle our bets. He passed me detailed work on complete global restructuring of chemical manufacture, asked me to pay up and then sunk two bottles of red before you can say General Belgrano. Hayley rang on the mobile to say emergency Board meeting had been called for that afternoon. Apparently competitor's new toothpaste turns stools fluorescent (possible youth niche market but total disaster for your ABC1s). Bill had resumed his customary management position under the table, so I faced Sir Marcus alone.

In the meeting I reassured Sir Marcus that we'd spent all week looking at the toothpaste market. In my considered opinion the best course of action was to do nothing and use the opportunity to restructure our chemical division for which I had with me some comprehensive proposals. Sir Marcus said I must have been working very hard indeed. I told him it's all about working smarter not harder. He liked that.

Saturday November 17

Immediately I woke up I knew there was something strange going on. Sadly, it wasn't Emma humping my brains out. In fact Emma was nowhere to be seen. Instead it was snowing. I looked out of the window and the snow was deep and crisp and even. I began to feel really excited especially as it meant I couldn't possibly get round to Kate's to look after the kids. At that moment I heard the sound of a turbo diesel and Kate's dad arrived in his Range Rover to drop the kids off.

After I'd got up we played a wonderful game called 'Captain Scott gets the papers'. When we got back I got them to build a big Snow Malcolm in the back garden. They wanted to come in a couple of times but I told them that Malcolm needed to be a lot taller. That kept them busy until I'd finished the papers and then it was time to play Captain Scott goes to the Blue Boar for lunch.

Becky was on duty and made a big fuss of the kids as if to say play your cards right, John, and I could give you a couple more like this. Why I'd want a couple of kids with big arses I couldn't imagine. Mike, Barney and Evan were all there and we got into a bit of discussion on why the Samoans were a funny old lot. We had a few pints for the purpose of central heating and I noticed that Mike can't get served by Becky any more. This could mean that the marriage plans are on the rocks or it could just as well mean that they're settling down into married life very quickly. Barney and Evan still getting on like a house on fire. Lovely to see. Maybe I should have a crack at Beryl (just to improve my friendship with Evan you understand). Got home quite late but very happy. Finished the evening by knocking the head off Snow Malcolm with a shovel. Very satisfying.

Sunday November 18

Woke up and realised I'd left the bloody kids at the pub again. I called Becky and, as I suspected, she was holding them hostage for me to come and collect. I said I would be round that afternoon. Might as well get some babysitting out of her. Spent the morning reading the papers and thinking through the rapidly approaching launch of Snifters. Something in my water told me that they were going to be a very, very big hit.

Kate and her dad came round at midday to get the kids because they were worried that the snow was going to get worse. I had to admit that the kids were down the pub which is not necessarily what you want to hear about a four- and six-year-old. For a fleeting second I thought Kate's dad was going to attack me. Kate smoothed things over by saying they were probably safer there than with me. I apologised profusely but I didn't really have a leg to stand on.

I went with them to find Becky. Of course she was as nice as pie to Kate and as the kids seemed very happy it all passed off peacefully. I made sure I left with Kate in case Becky demanded a session in the cold store as payment. Once I got home my first thought was that I needed to get down to the Blue Boar for a drink. Instead I had a few lagers at home and went to bed wondering where the hell Emma was. Shouldn't she be at home watching Coronation Street with an industrial size tub of ice-cream like all normal women?

Monday November 19

Got in rather early for me and spent the extra time chatting to Shirley on reception about our respective weekends in the snow. We saw Fulbright coming through the car park and I asked Shirley how she could bear asking him how his weekend was in case he went into all the sordid shirt lifting stuff. Fulbright came in at that moment and Shirley asked him how his weekend was. Fulbright gave me a searching look and said it was very good. He'd been to a country hotel with his lover and the snow had made it the perfect romantic break. How lovely I thought as I edged out of reception with my back to the wall. Got to my desk, deleted my e-mails, had a cup of coffee and looked out of the window at a big yellow JCB ripping up some concrete for the new reception. Perhaps they should keep the old one as a separate entrance (as it were) for our light-footed friends.

Tuesday November 20

Got in rather late and knew something was up because Shirley was radiating energy. She always does this when there's good gossip because she gets to tell everybody first on their way in.

Apparently the builders had unearthed the remains of some medieval stocks and a team of archaeologists were hot-sandalling it over to have a look at them. If I was a builder and found some rotting old rubbish I'd have it in the skip sharpish before it became Grade 1 listed rotting old rubbish and a protected World Heritage Site.

Fulbright called and asked whether I could do lunch to talk through some sales difficulties with him. Normally I wouldn't have lunch with Fulbright unless it was in a brightly lit area with multiple escape routes but there was something about the word difficulties and sales being together that I couldn't really say no to.

Wednesday November 21

Lots of plastic sheeting up all round the car park. Shirley brought me up to speed with the fact that they were an intact set of standing stocks, very unusual according to the bearded sandal wearers. Sir Marcus called me in and asked me from a marketing standpoint how having a pair of stocks for ritual humiliation outside the front door was consistent with the Smokehouse brand image. The words 'company culture' sprang to my lips but were fortunately diverted out through my nostrils at the last moment. I promised him a report by the end of the week and got out.

I told Deborah Wills in my department to work on stocks cultural impact report and then went to lunch with Ross Fulbright. Got a couple of funny looks on the way out but that's to be expected. We settled down for lunch and Fulbright was an absolute pack of nerves. He must have been lying about his sales results for the last five years I thought hopefully. Fulbright was just on the point of coming out with it (his results that is) when bloody Clare O'Keefe Operations Director sat at the table next to us. Fulbright closed up quicker than an electric umbrella and the rest of the lunch was arse-aching (metaphorically speaking) small talk.

Thursday November 22

Fulbright asked me out for lunch again. He was wringing his hands and shaking his head and generally in a right state. To help him out I asked him whether he'd made a massive cock-up and then immediately regretted it. I got another glass of wine down him and he finally said, 'John there's something I've got to tell you.' Warning lights started flashing as soon as he opened his mouth and I knew this was not going to be about sales figures. I was also very worried that he'd called me John. Suddenly the awful truth dawned on me. The bloody man was in love with me!! He wanted to lift my Jermyn Street double-cuffed shirt. Aaaaaarrggghhhh!!!!!!!

I had to try and think of what the politically correct response was when a pink wafer propositions you. I also made damn sure that I was getting the hell out of the restaurant and back to the safety of the office as I did this thinking. I called Bill Peters for moral support as soon as I got back and we immediately adjourned to the pub. He was all in favour of doing Fulbright for sexual harassment. I didn't know which way to turn (apart from keeping my back to the wall).

Friday November 23

Got in rather late and I could see Shirley in reception was positively aglow with gossip. As I walked into reception she suddenly went quiet and embarrassed. She muttered something about big new discoveries and I carried on to the lifts. Very odd. Fulbright was waiting for me in my office. It was obvious that we had to have it out (as it were) there and then. He asked me to close the door which I did, leaving it slightly ajar so that Hayley could see we didn't get naked at any point.

Fulbright then told me he wanted to tell me something straight. That would be a first from him I thought. He then told me he was having an affair with Emma, they had been going at it hammer and tongs for the last two months, they were in love and wanted to get married. I sat there a bit shell-shocked. All I could remember was how much he'd stressed the hammer and tongs bit. Two things immediately struck me: Firstly, I thought he was a nine bobber so why was he sleeping with my wife? And, secondly, the door was open. My phone went, Fulbright said he'd let me get it and then shot out of the room. It was Sir Marcus wondering how I was getting on with the ritual humiliation.

Saturday November 24

Woke up with the sun on my face and a fantastic sense of jubilation in my heart. This soon went (along with the sun) and I started to pick through the debris of yesterday. The big headline as far as I was concerned was that someone had been sleeping with my gorgeous wife; someone from the office had been sleeping with my wife; someone in Sales had been sleeping with my wife; someone who was a raging homosexual had been sleeping with my wife. Any one of these would have been bad enough but all rolled into the same affair was actually quite funny. I felt a strange sensation in my chest which at first I took to be indigestion so I popped a couple of Rennies. It didn't go so I realised it must be some kind of non-alcohol related emotion. A quick shower, shave and shit shifted it and I went out to get the papers.

In the paper shop there was this rather brassy looking brunette wearing something low cut for a top or high cut for a bottom. I realised that I was now free to ask her back for a damn good seeing to. Of course I would have asked her back for a damn good seeing to before but it would have had to have been at her place. I whistled all the way to the Blue Boar and toasted my new situation with a number of therapeutic beverages. Becky gave me the glad eye and I thought about giving her a quick one in the cold store but I remembered that I only did that when I was feeling low. All the boys were there so we had a detailed discussion as to why the Portuguese never really squared up in the personality department and generally got tucked into some serious refreshment.

Sunday November 25

I was woken up by crashing and banging downstairs. Emma had come to take her stuff. I made her a cup of tea and we got on like a house on fire. We agreed that out of everyone Colin was likely to be the most upset and that made me feel even better. Ross could make it with both sexes, Colin with neither. That's what you get for having a manky knapsack. Emma took all morning to pack and then she finally went with my parting gift of her grapefruit knife. It took me half an hour just to wander round the house and marvel at all the liberated space in the bathroom, bedroom and everywhere else. Things were looking up.

I was just about to hot-foot it down to the Blue Boar when the phone rang. It was some bloke I'd never heard of claiming to be Ross's boyfriend. He was terribly weepy and asked whether we wanted to meet up for a team hug. As he wasn't an employee of Smokehouse and covered by our strict corporate code of ethics governing interpersonal relationships, I told him where he could go for his team hug. Finally I strolled down to the Blue Boar thinking of Emma and Fulbright and for a moment I almost felt sorry for Fulbright. At the bar Mike was talking about possible locations for his honeymoon and we were helping out with names of fat farms etc.

Evan and Barney were buying each other drinks left right and centre. I realised the feeling of escape Evan must be feeling so I got the next few rounds and told them all about Emma and Fulbright. They took it all in their stride, admitted to a man they thought she was a twittering airhead and also admitted to a man that they wouldn't have minded giving her one. We also agreed unanimously that for shirt lifters to suddenly become skirt lifters just wasn't cricket. But by that time we were all richly leathered, so we lifted our glasses and wished Fulbright the very best of luck.

Monday November 26

It's payback time. No one messes with John Arthur Weak and gets away with it. Stopped at reception first thing and invited Shirley out for lunch as I needed to talk things through with her. She could barely contain her excitement at the amount of first-hand dirt she thought I was going to dish out to her. I knew she'd hold the front page until I'd given her the latest news so I was confident that I'd taken control of the main source of information in the company.

I then got to work on the other one, trotting downstairs to see Gary Johnson, the editor of *Smoke Signals* our company magazine. Gary is a man with no interest, excitement or personality whatsoever and the magazine accurately reflects this. I'd noticed in the last issue as I was checking for new secretarial totty that there had been a pathetic attempt at redesign, the net effect of which had been to make the magazine virtually illegible. I told Gary I'd just popped down to tell him what a triumph of marketing the redesign had been and we really needed people like him to get involved in advertising campaigns in Barbados etc. Funnily enough he agreed that closer links between internal and external marketing would be a good thing.

I suggested we started off by having Rob Drewitt from my department do some work experience in his. (Rob's a no-questions-asked kind of guy who does my dirty work in return for me not noticing that he doesn't do any other work.) Gary agreed and I was finally able to get away from him and his squalid little desk.

Tuesday November 27

Asked Hayley to send Martin Hooper up to my office. He's the office revolutionary working against capitalism from within. Naturally I've been working against him from within personnel since he first arrived but he probably thinks it's the nameless fascistic forces of capitalism oppressing him. He slouched into my office probably preparing for his redundancy. I said I'd always respected his work and how he'd maintained his integrity (i.e. he still dressed like a student and didn't do any work). He grunted. I then told him that I believed that the rights of women and gays were vitally important in the company and I wanted to voice my opinions in *Smoke Signals*. Would he mind writing the article for me because he was so much more attuned to these issues and could I have it before his appraisal. I could see the penny dropping down the long empty slot in his mind and he agreed.

Took Shirley out for lunch and told her that she'd always been someone I could talk to, that I was very emotionally vulnerable and fragile (thank you Colin) and something deep inside told me she was the person I could bare my soul to. She virtually imploded with sympathy. I then told her that I would very much like to see her after work to talk things through in great depth perhaps over dinner for two in the world's most expensive and tactfully lit restaurant. She was so happy to help that I almost expected her to suggest going to the restaurant immediately.

Wednesday November 28

Shirley was noticeably not talking to anybody about the Fulbright affair. It's funny how when you have your own secrets you cut down on communication in general in case you let anything about yourself slip. Rang Rob Drewitt for a meeting and gave him some specific editorial instructions for the magazine. Then called up Fulbright and said we should have lunch to talk through the situation like mature adults.

We sat down at the same table in the same restaurant where he'd tried to tell me that he was shunting my wife round the carpet. I told him that more than anything we didn't want Emma to get hurt and he agreed like the big woofter he is. I asked him not to say anything about it publicly until Friday so I had a chance to come to terms with my pain. He agreed and for a nasty moment I thought he was going to try and hug me.

Thursday November 29

Got the marketing department together and revealed my new idea of a bounty pack for students. We would give them an emergency kit of chocolate bars, soup, shampoo, soap etc for their first term at college to get them hooked on our products. Everyone agreed that this was a fantastic idea so I instructed them to get down to the warehouse and organise 500 trial bounty packs to see whether we'd got the mix of products right.

Had lunch with Bill Peters and we checked the final details of my strategy. We just had the one bottle of red because he knew I was on a mission. He was going to do the bulk of his drinking that night when he took Fulbright out for a man-to-man to help Fulbright understand the depth of my hurt and how to best manage it in his announcement to the company the next day. I took Shirley out for dinner and made up the biggest pack of lies about my emotional condition I've ever heard even from myself. She was so willing to take everything on board that it was all I could do not to sleep with her.

Friday November 30

Arrived at the office at the crack of dawn and made sure everyone who was anyone had a bounty pack of free goodies on their desk courtesy of their generous best mate John Weak. Spent the morning taking calls of thanks and gratitude. Half-way through the morning the new issue of *Smoke Signals* was delivered around the company. Top story was 'Sales Figures Shock Collapse' composed by ace reporter Rob Drewitt. Bottom half was 'Weak Champions Gay Rights' plus photo of me and kids taken in rare happy moment when they had just been told they were allowed home.

I sneaked into reception to overhear Shirley telling the world and his wife that she was not surprised sales were collapsing when Fulbright was so busy stealing other men's wives even when the man involved was championing the rights of gays which was what Fulbright was supposed to be anyway. I couldn't have scripted it better myself. Had long lunch with Bill Peters to celebrate total rout of Fulbright. Bill was still quite merry after drinking Fulbright under the table the night before. From what I gathered from Shirley in bed that night, Sir Marcus was not impressed by Fulbright's explanations of sales figures/team playing/sexuality shift especially when they ended with Fulbright vomiting into his waste bin.

DECEMBER

Saturday December 1

The good thing about older women is that they know what they want and they're also pathetically grateful to get it. Shirley wasn't up there with Kim in the Premier League of Filth but wasn't in the Conference with Emma either. When I got home there was a 15-page letter from Emma talking me through the last two months. It must have taken her most of that time to write the letter. She started on about personal growth so I skimmed through the rest looking for financial demands. There weren't any so I binned the letter and made myself a cup of coffee. Thinking through the divorce I wondered if there was a way that I could give her custody of the children even though they weren't hers. That really would be a big win all round for me.

Just as I was thinking about children the doorbell rang. It was Emma's dad Maurice with Uncle Nathan hidden behind him. Maurice gave me a handshake which simultaneously rearranged most of the small bones in my hand, communicated just how many rings he was wearing and what an unpleasant effect they would have on my face. As I thought, they'd come about the grandchildren situation and the fact that they hadn't heard from Emma for a while. I talked them through the situation with Fulbright, his sexual journey of discovery and how happy they now were together. Maurice was not at all happy. As they left I mentioned that it was all very unfortunate timing because I thought Emma and I might have made some progress on the grandchild front. Maurice shook my hand in a manner which amounted to a caress in comparison to his greeting and promised to sort matters out. Nice little present for the loving couple from me I thought.

Sunday December 2

Woke up early with Shirley. Got up a lot later. I love her to pieces obviously but Shirley is the loudest woman I've ever been in bed with. I'm sure it's a great reflection on my technique but it does begin to sound like the chorus of 'Old

MacDonald Had a Farm' once she gets going. Looked through the sports section of the paper, had another crack at Shirley and made my way to the Blue Boar. Barney and The Terminator arrived at the same time as I did and we matched each other pint for pint for the next 12 hours. He'd given Beryl a good seeing to the previous night and we agreed that older women were like ripe apples in that they were very tasty indeed if you could just catch them between cider and compost.

Monday December 3

Shirley accused me of being late in again which was pretty rich considering we'd only just finished at Old MacDonald's farm a few minutes earlier. Big week this week. It's Snifters launch week with the national roll out backed up by millions of quid worth of advertising. It's my idea, my name, my advertising and if it goes well it'll be the making of me.

Went for a celebratory lunch with Bill Peters and we wondered over a bottle of red whether Snifters would change the face of long lunches. We decided to pack in as many long lunches as possible just in case. Got back to big news. Fulbright has resigned. Officially because of the sales figures but unofficially because he doesn't want to be in the same company as me. I sent him a little e-mail which said that there really was no need for him to go and wished him all the very best in the future. That should make him feel even sicker with a bit of luck. I could almost get used to this being nice lark.

Tuesday December 4

Shirley avoided eye contact this morning which was a bad sign. I suppose it's to be expected though. You can't have an affair with any woman for more than three days before they start exhibiting all sorts of excessive emotional reactions. Visited the warehouse to check preparations for Snifters launch. Everyone in the warehouse seemed to be very happy with the way things were shaping up so I assumed they were all nicking the product. As promised I got Bill a couple of crates of product for his help in the past.

My mobile phone went calling me back to the office for emergency Board meeting because of sudden catastrophic share price dive. Apparently someone in the City had got hold of a copy of *Smoke Signals*, seen the fictional sales results, and put the word out to sell Smokehouse. Sir Marcus told me to organise an immediate internal inquiry which fortunately took the heat off me instantly. No one's likely to find themselves guilty in their own inquiry.

Wednesday December 5

Began immediate and thorough Internal Inquiry. I called no-questions-asked Rob Drewitt into my office and thanked him profusely for all the great undercover work he'd done for me at *Smoke Signals*. I then told him that he was going to have to fall on his sword, take the blame for the sales figures fiasco, and did he have any questions. He said he would do it, he didn't have any questions (that's the thing I like best about Drewitt) but that I would owe him a big one. I couldn't imagine any favour was going to be as big as saving my corporate bacon so I agreed like a shot.

Asked Shirley out for dinner but she was very snitty with me. I think Fulbright may have got to her and done some of his sensitivity stuff. Went to the gym with Howard instead. We had a couple of G&Ts and then made a bet that we could spend an hour in the gym doing nothing but looking in the mirror. We both managed it and we discovered that an alarming number of other people seemed to be doing it too.

Thursday December 6

I had a call from Sir Marcus first thing saying that he'd found the sources of the fake sales figures. Apparently it was Rob Drewitt who had confessed to Sir Marcus personally that it was revenge for Fulbright consistently making unwanted advances on his wife. (Best Supporting Actor goes to Rob Drewitt for his role in Twist of the Knife.) Sir Marcus was shocked as Rob was always such a reliable conscientious sort. He'd be more shocked to know that Rob isn't married. As I stifled my laughter Sir Marcus said he was off to pacify the City.

Long, long lunch with Bill to celebrate successful despatch of Fulbright and neat passing of buck to Drewitt. We toasted tomorrow's launch of Snifters and got so nostalgic for alcohol in bottles that we had to have another two before we left. Very happy day all round.

Friday December 7

Got in late and Hayley sent me straight up to Sir Marcus's office. Very bad sign. I went in and before I could sit down he told me that the share price hadn't recovered because the City boys didn't like uncertainty and didn't have the wit to cope with any shares that weren't heading steadily skywards. The City boys had also discovered that Fulbright was now Sales Director of our major competitor. As our real sales results were actually bloody good they all assumed that without Fulbright they were now going to be diabolical. Fair point. Sir Marcus was therefore taking drastic action to reduce costs which meant that the Snifters launch was cancelled. I tried to argue but found there was suddenly a door between me and him

Sitting in my office trying to recover from this body blow I had a call from Rob Drewitt asking for his favour. He'd heard what had passed between me and Sir Marcus (God knows how – he must be knocking off Clare Bridport) and asked if he could have the entire Snifters stock sitting in the warehouse. Couldn't really say no and I sensed the Drewitt had me by the knackers anyway. I told him to help himself and then had this uncanny premonition of Rob Drewitt being a millionaire within weeks.

Saturday December 8

Woke up with this crushing weight on my chest. Thought at first it might be Becky trying out a position for which she's anatomically unsuited but I soon realised it was grief and shock and horror at the loss of Snifters and the possible loss of whole struggle against Fulbright, Emma, Colin and the liberal hordes. If in doubt drink something or shag something. I had a final packet of Snifters by my bed but I was too depressed to look at them. Called Shirley for option two and she told me that she was seeing Fulbright and Emma later that day. She put the phone down in a right old snit and I could just imagine the three of them forming their victim support group. No doubt Colin will be included as well.

The mention of Emma made me realise that I'd also lost my wife in all this, so there was a bright spot. Suddenly remembered that duty called and it was my turn for the kids. Given the circumstances I was almost pleased to see them. I needed a couple of things for the house so I took them to B&Q World of Adventure. Went down to the Blue Boar and told the boys what had happened that week. I actually made it sound like a total triumph for me on all fronts and by the time I staggered home I nearly believed it.

Sunday December 9

I was still in bed at eleven o'clock when my sister Karen and her Reverend boyfriend arrived for lunch. This is something I'd arranged apparently but I sensed that the grapevine had been humming and they'd come to assess my emotional damage. I sent them out to get the papers while I got myself showered, shaved and shitted and then we trolled down to the Blue Boar. While Paul got the drinks in I apologised profusely to Karen about forgetting the lunch which obviously I'd been looking forward to for weeks. She then admitted they'd made up the invitation and just wanted to pop in and see me.

I thought I'd better make a clean breast of it and told them that Emma had left me for a gay man, that our marriage had never worked, and that I wouldn't advise anybody to get married in a hurry ever again. At that moment Tony the barman brought a bucket of champagne to our table. I was a bit nonplussed until Paul said they'd actually come down to announce their engagement. I thought for a moment this would be cue for tears but Karen was absolutely fascinated by the Emma story and wanted to know all the gory details. In the end I think Paul got a bit narked that she wasn't in tears. We had a couple of bottles of champagne to ease things along and I volunteered to do the wedding service for Paul as he obviously couldn't do it himself. He said he'd come back to me after he'd asked every other human being in the world.

Monday December 10

Got to work late and Shirley made a big point of ignoring me. I almost asked her for the minutes from her victim support group meeting as I'm sure they would have made fascinating reading. Sat down at my desk and pondered the fallout from last week. I'd made a pretty good job of passing the buck but I had a nasty feeling that the buck hadn't yet stopped anywhere and I hadn't heard the last of it.

As I was just mulling over my future I got a call on my mobile from a headhunter asking me whether I was interested in a very tasty opportunity. The timing couldn't have been better so I agreed to meet him in a nearby hotel on Wednesday. After work met up with Howard in the gym to work out my frustrations with some serious table football. For some unaccountable reason Howard pulverised me 89–7. I seemed to be doing a hell of a lot of spinning and very little kicking. I'm sure there's a significant metaphor in there somewhere.

Tuesday December 11

Day filled with interviews for new Smokehouse Sales Director to replace Ross 'Quite Shaggable After All' Fulbright. I'm on the panel of course because Marketing and Sales have traditionally worked very closely together. But not closely enough to notice him shunting my wife half-way round Europe.

The first interviewee was the widest wide boy from the widest part of Widesville. He's the first person I've ever met who could strut sitting down. We asked him a series of probing questions about business development in a global matrix managed environment to which his standard answer was 'piece of piss'. I began to warm to him but the rest of the panel were drawing huge crosses on their papers. Then we had some woman with an incredibly soft voice and more degrees than an industrial thermometer. Renton-Willets asked her about her soft skills and I think she actually blushed. I got a bit fed up and said that it was more important to have hard skills when it came to managing hundreds of hairy arsed sales execs. Was slapped down by rest of panel so didn't bother much with the rest. We looked at another couple of losers and then called it a day. It's amazing the rubbish headhunters send you.

Wednesday December 12

Felt unaccountably nervous about meeting with the headhunter. Hayley asked if she could leave early as I wouldn't be needing her. I was a bit distracted so I said yes instead of making up a lot of unnecessary things for her to do. She disappeared and I drove to an out-of-the-way hotel for my meeting. In general I'm a bit wary of headhunters because like traditional native headhunters, they take your head and, through a process of getting you rejected for a series of low level jobs, seriously reduce the size of it.

The headhunter turned up rather late because he wanted to get more details about the position he had in mind for me. We got talking and it really did sound like an ideal job for me. So ideal that it began to sound suspiciously like my own job. When it got down to location I realised that he was indeed offering me my own job. Or more to the point Sir Marcus had asked him to offer people my job. His face suddenly went a deep red, he realised what he'd done and he tried to get me to promise that I wouldn't tell anybody. I told him he owed me a big favour and he left in a hurry. Then I sat perfectly still listening to the sound of my world coming apart. It was clearly time for a drink so I settled into the bar and eventually had to stay the night at the hotel because I was in no fit state.

Thursday December 13

Got downstairs for an early breakfast with a horrible sinking feeling in my stomach that had nothing to do with the horrible hammering feeling in my head. Then amazingly I saw Hayley come into the restaurant. I thought she'd come to deliver the bad news to me but then I saw she was closely followed by Sir Marcus who had his hand unethically close to her rear end. Watching them from behind my newspaper, everything about their body language made it abundantly clear that they had just spent the night playing hunt the sausage.

Sometimes I think I lead a charmed life. I had the world's longest breakfast behind my newspaper until they'd both gone and then drove to work. Said a very cheery hello to Shirley who replied equally cheerily before she remembered who's side she was on. Had lunch with Bill Peters to share the good news about Sir Marcus and Hayley. He then admitted in a moment of candour that the reason he still had his job was he knew about Sir Marcus's five other non-executive relationships. My admiration for Sir Marcus soared but not quite to the level that I wasn't going to blackmail the living daylights out of him.

Friday December 14

Shirley had recovered her poise and tried to ignore me again, so I strode up to her desk and told her that despite everything I loved her. That'll give them something interesting to talk about in their victims' support group. I joked with Hayley that she looked radiant and that she must have a love interest in her life. The lying little minx said she wished she did. Soon she's going to wishing very, very hard she didn't.

Got on the phone to Sir Marcus saying I wanted an urgent discussion about my position. He agreed that was a good idea so I went up and told him about my position behind the newspaper. Naturally he asked me what I was doing there and I told him I was talking to the headhunter about a very interesting marketing job in a company very similar to this one. The penny dropped like a clanger and he said he'd make every effort to persuade me to stay on in my current role. How cute. As I got back to my desk I got a call from Rob Drewitt saying he'd shifted the entire stock of Snifters and would I like to go into business with him. Interesting day all round.

Saturday December 15

Woke up with a smile on my face. Weak pulls it off once more. There really is no stopping me. I'm going to hire someone for the day to walk round patting me on the back and lighting big cigars for me. Went round to pick up the kids and decided to give them a really good time for once. I asked them what they most wanted to do in the world. The answer was dunno. So I took them both for a completely unnecessary haircut, bought them a whole set of new clothes each and then took them back to their mother saying I'd exchanged the children for two others. Kate was spectacularly unamused but the kids said it was the best day out they'd ever had. I'm not sure which I understand less, kids or women.

Strolled down to the Blue Boar in a rare good mood but that went the moment I stepped into the bar. I knew something was terribly, terribly wrong and I could only think that someone had died. Mike and Barney were slumped at one end of the bar. They told me that Evan had run off with

Becky. My immediate thought was good for Evan, it's about time he got his bat out, but then I remembered that Mike was supposed to be marrying the silly tart. I couldn't understand why Barney was so miserable until Mike told me that they'd taken The Terminator with them. It was such a fantastic masterstroke by Evan that I almost cheered. Somehow I managed to look suitably grim. We had a desultory conversation about what an absolute shower the Welsh were, but as Evan had spectacularly poked both Barney and Mike in the eye, it didn't really get going.

Sunday December 16

Woke up early, laughed out loud and went back to sleep. Got up two hours later and walked down to the paper shop whistling all the way. Saw the brassy looking woman with the low-cut top and wondered what sort of woman would want to display her naked cleavage in the middle of winter. The answer was my kind of woman and I decided that next time I saw her I would slide in there and give her some high-octane chat.

Read the paper from cover to cover, including how a large demonstration for improved patient care had got out of control. A man being released from hospital had been caught in the stampede, badly crushed and rushed back to hospital. This was Martin Padley. If he doesn't want to play rugby he should just say so. Cooked myself a monstrous breakfast/lunch and then made my way to the Blue Boar for some serious refreshment. Inside there were three men I'd never seen before in my life standing at our end of the bar. There wasn't a sign of Mike or Barney or Evan or Becky or The Terminator. I didn't even recognise the barmaid. It was like I'd stepped into a completely different pub. The three blokes at the end were drinking away like they owned the place and the sight of them in our spot put me right off my beer. I went home, got some lager out of the fridge and watched a couple of Emma's more explicit exercise videos.

Monday December 17

Have decided to cheer myself up by overdosing on Christmas spirit. There's one week to go before the Christmas party. Top of mistletoe list is scorching Emily Reimbold from research department who's built entirely from gravity defying materials. Have tried to use the legendary Weak charm on her more than once but having a conversation with her is like continually serving into the net. Absolutely no sense of humour that girl. Will just have to get totally bladdered at party and let nature take its course.

Giles Renton-Willets (weirdo HR Director) popped by with Christmas bonus calculations for my team. I really don't know why he bothers. I decide who gets the bonuses in my department based on ability alone (the ability to brown nose yours truly). On the bright side I had a good haul of supplier gifts this year. Sent back tacky promotional items with standard 'can't possibly accept' letter with Drinks Direct number lightly pencilled on top.

Tuesday December 18

Brand Manager Kevin Spears is organising some kind of revue for the Christmas party. Thinks he's a bit of a whiz on impressions. He certainly does a good impression of a pillock when I've worked with him. Everyone got note from the thought police (HR department) written by Victoria 'politically correct' Prothero (walking chastity belt). In amongst all the nurturing supportive HR jargon it managed to communicate that inappropriate behaviour would not be tolerated at Christmas party. That's OK by me as I can't imagine any behaviour that wouldn't be appropriate at a Christmas party. After work went to gym with Howard and spent a good hour in the mixed sauna swapping techniques for getting kit off totty. Had to stop when some woman came in and sat there naked. Not very pleasant.

Wednesday December 19

Cleared my desk and practised my skit for the revue, the great rugby song 'Bestiality's best'. Sensitivity guidelines don't mention animals so should be all right with the thought police. Put in a few extra verses about foxes, beaver etc. Should go down well especially with the totty. Had lunch with Bill Peters who was sitting at usual seat in Bojangles (he calls it benchmarking). He was pretty trolleyed when I got there and he told me he intends to keep drinking from now until January to miss Christmas completely. Has volunteered to do a trick with a pint of vodka and a pair of underpants for Christmas revue. PC Prothero is trying to get a court exclusion order to keep him away from party.

Thursday December 20

Christmas party!! Emily Reimbold almost wearing a dress. Had a couple of glasses of fizz and asked her if she wanted to work with me on a 'positioning' project. She told me where I could position myself. Great sense of humour that girl!! Had a couple more drinks. Spears then got up and did impressions of various people in the company who all sounded amazingly like Spears. Finished with one of a loud director with a Porsche that brought the house down. Made a little note of anyone laughing too hard. Haven't signed off their bonuses yet. Had a couple more drinks and then got up with a jock strap on my head for 'Bestiality's best'. Started well but for some reason room went deathly quiet. All a bit odd as sheep verse is usually a winner on the rugby coach. Half way through Bill Peters walked onto stage buck naked with a pint of vodka in his hand and his underpants over his head. Finished song together. Entire HR department imploded. All got a bit hazy after that.

Friday December 21

Arrived at work just before lunch. Only person in the building without hangover was Clare O'Keefe who really let her hair down with a tomato juice. She barged into my office saying that all Christmas cards to our suppliers had to be signed by end of play. I pointed Hayley to the pile of envelopes and told her to sign them (she does my signature better than I do) while I got seven coffees and a cooked breakfast for myself. Everyone in the office was giving me very funny looks for some reason.

Bill Peters called from Mr Bojangles to break the news. Shitty death!!! Apparently I got off with PC Prothero from HR last night. How I ever managed to torch off the rivets on her chastity belt I'll never know. Got back to office and found another pile of envelopes on my desk which turned out to be supplier Christmas cards. The first lot were the bonuses all of which Hayley had signed off and distributed without me even looking at them! Mine wasn't enough for the bus fare home. At the bottom it said in case of complaint contact Victoria Prothero in HR. I called HR immediately only to be told that she was at home with a stress related disorder. The tone of voice of the little HR girly implied that I was that stress related disorder. I suddenly decided that I'd had enough of the working year and left. Shirley snatched the mistletoe from reception as I passed in case I tried anything. Happy bloody Christmas.

Saturday December 22

Stayed in bed for a long time because I couldn't think of any pressing reason to be out of bed. Eventually my bladder got quite pressing and I got up. Went out for the papers and over breakfast I discovered that there were three days to Christmas and if I didn't watch out I was going to be spending Christmas Eve without any totty on hand. Flicking through my filofax I came across the list of responses to my personal ad at the beginning of the year. They'd all been crossed off apart from one right at the bottom called Pam who had come last for a number of reasons. One of the big reasons was that she lived in the north, an area of the country I take great pains to avoid because of the persistent cases of cap on head disease.

I gave Pam a call and apologised for taking so long to get in touch but that I had taken all year to pluck up my courage. She said she quite understood as she was also a bit like that. She was still single – which was good and bad news – and was free that evening. I told her it would take me five hours to drive up from London but she said that was fine as it would just about give her time to get ready. In five hours she should be able to rebuild herself from the ground up which, as I got further north, I was praying she had. We went to what Pam said was the best hotel in town which in terms of stars wasn't even a cloud of hot gases. The most extraordinary thing about Pam was that everything about her was utterly plain. Plain looks, plain clothes, plain job, plain hair, plain life. It was also pretty plain that she would be quite happy to indulge in a little plain bonkage. But however much I drank I just couldn't get to the point where her features blurred into something I could jump on. Eventually her sense of disappointment became overwhelming so I gave her a kiss on the cheek and put her in a taxi.

Sunday December 23

At four in the morning I was woken by a knocking on my hotel door. I could only imagine it was some kind of fire drill so I went and opened it. Immediately Pam barged her way in, took off her clothes and got into bed. She whispered to me that I couldn't come all this way and then go back empty handed. And then boy did I have my hands full. I was still virtually asleep but she attacked me like a chicken drumstick. When I woke up she was gone and I suddenly felt cheated. This one was supposed to last me over Christmas.

As I drove home I saw all the northern guest workers streaming out of London heading north for their Christmas offal. I finally got back home and out of sheer force of habit went to the Blue Boar. None of the boys were there and of course there was no Becky. I asked Tony what the news was and he said that as far as he knew Evan and Becky had gone off somewhere sunny. The penny dropped and I suddenly realised that I should go to the Caribbean for Christmas. I shot into town but just as I was setting foot inside the travel agent my mobile went. It was Kate. Malcolm The Talcum had decided to spend Christmas with his mother (I suspect she probably wanted her picnic blanket back). Would I mind coming over and looking after the kids with her for Christmas. I put the exotic islands brochure down and told her I couldn't think of anything nicer.

Christmas Eve

Met Howard at gym for table football marathon. We started at 11.00 in the morning and finished at 11.00 at night. In between bouts of skilful Italian style football we had a few drinks so by the end we could hardly see the table let alone the ball. The final score was 211–189 to yours truly. Possibly high point of my year. Howard immediately asked for a rematch. Management asked us to leave the building and told us they would not be renewing our membership next year. Howard tried to take the table football with him on the way out but didn't have the co-ordination, strength, sense of direction or anything else required to carry it off. Nice thought though.

Christmas Day

Got up late and collected together all the sensitive, well thought out Christmas presents I had bought from the newsagents just before they closed the night before. Drove across to Kate's and parked in my old spot. The kids were pathetically grateful to see me. Kate gave me a lingering, passionate peck on the cheek and we went inside to plough through Christmas. I accidentally asked how 'that tosser Malcolm' was and, as I thought, was rewarded with the kids referring to 'that tosser Malcolm' throughout the day.

Drank half a bottle of sherry before Kate's parents arrived and was thus suitably immune to their special yuletide looks of withering contempt. I insisted on watching the Queen's speech because I knew they were ardent republicans and then spent the rest of the afternoon feeding them titbits of wisdom from Her Majesty. Eventually I retired to the spare room which had been kept just as it was when I spent my nights there during our marriage i.e. 500 pairs of shoes that had been worn once and were now completely unwearable.

Boxing Day

Kate went off to the sales courtesy of my maintenance payments and I took the kids round the park and then to McDonald's.

Thursday December 27

Woke up at seven o'clock and went into work. There was no one there I knew or wanted to know. What kind of sad people come in the office over Christmas? Sat down at my computer and commenced my annual reading of e-mails. I had deleted roughly five thousand over the course of the year and I just wanted to see if I'd missed anything.

There was a traffic warden in Sycamore Road so anybody who'd parked there should move their car; someone had found a purse in the women's lavatories and would anyone like to claim it (if it had been a wallet in the women's lavatories I would have claimed it just for the PR); would anyone like to be part of a Smokehouse Choir; volunteers needed for catering committee (after strange death of half the former members); someone with a green Fiat Uno left their lights on in the car park; ten Smokehouse runners in London Marathon looking for sponsors; kittens for sale to good family; EU Health & Safety directive regarding capacity of waste bins; green sock found in reception; holiday home available in Bosnia; apologies for virus circulated by IT department; accommodation required for Spanish student;

donations please for David Ratley after 42 years of service to Smokehouse; petition in support of Dalai Lama. By five o'clock I was only about half-way through so I called it a day and went home.

Friday December 28

Got back to my desk and ploughed through the second half of my deleted e-mails; traffic warden now in Cedar Road so move your cars if you've parked there; has anyone seen my purse; Smokehouse Choir tour of West Africa; more volunteers needed for catering committee; green Fiat Uno being removed by scrap men unless claimed; £789 raised by London Marathon team (that's a pathetic £3 per mile); more apologies for viruses circulated by IT department; yellow sock found in stationery cupboard; would people please stop binning EU Health & Safety directives; announcement of David Ratley's engagement to Conchita, Spanish student; would the Norwich City fan please stop changing in the stationery cupboard; has anyone heard last known whereabouts of Smokehouse Choir; thanks from Dalai Lama for kittens; still some weeks available in holiday home in Bosnia.

Permanently deleted all the year's e-mails and realised I was missing a whole layer of office life. Thank God. The whole e-mail experience is like lifting a big rock and seeing all the little crawling low life scurrying around doing unpleasant things in the mud. Could only be the result of IT people attempting to communicate.

Saturday December 29

Kate went off to see a friend in Cardiff, I took the kids round the park three times, McDonald's twice.

Sunday December 30

Howard and I have decided to have a monster bender to get the last year well and truly behind us. We decided to go on a pub crawl of every bar in town where we'd ever got lucky. After the first ten we were beginning to subscribe to the lightning never strikes twice theory. We soldiered on manfully and amazingly, about two in the morning, we bumped into Madeleine Eccles and some other classy looking totty in a club. Howard was snogging one of them before we'd even been introduced properly. She must have been as desperate as he was.

I got talking to Madeleine. She told me that she was really disappointed I hadn't finished my course of therapy because she was really beginning to like me. I perked up at this and she went on about how she thought my attitude to women was how women really wanted to be treated and that if only the younger generation realised this. She liked the way I'd kept my inner teenager completely intact but on top of that I also had a superficial layer of sophistication. I thought I've finally found a woman who talks sense.

I have to admit that I was spectacularly cabbaged at this point but I remember her very clearly talking about how she wanted to live out various sexual fantasies with me. One of them was that she'd always seen Nelson's Column in Trafalgar Square as being very phallic. As part of her fantasy would I mind standing naked with my arms round it. I thought this sounded like a tremendous idea so we got into a taxi. All the way there she was telling me all the details of what would happen after Trafalgar Square. I got so excited that I practically tore my clothes off and leapt out of the taxi. The last memory I have was of me standing stark naked hugging Nelson's Column with her driving off in the taxi waving my underpants through the window and laughing like a hyena.

Monday December 31

I woke up in a police cell wearing a blue overall. After about an hour the cell stopped spinning and I noticed I was sharing a cell with some other bloke. I suddenly remembered that it was my turn to take the kids so I banged on the cell door and asked for my phone call. I rang Kate and told her that I was unavoidably detained but that I would come round and have them all the following day. She said not to bother as Malcolm had been allowed out by his mother and was back with the picnic blanket.

When I got back to my cell the bloke had woken up and he told me that he'd also been fantastically drunk the night before and hadn't a clue what he had done. I said he sounded remarkably jolly for someone who'd been drinking to the point of oblivion. He told me he hadn't actually been drinking but had been taking these new alcohol pills called APs. Apparently APs were all the rage in the clubs amongst the kids who were tired of drugs. The way he described them, they sounded a lot like Snifters to me, rebranded by Drewitt for the youth market. He's a smart one Drewitt. I'll have to get in touch with him when I get out of prison. While I was waiting to be released I thought it might be a good idea to write myself a few New Year's resolutions. I lit a cigarette and started writing.

- Give up smoking
- Engage with women on a new level (groin)
- Show ex-wives magnitude of their errors
- Make a big splash in new job
- Get six pack (from exercise not off-licence)
- Work smarter not harder (Or just take it easy – whatever's easiest)
- Be myself

Follow the continuing corporate dominance of John Weak in the back of *Management Today* magazine every month.